RANDOM HOUSE

LARGE PRINT

HANNIBAL RISING

Also by Thomas Harris
available from Random House Large Print

Hannibal

HANNIBAL RISING

a novel by

THOMAS HARRIS

RANDOM HOUSE
LARGE PRINT

Published in the United States of America
by Random House Large Print in association
with Delacorte Press, New York.
Distributed by Random House, Inc., New York.

Title page image, "Ink Drawing of a Shrike on a Twig" by Musashi, Kuboso Memorial Museum of Arts, Izumi, Japan

The Library of Congress has established a Cataloging-in-Publication record for this title.

ISBN-13: 978-0-375-43541-6
ISBN-10: 0-375-43541-7

www.randomlargeprint.com

FIRST LARGE PRINT EDITION

10 9 8 7 6 5 4 3 2 1

This Large Print edition published in accord
with the standards of the N.A.V.H.

HANNIBAL RISING

PROLOGUE

THE DOOR TO DR. HANNIBAL LECTER'S memory palace is in the darkness at the center of his mind and it has a latch that can be found by touch alone. This curious portal opens on immense and well-lit spaces, early baroque, and corridors and chambers rivaling in number those of the Topkapi Museum.

Everywhere there are exhibits, well-spaced and lighted, each keyed to memories that lead to other memories in geometric progression.

Spaces devoted to Hannibal Lecter's earliest years differ from the other archives in being incomplete. Some are static scenes, fragmentary, like painted Attic shards held together by blank plaster. Other rooms hold sound and motion, great snakes wrestling and heaving in the dark and lit in flashes. Pleas and screaming fill some places on the grounds where Hannibal himself cannot go. But the corridors do not echo screaming, and there is music if you like.

The palace is a construction begun early in Hannibal's student life. In his years of confinement he improved and enlarged his palace, and its riches sustained him for long periods while warders denied him his books.

Here in the hot darkness of his mind, let us feel together for the latch. Finding it, let us elect for music in the corridors and, looking neither left nor right, go to the Hall of the Beginning where the displays are most fragmentary.

We will add to them what we have learned elsewhere, in war records and police records, from interviews and forensics and the mute postures of the dead. **Robert Lecter's letters, recently unearthed, may help us establish the vital statistics of Hannibal, who altered dates freely to confound the authorities and his chroniclers. By our efforts we may watch as the beast within turns from the teat and, working upwind, enters the world.**

I

This is the first thing
I have understood:
Time is the echo of an axe
Within a wood.

——Philip Larkin

1

HANNIBAL THE GRIM (1365–1428) built Lecter Castle in five years, using for labor the soldiers he had captured at the Battle of Žalgiris. On the first day his pennant flew from the completed towers, he assembled the prisoners in the kitchen garden and, mounting his gallows to address them, he released the men to go home, just as he had promised. Many elected to stay in his service, owing to the quality of his provender.

Five hundred years later Hannibal Lecter, eight years old and eighth of the name, stood in the kitchen garden with his little sister Mischa and threw bread to the black swans on the black water of the moat. Mischa held on to Hannibal's hand to steady herself and missed the moat entirely on several throws. Big carp stirred the lily pads and sent the dragonflies soaring.

Now the Alpha swan came out of the water, stumping toward the children on his short legs, hissing his challenge. The swan had known Hannibal all his life and still he came, his black wings shutting out part of the sky.

"Ohh, Anniba!" Mischa said and hid behind Hannibal's leg.

Hannibal raised his arms to shoulder height as his father had taught him to do, his reach augmented with willow branches held in his hands. The swan stopped to consider Hannibal's greater wingspan, and retired to the water to feed.

"We go through this every day," Hannibal told the bird. But today was not every day and he wondered where the swans could flee.

Mischa in her excitement dropped her bread on the damp ground. When Hannibal stooped to help her, she was pleased to daub mud on his nose with her little star-shaped hand. He daubed a bit of mud on the end of her nose and they laughed at their reflections in the moat.

The children felt three hard thumps in the ground and the water shivered, blurring their faces. The sound of distant explosions rolled across the fields. Hannibal grabbed up his sister and ran for the castle.

The hunting wagon was in the courtyard,

hitched to the great draft horse Cesar. Berndt in his hostler's apron and the houseman, Lothar, loaded three small trunks into the wagon box. Cook brought out a lunch.

"Master Lecter, Madame wants you in her room," Cook said.

Hannibal passed Mischa along to Nanny and ran up the hollowed steps.

Hannibal loved his mother's room with its many scents, the faces carved in the woodwork, its painted ceiling—Madame Lecter was of the Sforza on one side and a Visconti on the other, and she had brought the room with her from Milan.

She was excited now and her bright maroon eyes reflected the light redly in sparks. Hannibal held the casket as his mother pressed the lips of a cherub in the molding and a hidden cabinet opened. She scooped her jewels into the casket, and some bundled letters; there was not room for them all.

Hannibal thought she looked like the cameo portrait of her grandmother that tumbled into the box.

Clouds painted on the ceiling. As a baby nursing he used to open his eyes and see his mother's bosom blended with the clouds. The feel of the edges of her blouse against his face. The wet nurse too—her gold cross

gleamed like sunlight between prodigious clouds and pressed against his cheek when she held him, she rubbing the mark of the cross on his skin to make it go away before Madame might see it.

But his father was in the doorway now, carrying the ledgers.

"Simonetta, we need to go."

The baby linens were packed in Mischa's copper bathtub and Madame put the casket among them. She looked around the room, and took a small painting of Venice from its tripod on the sideboard, considered a moment, and gave it to Hannibal.

"Take this to Cook. Take it by the frame." She smiled at him. "Don't smudge the back."

Lothar carried the bathtub out to the wagon in the courtyard, where Mischa fretted, uneasy at the stir around her.

Hannibal held Mischa up to pat Cesar's muzzle. She gave the horse's nose a few squeezes as well to see if it would honk. Hannibal took grain in his hand and trailed it on the ground in the courtyard to make an "M." The pigeons flocked to it, making an "M" in living birds on the ground. Hannibal traced the letter in Mischa's palm—she was approaching three years old and he despaired of her ever learning to read. " 'M' for Mischa!" he said. She ran among the birds laughing and they flew up around her, circling the towers, lighting in the belfry.

Cook, a big man in kitchen whites, came out carrying a lunch. The horse rolled an eye at Cook and followed his progress with a rotating ear—when Cesar was a colt, Cook had run him out of the vegetable garden on a number of occasions, yelling oaths and swatting his rump with a broom.

"I'll stay and help you load the kitchen," Mr. Jakov said to Cook.

"Go with the boy," Cook said.

Count Lecter lifted Mischa into the wagon and Hannibal put his arms around her. Count Lecter cupped Hannibal's face in his hand. Surprised by the tingle in his father's hand, Hannibal looked closely into Count Lecter's face.

"Three planes bombed the rail yards. Colonel Timka says we have at least a week, if they reach here at all, and then the fighting will be along the main roads. We'll be fine at the lodge."

It was the second day of Operation Barbarossa, Hitler's lightning sweep across Eastern Europe into Russia.

2

BERNDT WALKED AHEAD of the wagon on the forest path, careful of the horse's face, hacking back the overgrown branches with a Swiss half-pike.

Mr. Jakov followed on a mare, his saddlebags full of books. He was unused to horseback and he hugged the horse's neck to pass beneath the limbs. Sometimes where the trail was steep, he dismounted to push along with Lothar and Berndt and Count Lecter himself. Branches snapped back behind them to close the trail again.

Hannibal smelled greenery crushed by the wheels and Mischa's warm hair beneath his chin as she rode on his lap. He watched the German bombers pass over high. Their vapor trails made a musical staff and Hannibal hummed to his sister the notes the black puffs of flak made in the sky. It was not a satisfying tune.

"No," Mischa said. "Anniba sing **'Das Mannlein'**!" And together they sang about the mysterious little man in the woods, Nanny joining in in the swaying wagon and Mr. Jakov singing from horseback, though he preferred not to sing in German.

> **Ein Mannlein steht im Walde ganz still**
> **und stumm,**
> **Es hat von lauter Purpur ein Mantlein**
> **um,**
> **Sagt, wer mag das Mannlein sein**
> **Das da steht im Walde allein**
> **Mit dem purporroten Mantelein—**

Two hard hours brought them to a clearing beneath the canopy of the high forest.

The hunting lodge had evolved over three hundred years from a crude shelter into a comfortable forest retreat, half-timbered with a steep roof to shed the snow. There was a small barn containing two stalls and a bunkhouse and, behind the lodge, a Victorian privy with gingerbread carvings, its roof just visible over the screening hedge.

Still visible in the foundations of the lodge are

the stones of an altar built in the Dark Ages, by a people who venerated the grass snake.

Now Hannibal watched a grass snake flee that ancient place as Lothar cut back some vines so Nanny could open windows.

Count Lecter ran his hands over the big horse while it drank a gallon and a half from the well bucket. "Cook will have the kitchen packed by the time you get back, Berndt. Cesar can rest in his own stall overnight. You and Cook start back here at first light, no later. I want you well clear of the castle by morning."

Vladis Grutas entered the courtyard of Lecter Castle with his most pleasant expression, scanning the windows as he came. He waved and called out "Hello!"

Grutas was a slight figure, dirty blond, in civilian clothes, with eyes so pale and blue they looked like discs of the empty sky. He called out "Hello in the house!" When there was no reply he went in the kitchen entrance and found cases of supplies packed on the kitchen floor. Quickly he put coffee and sugar in his pack. The cellar door was open. He looked down the long stairs and saw a light.

Violating another creature's den is the oldest

taboo. To certain warps, slipping in offers the freezing feeling of arousal, as it did now.

Grutas went down the staircase into the cool cave air of the castle's vaulted dungeons. He peered through an arch and saw that the iron grate securing the wine room was open.

A rustling noise. Grutas could see labeled wine racks floor to ceiling filled with bottles and the cook's big shadow moving around the room as he worked by the light of two lanterns. Square wrapped packages were on the tasting table in the center of the room and, with them, a single small painting in an ornate frame.

Grutas showed his teeth when that big bastard of a cook came into view. Now the cook's wide back was to the door as he worked over the table. A rustling of paper.

Grutas flattened himself against the wall in the shadow of the steps.

The cook wrapped the painting in paper and wrapped it in kitchen string, making a parcel like the others. With a lantern in his free hand, he reached up and pulled on an iron chandelier above the tasting table. A click and at the back of the wine cellar one end of a wine rack swung a few inches away from the wall of the room. Cook swung the rack away from the wall with a groan of hinges. Behind it was a door.

Cook went into the concealed room behind

the wine cellar and hung one of his lanterns back there. Then he carried the parcels inside.

As he was swinging the wine rack closed, his back to the door, Grutas started up the steps. He heard a shot fired outside, and then the cook's voice below him.

"Who's that!"

Cook came behind him, fast on the stairs for a big man.

"Stop you! You were never to come here."

Grutas ran through the kitchen and into the courtyard waving and whistling.

Cook grabbed a stave from the corner and ran across the kitchen toward the courtyard when he saw a silhouette in the doorway, an unmistakable helmet shape, and three German paratroopers with submachine guns came into the room. Grutas was behind them.

"Hi, Cookie," Grutas said. He picked up a salted ham from the crate on the floor.

"Put back the meat," the German corporal said, pointing his weapon at Grutas as readily as he did at the cook. "Get outside, go with the patrol."

The trail was easier descending to the castle, Berndt making good time with the empty wagon, wrapping the reins around his arm while he lit his pipe. As he approached the edge of the forest he thought he saw a big stork taking off from high in a tree. As he got closer he saw the flapping white was fabric, a parachute caught in high limbs, the risers cut. Berndt stopped. He put down his pipe and slid off the wagon. He put his hand over Cesar's muzzle and spoke quietly into the horse's ear. Then he moved forward on foot, cautious.

Suspended from a lower limb was a man in rough civilian clothes, newly hanged with the wire noose well into his neck, his face blue-black, his muddy boots a foot above the ground. Berndt turned back fast toward the wagon, looking for a place to turn around on the narrow trail, his own boots looking strange to him as he found footing on the rough ground.

They came out of the trees then, three German soldiers under a sergeant and six men in civilian clothes. The sergeant considered, drew back the bolt of his machine pistol. Berndt recognized one of the civilians.

"Grutas," he said.

"Berndt, goody Berndt, who always got up his lessons," Grutas said. He walked up to Berndt with a smile that seemed friendly enough.

"He can handle the horse," Grutas said to the German sergeant.

"Maybe he is your friend," the sergeant said.

"Maybe not," Grutas said, and spit in Berndt's face. "I hung the other one, didn't I? I knew him too. Why should we walk?" And softly, "I'll shoot him at the castle if you will lend me back my gun."

3

BLITZKRIEG, HITLER'S lightning war, was faster than anyone imagined. At the castle Berndt found a company of the Totenkopf Death's Head Division, Waffen-SS. Two Panzer tanks were parked near the moat with a tank destroyer and some half-track trucks.

The gardener Ernst lay facedown in the kitchen yard with blowflies on his head.

Berndt saw this from the wagon box. Only the Germans rode in his wagon. Grutas and the others had to walk behind. They were only **Hilfswillige,** or Hiwis, locals who volunteered to help the invading Nazis.

Berndt could see two soldiers, high on a tower of the castle, running down the Lecters' wild-boar pennant and putting up a radio aerial and a swastika flag in its place.

A major wearing SS black and the Totenkopf skull insignia came out of the castle to look at Cesar.

"Very nice, but too wide to ride," he said regretfully—he had brought his jodhpurs and spurs to ride for recreation. The other horse would do. Behind him two storm troopers came out of the house, hustling Cook along between them.

"Where is the family?"

"In London, sir," Berndt said. "May I cover Ernst's body?"

The major motioned to his sergeant, who stuck the muzzle of the Schmeisser under Berndt's chin.

"And who will cover yours? Smell the barrel. It's still smoking. It can blow your fucking brains out too," the major said. "Where is the family?"

Berndt swallowed. "Fled to London, sir."

"Are you a Jew?"

"No, sir."

"A Gypsy?"

"No, sir."

He looked at a wad of letters from a desk in the house. "There is mail for a Jakov. Are you the Jew Jakov?"

"A tutor, sir. Long gone."

The major checked Berndt's earlobes to see if

they were pierced. "Show the sergeant your dick." Then, "Shall I kill you or will you work?"

"Sir, these people all know each other," the sergeant said.

"Is that so? Perhaps they like each other." He turned to Grutas. "Perhaps your fondness for your landsmen is more than you love us, **hem,** Hiwis?" The major turned to his sergeant. "Do you think we really need any of them?" The sergeant leveled the gun at Grutas and his men.

"The cook is a Jew," Grutas said. "Here is useful local knowledge—you let him cook for you, you would be dead within the hour from Jew poison." He pushed forward one of his men. "Pot Watcher can cook, and forage and soldier too."

Grutas went to the center of the courtyard, moving slowly, the muzzle of the sergeant's machine pistol tracking him. "Major, you wear the ring and the scars of Heidelberg. Here is military history, of the kind you yourself are making. This is the Ravenstone of Hannibal the Grim. Some of the most valiant Teutonic Knights died here. Is it not time to wash the stone with Jew blood?"

The major raised his eyebrows. "If you want to be SS, let's see you earn it." He nodded to his sergeant. The SS sergeant took a pistol from his flap holster. He shucked all the bullets but one from the clip and handed the pistol to Grutas. Two storm troopers dragged the cook to the Ravenstone.

The major seemed more interested in examining the horse. Grutas held the pistol to the cook's head and waited, wanting the major to watch. Cook spit on him.

Swallows started from the towers at the shot.

Berndt was put to moving furniture for the officers' billet upstairs. He looked to see if he had wet himself. He could hear the radio operator in a small room under the eaves, both code and voice transmissions in heavy static. The operator ran down the stairs with his pad in his hand and returned moments later to break down his equipment. They were moving east.

From an upper window Berndt watched the SS unit passing a backpack radio out of the Panzer to the small garrison they were leaving behind. Grutas and his scruffy civilians, issued German weapons now, carried out everything from the kitchen and piled the supplies into the back of a half-track truck with some support personnel. The troops mounted their vehicles. Grutas ran out of the castle to catch up. The unit moved toward Russia, taking Grutas and the other Hiwis. They seemed to have forgotten Berndt.

A squad of Panzergrenadiers with a machine gun and the radio were left behind at the castle. Berndt waited in the old tower latrine until dark. The small German garrison all ate in the kitchen, with one sentry posted in the court-yard. They had found some schnapps in a kitchen cabinet. Berndt came out of the tower latrine, thankful the stone floors did not creak.

He looked into the radio room. The radio was on Madame's dresser, scent bottles pushed off on the floor. Berndt looked at it. He thought about Ernst dead in the kitchen yard and Cook spitting on Grutas with his last breath. Berndt slipped into the room. He felt he should apolo-gize to Madame for the intrusion. He came down the service stairs in his stocking feet car-rying his boots and the two packs of the radio and charger and slipped out a sally port. The ra-dio and hand-cranked generator made a heavy load, more than twenty kilos. Berndt humped it into the woods and hid it. He was sorry he could not take the horse.

Dusk and firelight glowing on the painted tim-bers of the hunting lodge, shining in the dusty eyes of trophy animals as the family gathered around the fireplace. The animal heads were old, patted bald years ago by generations of children reaching through the banister of the upper landing.

Nanny had Mischa's copper bathtub in a corner of the hearth. She added water from a kettle to adjust the temperature, made suds and lowered Mischa into the water. The child batted happily at the foam. Nanny fetched towels to warm before the fire. Hannibal took Mischa's baby bracelet off her wrist, dipped it in the suds and blew bubbles for her through the bracelet. The bubbles, in their brief flight on the draft, reflected all the bright faces before they burst above the fire. Mischa liked to grab for the bubbles, but wanted her bracelet back, and was not satisfied until it was on her arm again.

Hannibal's mother played baroque counterpoint on a small piano.

Tiny music, the windows covered with blankets as night fell and the black wings of the forest closed around them. Berndt arrived exhausted and the music stopped. Tears stood in Count Lecter's eyes as he listened to Berndt. Hannibal's mother took Berndt's hand and patted it.

The Germans began at once to refer to Lithuania as Ostland, a German minor colony, which in time could be resettled with Aryans after the lower Slavic life forms were liquidated. German columns were on the roads, German trains on the railways carrying artillery east.

Russian fighter-bombers bombed and strafed the columns. Big Ilyushin bombers out of Russia pounded the columns through heavy flak from the anti-aircraft guns mounted on the trains.

The black swans flew as high as they could comfortably go, the four black swans in echelon, their necks extended, trying for the south, the roar of airplanes above them as dawn broke.

A burst of flak and the lead swan crumpled in mid-stroke and began the long plunge to earth, the other birds turning, calling down the air, losing altitude in great circles. The wounded swan thumped heavily in an open field and did not move. His mate swooped down beside him, poked him with her beak, waddled around him with urgent honks.

He did not move. A shellburst in the field, and Russian infantry were visible moving in the trees at the edge of the meadow. A German Panzer tank jumped a ditch and came across the meadow, firing its coaxial machine gun into the trees, coming, coming. The swan spread her wings and stood her ground over her mate even though the tank was wider than her wings, its engine loud as her wild heart. The swan stood over her mate hissing, hitting the tank with hard blows of her wings at the last, and the tank rolled over them, oblivious, in its whirring treads a mush of flesh and feathers.

4

THE LECTER FAMILY survived in the woods for the terrible three and a half years of Hitler's eastern campaign. The long forest path to the lodge was filled with snow in winter and overgrown in spring, the marshes too soft in summer for tanks.

The lodge was well stocked with flour and sugar to last through the first winter, but most importantly it had salt in casks. In the second winter they came upon a dead and frozen horse. They were able to cut it up with axes and salt the meat. They salted trout as well, and partridges.

Sometimes men in civilian clothes came out of the forest in the night, quiet as shadows. Count Lecter and Berndt talked with them in Lithuanian, and once they brought a man with blood soaked through his shirt, who died on a pallet in the corner while Nanny was mopping his face.

Every day when the snow was too deep to forage, Mr. Jakov gave lessons. He taught English, and very bad French, he taught Roman history with a heavy emphasis on the sieges of Jerusalem, and everyone attended. He made dramatic tales out of historical events, and Old Testament stories, sometimes embellishing them for his audience beyond the strict bounds of scholarship.

He instructed Hannibal in mathematics privately, as the lessons had reached a level inaccessible to the others.

Among Mr. Jakov's books was a copy bound in leather of Christiaan Huyghens' **Treatise on Light,** and Hannibal was fascinated with it, with following the movement of Huyghens' mind, feeling him moving toward discovery. He associated the **Treatise on Light** with the glare of the snow and the rainbow distortions in the old windowpanes. The elegance of Huyghens' thought was like the clean and simplified lines of winter, the structure under the leaves. A box opening with a click and inside, a principle that works every time. It was a dependable thrill, and he had been feeling it since he could read.

Hannibal Lecter could always read, or it

seemed that way to Nanny. She read to him for a brief period when he was two, often from a Brothers Grimm illustrated with woodcuts where everyone had pointed toenails. He listened to Nanny reading, his head lolling against her while he looked at the words on the page, and then she found him at it by himself, pressing his forehead to the book and then pushing up to focal distance, reading aloud in Nanny's accent.

Hannibal's father had one salient emotion—curiosity. In his curiosity about his son, Count Lecter had the houseman pull down the heavy dictionaries in the castle library. English, German, and the twenty-three volumes of the Lithuanian dictionary, and then Hannibal was on his own with the books.

When he was six, three important things happened to him.

First he discovered Euclid's **Elements,** in an old edition with hand-drawn illustrations. He could follow the illustrations with his finger, and put his forehead against them.

That fall he was presented with a baby sister, Mischa. He thought Mischa looked like a wrinkled red squirrel. He reflected privately that it was a pity she did not get their mother's looks.

Usurped on all fronts, he thought how convenient it would be if the eagle that sometimes soared over the castle should gather his little sister up and gently transport her to some happy peasant home in a country far away, where the residents all looked like squirrels and she would fit right in. At the same time, he found he loved her in a way he could not help, and when she was old enough to wonder, he wanted to show her things, he wanted her to have the feeling of discovery.

Also in the year Hannibal was six, Count Lecter found his son determining the height of the castle towers by the length of their shadows, following instructions which he said came directly from Euclid himself. Count Lecter improved his tutors then—within six weeks arrived Mr. Jakov, a penniless scholar from Leipzig.

Count Lecter introduced Mr. Jakov to his pupil in the library and left them. The library in warm weather had a cold-smoked aroma that was ingrained in the castle's stone.

"My father says you will teach me many things."

"If you wish to learn many things, I can help you."

"He tells me you are a great scholar."

"I am a student."

"He told my mother you were expelled from the university."

"Yes."

"Why?"

"Because I am a Jew, an Ashkenazi Jew to be precise."

"I see. Are you unhappy?"

"To be a Jew? No, I'm glad."

"I meant are you unhappy to be out of school?"

"I am glad to be here."

"Do you wonder if I am worth your time?"

"Every person is worth your time, Hannibal. If at first appearance a person seems dull, then look harder, look **into** him."

"Did they put you in the room with an iron grate over the door?"

"Yes, they did."

"It doesn't lock anymore."

"I was pleased to see that."

"That's where they kept Uncle Elgar," Hannibal said, aligning his pens in a row before him. "It was in the 1880s, before my time. Look at the windowpane in your room. It has a date he scratched with a diamond into the glass. These are his books."

A row of immense leather tomes occupied an entire shelf. The last one was charred.

"The room will have a smoky smell when it rains. The walls were lined with hay bales to muffle his utterances."

"Did you say his utterances?"

"They were about religion, but—do you know the meaning of 'lewd' or 'lewdness'?"

"Yes."

"I'm not clear on it myself, but I believe it means the sort of thing one wouldn't say in front of Mother."

"That's my understanding of it as well," Mr. Jakov said.

"If you'll look at the date on the glass, it's exactly the day direct sunlight reaches his window every year."

"He was waiting for the sun."

"Yes, and that's the day he burned up in there. As soon as he got sunlight, he lit the hay with the monocle he wore as he composed these books."

Hannibal further acquainted his tutor with Lecter Castle with a tour of the grounds. They passed through the courtyard, with its big block of stone. A hitching ring was in the stone and, in its flat top, the scars of an axe.

"Your father said you measured the height of the towers."

"Yes."

"How high are they?"

"Forty meters, the south one, and the other is a half-meter shorter."

"What did you use for a gnomon?"

"The stone. By measuring the stone's height and its shadow, and measuring the shadow of the castle at the same hour."

"The side of the stone is not exactly vertical."

"I used my yo-yo as a plumb."

"Could you take both measurements at once?"

"No, Mr. Jakov."

"How much error might you have from the time between the shadow measurements?"

"A degree every four minutes as the earth turns. It's called the Ravenstone. Nanny calls it the **Rabenstein.** She is forbidden to seat me on it."

"I see," Mr. Jakov said. "It has a longer shadow than I thought."

They fell into a pattern of having discussions while walking and Hannibal, stumping along beside him, watched his tutor adjust to speaking to someone much shorter. Often Mr. Jakov turned his head to the side and spoke into the air above Hannibal, as though he had forgotten he was talking with a child. Hannibal wondered if he missed walking and talking with someone his own age.

Hannibal was interested to see how Mr. Jakov got along with the houseman, Lothar, and

Berndt the hostler. They were bluff men and shrewd enough, good at their jobs. But theirs was a different order of mind. Hannibal saw that Mr. Jakov made no effort to hide his mind, or to show it off, but he never pointed it directly at anyone. In his free time, he was teaching them how to survey with a makeshift transit. Mr. Jakov took his meals with Cook, from whom he extracted a certain amount of rusty Yiddish, to the surprise of the family.

The parts of an ancient catapult used by Hannibal the Grim against the Teutonic Knights were stored in a barn on the property, and on Hannibal's birthday Mr. Jakov, Lothar and Berndt put the catapult together, substituting a stout new timber for the throwing arm. With it they threw a hogshead of water higher than the castle, it falling to burst with a wonderful explosion of water on the far bank of the moat that sent the wading birds flapping away.

In that week, Hannibal had the keenest single pleasure of his childhood. As a birthday treat Mr. Jakov showed him a non-mathematical proof of the Pythagorean theorem using tiles and their impression on a bed of sand. Hannibal looked at it, walked around it. Mr. Jakov lifted one of the tiles and raised his eyebrows, asking if Hannibal wanted to see the proof again. And Hannibal got it. He got it with a rush that felt like he was being launched off the catapult.

Mr. Jakov rarely brought a textbook to their discussions, and rarely referred to one. At the age of eight, Hannibal asked him why.

"Would you like to remember everything?" Mr. Jakov said.

"Yes."

"To remember is not always a blessing."

"I would like to remember everything."

"Then you will need a mind palace, to store things in. A palace in your mind."

"Does it have to be a palace?"

"It will grow to be enormous like a palace," Mr. Jakov said. "So it might as well be beautiful. What is the most beautiful room you know, a place you know very well?"

"My mother's room," Hannibal said.

"Then that's where we will begin," Mr. Jakov said.

Twice Hannibal and Mr. Jakov watched the sun touch Uncle Elgar's window in the spring, but by the third year they were hiding in the woods.

5

Winter, 1944–45

WHEN THE EASTERN FRONT collapsed, the Russian Army rolled like lava across Eastern Europe, leaving behind a landscape of smoke and ashes, peopled by the starving and the dead. From the east and from the south the Russians came, up toward the Baltic Sea from the 3rd and 2nd Belorussian Fronts, driving ahead of them broken and retreating units of the Waffen-SS, desperate to reach the coast where they hoped to be evacuated by boat to Denmark.

It was the end of the Hiwis' ambitions. After they had faithfully killed and pillaged for their Nazi masters, shot Jews and Gypsies, none of them got to be SS. They were called Osttruppen, and were barely considered as soldiers. Thousands were put in slave labor battalions and worked to death.

But a few deserted and went into business for themselves. . . .

A handsome Lithuanian estate house near the Polish border, open like a dollhouse on one side where an artillery shell had blown the wall away. The family, flushed from the basement by the first shellburst and killed by the second, were dead in the ground-floor kitchen. Dead soldiers, German and Russian, lay in the garden. A German staff car was on its side, blown half in two by a shell.

An SS major was propped on a divan in front of the living room fireplace, blood frozen on the legs of his trousers. His sergeant pulled a blanket off a bed and put it over him and got a fire going, but the room was open to the sky. He got the major's boot off and his toes were black. The sergeant heard a noise outside. He unslung his carbine and went to the window.

A half-track ambulance, a Russian-made ZiS-44 but with International Red Cross markings, rumbled up the gravel drive.

Grutas got out of the ambulance first with a white cloth.

"We are Swiss. You have wounded? How many are you?"

The sergeant looked over his shoulder. "Medics, Major. Will you go with them, sir?" The major nodded.

Grutas and Dortlich, a head taller, pulled a stretcher out of the half-track.

The sergeant came out to speak to them. "Easy with him, he's hit in the legs. His toes are frozen. Maybe frostbite gangrene. You have a field hospital?"

"Yes, of course, but I can operate here," Grutas told the sergeant and shot him twice in the chest, dust flying off the uniform. The man's legs collapsed and Grutas stepped over him through the doorway and shot the major through the blanket.

Milko, Kolnas, and Grentz piled out of the back of the half-track. They wore a mix of uniforms—Lithuanian police, Lithuanian medics, Estonian medical corps, International Red Cross—but all wore large medical insignia on their armbands.

There is much bending involved in stripping the dead; the looters grunted and bitched at the effort, scattering papers and wallet photos. The major still lived, and he raised his hand to Milko. Milko took the wounded man's watch and stuffed it into his pocket.

Grutas and Dortlich carried a rolled tapestry out of the house and threw it into their half-track truck.

They put the canvas stretcher on the ground and tossed onto it watches, gold eyeglasses, rings.

A tank came out of the woods, a Russian T-34 in winter camouflage, its cannon traversing the field, the machine gunner standing up in the hatch.

A man hiding in a shed behind the farmhouse broke from cover and ran across the field toward the trees, carrying in his arms an ormolu clock, leaping over bodies.

The tank's machine gun stuttered and the running looter pitched forward, tumbling to fall beside the clock, his face smashed and the clock's face smashed too; his heart and the clock beat once and stopped.

"Grab a body!" Grutas said.

They threw a corpse on top of the loot on the stretcher. The tank's turret turned toward them. Grutas waved a white flag and pointed to the medical insignia on the truck. The tank moved on.

A last look around the house. The major was still alive. He gripped Grutas' pants leg as he passed. He got his arms around Grutas' leg and would not let go. Grutas bent to him, seized the insignia on his collar.

"We were supposed to get these skulls," he said. "Maybe the maggots can find one in your face." He shot the major in the chest. The man let go of Grutas' pants leg and looked at his own bare wrist as though curious about the time of his death.

The half-track truck bounced across the field, its tracks mushing bodies, and as it reached the woods, the canvas lifted on the back and Grentz threw the body out.

From above, a screaming Stuka dive bomber came after the Russian tank, cannon blazing. Under the cover of the forest canopy, buttoned up in the tank, the crew heard a bomb go off in the trees and splinters and shrapnel rang on the armored hull.

6

_____

"DO YOU KNOW what today is?" Hannibal
asked over his breakfast gruel at the lodge. "It's
the day the sun reaches Uncle Elgar's window."

"What time will it appear?" Mr. Jakov asked,
as though he didn't know.

"It will peep around the tower at ten-thirty,"
Hannibal said.

"That was in 1941," Mr. Jakov said. "Do you
mean to say the moment of arrival will be the
same?"

"Yes."

"But the year is more than 365 days long."

"But, Mr. Jakov, this is the year after leap year.
So was 1941, the last time we watched."

"Then does the calendar adjust perfectly, or
do we live by gross corrections?"

A thorn popped in the fire.

"I think those are separate questions," Hannibal said.

Mr. Jakov was pleased, but his response was just another question: "Will the year 2000 be a leap year?"

"No—yes, yes, it will be a leap year."

"But it is divisible by one hundred," Mr. Jakov said.

"It's also divisible by four hundred," Hannibal said.

"Exactly so," Mr. Jakov said. "It will be the first time the Gregorian rule is applied. Perhaps, on that day, surviving all gross corrections, you will remember our talk. In this strange place." He raised his cup. "Next year in Lecter Castle."

Lothar heard it first as he drew water, the roar of an engine in low gear and cracking of branches. He left the bucket on the well and in his haste he came into the lodge without wiping his feet.

A Soviet tank, a T-34 in winter camouflage of snow and straw, crashed up the horse trail and into the clearing. Painted on the turret in Russian were AVENGE OUR SOVIET GIRLS and WIPE OUT THE FASCIST VERMIN. Two soldiers in white rode on the back over the radiators. The turret swiveled to point the tank's cannon at the house. A hatch opened and a gunner in hooded winter white stood behind a machine gun. The tank commander stood in the other hatch with a megaphone. He repeated his message in Russian and in German, barking over the diesel clatter of the tank engine.

"We want water, we will not harm you or take your food unless a shot comes from the house. If we are fired on, every one of you will die. Now come outside. Gunner, lock and load. If you don't see faces by the count of ten, fire." A loud clack as the machine gun's bolt went back.

Count Lecter stepped outside, standing straight in the sunshine, his hands visible. "Take the water. We are no harm to you."

The tank commander put his megaphone aside. "Everyone outside where I can see you."

The count and the tank commander looked at each other for a long moment. The tank commander showed his palms. The count showed his palms.

The count turned to the house. "Come."

When the commander saw the family he said, "The children can stay inside where it's warm." And to his gunner and crew, "Cover them. Watch the upstairs windows. Start the pump. You can smoke."

The machine gunner pushed up his goggles and lit a cigarette. He was no more than a boy, the skin of his face paler around his eyes. He saw Mischa peeping around the door facing and smiled at her.

Among the fuel and water drums lashed to the tank was a small petrol-powered pump with a rope starter.

The tank driver snaked a hose with a screen filter down the well and after many pulls on the rope the pump clattered, squealed, and primed itself.

The noise covered the scream of the Stuka dive bomber until it was almost on them, the tank's gunner swiveling his muzzle around, cranking hard to elevate his gun, firing as the airplane's winking cannon stitched the ground. Rounds screamed off the tank, the gunner hit, still firing with his remaining arm.

The Stuka's windscreen starred with fractures, the pilot's goggles filled with blood and the dive bomber, still carrying one of its eggs, hit tree-tops, plowed into the garden and its fuel exploded, cannon under the wings still firing after the impact.

Hannibal, on the floor of the lodge, Mischa partly under him, saw his mother lying in the yard, bloody and her dress on fire.

"Stay here!" to Mischa and he ran to his mother, ammunition in the airplane cooking off now, slow and then faster, casings flying backward striking the snow, flames licking around the remaining bomb beneath the wing. The pilot sat in the cockpit, dead, his face burned to a death's head in flaming scarf and helmet, his gunner dead behind him.

Lothar alone survived in the yard and he raised a bloody arm to the boy. Then Mischa ran to her mother, out into the yard and Lothar tried to reach her and pull her down as she passed, but a cannon round from the flaming plane slammed through him, blood spattering the baby and Mischa raised her arms and screamed into the sky. Hannibal heaped snow onto the fire in his mother's clothes, stood up and ran to Mischa amid the random shots and carried her into the lodge, into the cellar. The shots outside slowed and stopped as bullets melted in the breeches of the cannon. The sky darkened and snow came again, hissing on the hot metal.

Darkness, and snow again. Hannibal among the corpses, how much later he did not know, snow drifting down to dust his mother's eyelashes and her hair. She was the only corpse not blackened and crisped. Hannibal tugged at her, but her body was frozen to the ground. He pressed his face against her. Her bosom was frozen hard, her heart silent. He put a napkin over her face and piled snow on her. Dark shapes moved at the edge of the woods. His torch reflected on wolves' eyes. He shouted at them and waved a shovel. Mischa was determined to come out to her mother—he had to choose. He took Mischa back inside and left the dead to the dark. Mr. Jakov's book was undamaged beside his blackened hand until a wolf ate the leather cover and amid the scattered pages of Huyghens' **Treatise on Light** licked Mr. Jakov's brains off the snow.

Hannibal and Mischa heard snuffling and growling outside. Hannibal built up the fire. To cover the noise he tried to get Mischa to sing; he sang to her. She clutched his coat in her fists.

"Ein Mannlein . . ."

Snowflakes on the windows. In the corner of a pane, a dark circle appeared, made by the tip of a glove. In the dark circle a pale blue eye.

7

THE DOOR BURST OPEN then and Grutas came in with Milko and Dortlich. Hannibal grabbed a boar spear from the wall and Grutas, with his sure instinct turned his gun on the little girl.

"Drop it or I'll shoot her. Do you understand me?"

The looters swarmed Hannibal and Mischa then.

The looters in the house, Grentz outside waved for the half-track truck to come up, the truck slit-eyed, its blackout lights picking up wolves' eyes at the edge of the clearing, a wolf dragging something.

The men gathered around Hannibal and his sister at the fire, the fire warming from the looters' clothes a sweetish stink of weeks in the field and old blood caked in the treads of their boots, they gathered close. Pot Watcher caught a small insect emerging from his clothes and popped its head off with his thumbnail.

They coughed on the children. Predator breath, ketosis from their scavenged diet of mostly meat, some scraped from the half-track's treads, made Mischa bury her face in Hannibal's coat. He gathered her inside his coat and felt her heart beating hard. Dortlich picked up Mischa's bowl of porridge and wolfed it down himself, getting the last wipe from the bowl on his scarred and webbed fingers. Kolnas extended his bowl, but Dortlich did not give him any.

Kolnas was stocky and his eyes took on a shine when he looked at precious metal. He slipped Mischa's bracelet off her wrist and put it in his pocket. When Hannibal grabbed at his hand, Grentz pinched him on the side of the neck and his whole arm went numb.

Distant artillery boomed.

Grutas said, "If a patrol comes—either side— we're setting up a field hospital here. We saved these little ones and we're protecting their family's stuff in the truck. Get a Red Cross off the truck and hang it over the door. Do it now."

"The other two will freeze if you leave them in the truck," Pot Watcher said. "They got us by the patrol, they may be useful again."

"Put them in the bunkhouse," Grutas said. "Lock them in."

"Where would they go?" Grentz said. "Who would they tell?"

"They can tell you about their sad fucking lives, in Albanian, Grentz. Get your ass out there and do it."

In the blowing snow, Grentz lifted two small figures out of the truck and prodded them toward the barn bunkhouse.

8

GRUTAS HAD A SLENDER chain, freezing against the children's skin as he looped it around their necks. Kolnas snapped on the heavy padlocks. Grutas and Dortlich chained Hannibal and Mischa to the banister on the upper landing of the staircase, where they were out of the way but visible. The one called Pot Watcher brought them a chamber pot and blanket from a bedroom.

Through the bars of the banister, Hannibal watched them throw the piano stool onto the fire. He tucked Mischa's collar underneath the chain to keep it off her neck.

The snow banked high against the lodge, only the upper panes of the windows admitted a grey light. With the snow blowing sideways past the windows and the wind squeal, the lodge was

like a great train moving. Hannibal rolled himself and his sister in the blanket and the landing
carpet. Mischa's coughs were muffled. Her forehead was hot against Hannibal's cheek. From
beneath his coat, he took a crust of stale bread
and put it in his mouth. When it was soft, he
gave it to her.

Grutas drove one of his men outside every few
hours to shovel the doorway, keeping a path to
the well. And once Pot Watcher took a pan of
scraps to the barn.

Snowed in, the time passing in a slow ache.
There was no food, and then there was food,
Kolnas and Milko carrying Mischa's bathtub to
the stove lidded with a plank, which scorched
where it overhung the tub, Pot Watcher feeding
the fire with books and wooden salad bowls.
With one eye on the stove, Pot Watcher caught
up on his journal and accounts. He piled small
items of loot on the table for sorting and counting. In a spidery hand he wrote each man's
name at the top of a page:

Vladis Grutas
Zigmas Milko
Bronys Grentz
Enrikas Dortlich
Petras Kolnas

And last he wrote his own name, **Kazys Porvik.**

Beneath the names he listed each man's share of the loot—gold eyeglasses, watches, rings and earrings, and gold teeth, which he measured in a stolen silver cup.

Grutas and Grentz searched the lodge obsessively, snatching out drawers, tearing the backs off bureaus.

After five days the weather cleared. They all put on snowshoes and walked Hannibal and Mischa out to the barn. Hannibal saw a wisp of smoke from the bunkhouse chimney. He looked at Cesar's big horseshoe nailed above the door for luck and wondered if the horse was still alive. Grutas and Dortlich shoved the children into the barn and locked the door. Through the crack between the double doors, Hannibal watched them fan out into the woods. It was very cold in the barn. Pieces of children's clothing lay wadded in the straw. The door into the bunkhouse was closed but not locked. Hannibal pushed it open. Wrapped in all the blankets off the cots and as close as possible to the small stove was a boy not more than eight years old. His face was dark around his sunken eyes. He wore a mixture of clothing, layer on layer, some of it girl's garments. Hannibal put Mischa behind him. The boy shrank away from him.

Hannibal said "Hello." He said it in Lithuanian, German, English and Polish. The boy did not reply. Red and swollen chilblains were on his ears and fingers. Over the course of the long cold day he managed to convey that he was from Albania and only spoke that language. He said his name was Agon. Hannibal let him feel his pockets for food. He did not let him touch Mischa. When Hannibal indicated he and his sister wanted half the blankets the boy did not resist. The young Albanian started at every sound, his eyes rolling toward the door, and he made chopping motions with his hand.

The looters came back just before sunset. Hannibal heard them and peered through the crack in the double doors of the barn.

They were leading a half-starved little deer, alive and stumbling, a tasseled swag from some looted mansion looped around its neck, an arrow sticking in its side. Milko picked up an axe.

"Don't waste the blood," Pot Watcher said with a cook's authority.

Kolnas came running with his bowl, his eyes shining. A cry from the yard and Hannibal covered Mischa's ears against the sound of the axe. The Albanian boy cried and gave thanks.

Late in the day when the others had eaten, Pot Watcher gave the children a bone to gnaw with a little meat and sinew on it. Hannibal ate a little and chewed up mush for Mischa. The juice got away when he transferred it with his fingers, so he gave it to her mouth to mouth. They moved Hannibal and Mischa back into the lodge and chained them to the balcony railing, and left the Albanian boy in the barn alone. Mischa was hot with fever, and Hannibal held her tight under the cold-dust smell of the rug.

The flu dropped them all; the men lay as close to the dying fire as they could get, coughing on one another, Milko finding Kolnas' comb and sucking the grease from it. The skull of the little deer lay in the dry bathtub, every scrap boiled off it.

Then there was meat again and the men ate with grunting sounds, not looking at one another. Pot Watcher gave gristle and broth to Hannibal and Mischa. He carried nothing to the barn.

The weather would not break, the sky low and granite grey, sounds of the woods hushed except for the crack and crash of ice-laden boughs.

The food was gone days before the sky cleared. The coughing seemed louder in the bright afternoon after the wind dropped. Grutas and Milko staggered out on snowshoes.

After the length of a fever dream, Hannibal heard them return. A loud argument and scuffling. Through the bars of the banister he saw

Grutas licking a bloody birdskin, throwing it to the others, and they fell on it like dogs. Grutas' face was smeared with blood and feathers. He turned his bloody face up to the children and he said, "We have to eat or die."

That was the last conscious memory Hannibal Lecter had of the lodge.

Because of the Russian rubber shortage the tank was running on steel road wheels that sent a numbing vibration through the hull and blurred the view in the periscope. It was a big KV-1 going hard along a forest trail in freezing weather, the front moving miles westward with every day of the German retreat. Two infantrymen in winter camouflage rode on the rear deck of the tank, huddled over the radiators, watching for the odd German Werewolf, a fanatic left behind with a Panzerfaust rocket to try to destroy a tank. They saw movement in the brush. The tank commander heard the soldiers on top firing, turned the tank toward their target to bring his coaxial machine gun to bear. His magnifying eyepiece showed a boy, a child coming out of the brush, bullets kicking up the snow beside him as the soldiers shot from the moving tank. The commander stood up in the hatch and stopped the shooting. They had killed a few children by mistake, the way it happens, and were glad enough not to kill this one.

The soldiers saw a child, thin and pale, with a chain locked around his neck, the end of the chain dragging in an empty loop. When they set him near the radiators and cut the chain off him, pieces of his skin came away on the links. He carried good binoculars in a bag clutched fiercely against his chest. They shook him, asking questions in Russian, Polish, and makeshift Lithuanian, until they realized he could not speak at all.

The soldiers shamed each other into not taking the field glasses from the boy. They gave him half an apple and let him ride behind the turret in the warm breath of the radiators until they reached a village.

9

A SOVIET MOTORIZED unit with a tank destroyer and heavy rocket launcher had sheltered at the abandoned Lecter Castle overnight. They were moving before dawn, leaving melted places in the snow of the courtyard with dark oil stains in them. One light truck remained at the castle entrance, the motor idling.

Grutas and his four surviving companions, in their medical uniforms, watched from the woods. It had been four years since Grutas shot the cook in the castle courtyard, fourteen hours since the looters fled the burning hunting lodge, leaving their dead behind them.

Bombs thudded far away and on the horizon anti-aircraft tracers arched into the sky.

The last soldier backed out the door, paying out fuse from a reel.

"Hell," Milko said. "It's about to rain rocks big as boxcars."

"We're going in there anyway," Grutas said.

The soldier unreeled fuse to the bottom of the steps, cut it and squatted at the end.

"The dump's been looted anyway," Grentz said. **"C'est foutu."**

"Tu débandes?" Dortlich said.

"Va te faire enculer," Grentz said. They had picked up the French when the Totenkopfs re-fitted near Marseilles, and liked to insult each other with it in the tight moments before action. The curses reminded them of pleasant times in France.

The Soviet trooper on the steps split the fuse ten centimeters from the end and stuck a match head in the split.

"What color's the fuse?" Milko said.

Grutas had the field glasses. "Dark, I can't tell."

From the woods, they could see the flare of a second match on his face as the trooper lit the fuse.

"Is it orange or is it green?" Milko said. "Does it have stripes on it?"

Grutas did not answer. The soldier walked to the truck, taking his time, laughing as his companions on the truck yelled at him to hurry, the fuse sparking behind him on the snow.

Milko was counting under his breath.

As soon as the vehicle was out of sight, Grutas and Milko ran for the fuse. The fire in the fuse crossing the threshold now as they reached it. They could not make out the stripes until they were close. **Burns at twominutesameter twominutesameter twominutesameter.** Grutas slashed it in two with his spring knife.

Milko muttered **"fuck the farm"** and charged up the steps and into the castle, following the fuse, looking, looking, for other fuses, other charges. He crossed the great hall toward the tower, following the fuse and saw what he was looking for, the fuse spliced onto a big loop of detonating cord. He came back into the great hall and called out, "It's got a ring main cord. That's the only fuse. You got it." Breeching charges were packed around the base of the tower to destroy it, coordinated by the single loop of detonating cord.

The Soviet troops had not bothered to close the front door, and their fire still burned on the hearth in the great hall. Graffiti scarred the bare walls and the floor near the fire was littered with droppings and bumwad from their final act in the relative warmth of the castle.

Milko, Grentz and Kolnas searched the upper floors.

Grutas motioned for Dortlich to follow him

and descended the stairs to the dungeon. The grate across the wine room door hung open, the lock broken.

Grutas and Dortlich shared one flashlight between them. The yellow beam gleamed off glass shards. The wine room was littered with empty bottles of fine vintages, the necks knocked off by hasty drinkers. The tasting table, knocked over by contesting looters, lay against the back wall.

"Balls," Dortlich said. "Not a swig left."

"Help me," Grutas said. Together they pulled the table away from the wall, crunching glass underfoot. They found the decanting candle behind the table and lit it.

"Now, pull on the chandelier," Grutas told the taller Dortlich. "Just give it a tug, straight down."

The wine rack swung away from the back wall. Dortlich reached for his pistol when it moved. Grutas went into the chamber behind the wine room. Dortlich followed him.

"God in Heaven!" Dortlich said.

"Get the truck," Grutas said.

10

Lithuania, 1946

HANNIBAL LECTER, thirteen, stood alone on the rubble beneath the moat's embankment at the former Lecter Castle and threw crusts of bread onto the black water. The kitchen garden, its bounding hedges overgrown, was now the People's Orphanage Cooperative Kitchen Garden, featuring mostly turnips. The moat and its surface were important to him. The moat was constant; on its black surface reflected clouds swept past the crenellated towers of Lecter Castle just as they always had.

Over his orphanage uniform Hannibal now wore the penalty shirt with the painted words NO GAMES. Forbidden to play in the orphans' soccer game on the field outside the walls, he did not feel deprived. The soccer game was interrupted when the draft horse Cesar and his Russian driver crossed the field with a load of firewood on the wagon. Cesar was glad to see Hannibal when he could visit the stable, but he did not care for turnips.

Hannibal watched the swans coming across the moat, a pair of black swans that survived the war. Two cygnets accompanied them, still fluffy, one riding on his mother's back, one swimming behind. Three older boys on the embankment above parted a hedge to watch Hannibal and the swans.

The male swan climbed out onto the bank to challenge Hannibal.

A blond boy named Fedor whispered to the others. "Watch that black bastard flap the dummy—he'll knock shit out of him like he did you when you tried to get the eggs. We'll see if the dummy can cry." Hannibal raised his willow branches and the swan went back into the water.

Disappointed, Fedor took a slingshot of red inner-tube rubber out of his shirt and reached into his pocket for a stone. The stone hit the mud at the edge of the moat, spattering Hannibal's legs with mud. Hannibal looked up at Fedor expressionless and shook his head. The next stone Fedor shot splashed into the water beside the swimming cygnet, Hannibal raising his branches now, hissing, shooing the swans out of range.

A bell sounded from the castle.

Fedor and his followers turned, laughing from their fun, and Hannibal stepped out of the hedge swinging a yard of weeds with a big dirt ball on the roots. The dirt ball caught Fedor hard in the face and Hannibal, a head shorter, charged and shoved him down the steep embankment to the water, scrambling after the stunned boy and had him in the black water, holding him under, driving the slingshot handle again and again into the back of his neck, Hannibal's face curiously blank, only his eyes alive, the edges of his vision red. Hannibal heaved to turn Fedor over to get to his face. Fedor's companions scrambled down, did not want to fight in the water, yelling to a monitor for help. First Monitor Petrov led the others cursing down the bank, spoiled his shiny boots and got mud on his flailing truncheon.

Evening in the great hall of Lecter Castle, stripped now of its finery and dominated by a big portrait of Joseph Stalin. A hundred boys in uniform, having finished their supper, stood in place at plank tables singing "The Internationale." Headmaster, slightly drunk, directed the singing with his fork.

First Monitor Petrov, newly appointed, and Second Monitor in jodhpurs and boots walked among the tables to be sure everyone was singing. Hannibal was not singing. The side of his face was blue and one of his eyes was half-closed. At another table Fedor watched, a bandage on his neck and scrapes on his face. One of his fingers was splinted.

The monitors stopped before Hannibal. Hannibal palmed a fork.

"Too good to sing with us, Little Master?" First Monitor Petrov said over the singing. "You're not Little Master here anymore, you're just another orphan, and by God you'll sing!"

First Monitor swung his clipboard hard against the side of Hannibal's face. Hannibal did not change his expression. Neither did he sing. A trickle of blood came from the corner of his mouth.

"He's mute," Second Monitor said. "No sense in beating him."

The song ended and First Monitor's voice was loud in the silence.

"For a mute, he can scream well enough at night," First Monitor said, and swung with his other hand. Hannibal blocked the blow with the fork in his fist, the tines digging into

First Monitor's knuckles. First Monitor started around the table after him.

"Stop! Do not hit him again. I don't want him marked." Headmaster might be drunk, but he ruled. "Hannibal Lecter, report to my office."

Headmaster's office contained an army surplus desk and files and two cots. It was here that the change in the castle's smell struck Hannibal most. Instead of lemon-oil furniture polish and perfume there was the cold stink of piss in the fireplace. The windows were bare, the only remaining ornament the carved woodwork.

"Hannibal, was this your mother's room? It has a sort of feminine feeling." Headmaster was capricious. He could be kind, or cruel when his failures goaded him. His little eyes were red and he was waiting for an answer.

Hannibal nodded.

"It must be hard for you to live in this house."

No response.

Headmaster took a cable from his desk. "Well, you won't be here much longer. Your uncle is coming to take you to France."

11

THE FIRE ON THE kitchen hearth gave the only light. Hannibal in shadow watched the cook's assistant asleep and drooling in a chair near the fire, an empty glass beside him. Hannibal wanted the lantern on the shelf just behind him. He could see the glass mantle gleam in the firelight.

The man's breathing was deep and regular with a rumble of catarrh. Hannibal moved across the stone floor, into the vodka-and-onion aura of the cook's assistant, and came close behind him.

The wire handle of the lantern would creak. Better to lift it by the base and the top, holding the glass mantle steady so that it would not rattle. Lift it straight up and off the shelf. He had it now in both hands.

A loud pop, as a piece of firewood, hissing steam, burst in the fireplace, sending sparks and small coals skipping across the hearth, a coal coming to rest an inch from the assistant cook's foot in its felt boot liner.

What tool was close? On the countertop was a canister, a 150-mm shell casing full of wooden spoons and spatulas. Hannibal set the lantern down and, with a spoon, flipped the coal to the center of the floor.

The door to the dungeon stairs was in the corner of the kitchen. It swung open quietly at Hannibal's touch, and he went through it into absolute darkness, remembering the upper landing in his mind, and closed the door behind him. He struck a match on the stone wall, lit the lantern and went down the familiar stairs, the air cooling as he descended. The lantern light jumped from vault to vault as he passed through low arches to the wine room. The iron gate stood open.

The wine, long ago looted, had been replaced on the shelves with root vegetables, primarily turnips. Hannibal reminded himself to put a few sugar beets in his pocket—as Cesar would eat them in the absence of apples, though they turned his lips red, and gave him the appearance of wearing lipstick.

In his time in the orphanage, seeing his house violated, everything stolen, confiscated, abused, he had not looked here. Hannibal put the lantern on a high shelf and dragged some sacks of potatoes and onions from in front of the rear wine shelves. He climbed onto the table, gripped the chandelier and pulled. Nothing. He released the chandelier and tugged it again. Now he swung from it with his full weight. The chandelier dropped an inch with a jar that made the dust fly off it, and he heard a groan from the rear wine shelves. He scrambled down. He could get his fingers in the gap and pull.

The wine shelves came away from the wall with a considerable squeal of hinges. He went back to his lantern, ready to blow it out if he heard a sound. Nothing.

It was here, in this room, that he had last seen Cook, and for a moment Cook's great round face appeared to him in vital clarity, without the scrim time gives our images of the dead.

Hannibal took his lantern and went into the hidden room behind the wine room. It was empty.

One large gilt picture frame remained, threads of canvas sticking out of it where the painting had been cut out of the frame. It had been the largest picture in the house, a romanticized view of the Battle of Žalgiris emphasizing the achievements of Hannibal the Grim.

Hannibal Lecter, last of his line, stood in the looted castle of his childhood looking into the empty picture frame in the knowledge that he was of his line and not of his line. His memories were of his mother, a Sforza, and of Cook and Mr. Jakov from a tradition other than his own. He could see them in the empty frame, gathered before the fire at the lodge.

He was not Hannibal the Grim in any way he understood. He would conduct his life beneath the painted ceiling of his childhood. But it was as thin as Heaven, and nearly as useless. So he believed.

They were all gone, the paintings with faces that were as familiar to him as his family.

There was an oubliette in the center of the room, a dry stone well into which Hannibal the Grim could cast his enemies and forget them. It had been fenced round in later years to prevent accidents. Hannibal held his lantern over it and the light gave out halfway down the shaft. His father had told him that in his own childhood a jumble of skeletons remained at the bottom of the oubliette.

Once as a treat, Hannibal had been lowered

into the oubliette in a basket. Near the bottom, a word was scratched into the wall. He could not see it now by lantern light, but he knew it was there, uneven letters scratched in the dark by a dying man—the word **"Pourquoi?"**

12

IN THE LONG dormitory the orphans were sleeping. They were in the order of their age. The youngest end of the dormitory had the brooder-house smell of a kindergarten. The youngest hugged themselves in sleep and some called out to their remembered dead, seeing in the dreamed faces a concern and tenderness they would not find again.

Further along some older boys masturbated under their covers.

Each child had a footlocker and on the wall above each bed was a space to put drawings or, rarely, a family photograph.

Here is a row of crude crayon drawings above the successive beds. Above Hannibal Lecter's bed is an excellent chalk and pencil drawing of a baby's hand and arm, arresting and appealing in its gesture, the plump arm foreshortened as the baby reaches to pat. There is a bracelet on the arm. Beneath the drawing, Hannibal sleeps, his eyelids twitching. His jaw muscles bunch and his nostrils flare and pinch at a dreamed whiff of cadaverine breath.

The hunting lodge in the forest. Hannibal and Mischa in the cold-dust smell of the rug rolled around them, ice on the windows refracting the light green and red. The wind gusts and for a moment the chimney does not draw. Blue smoke hangs in tiers under the peaked roof, in front of the balcony railing, and Hannibal hears the front door blast open and looks through the railing. Mischa's bathtub is on the stove where the Cooker boils the little deer's horned skull with some shriveled tubers. The roiling water bangs the horns against the metal walls of the tub as though the little deer is making a last effort to butt. Blue-Eyes and Web-Hand come in with a blast of cold air, knocking off their snowshoes and leaning them against the wall. The others crowd them, Bowl-Man stumping from the corner on frostbitten feet. Blue-Eyes

takes from his pocket the starved bodies of three small birds. He puts a bird, feathers and all, into the water until it is soft enough to rip off the skin. He licks the bloody bird-skin, blood and feathers on his face, the men crowding around him. He flings the skin to them and they fall on it like dogs.

He turns his blood-smeared face to the balcony, spits out a feather and speaks. "We have to eat or die."

They put into the fire the Lecter family album and Mischa's paper toys, her castle, her paper dolls. Hannibal is standing on the hearth now, suddenly, no sense of descending, and then they are in the barn, where clothing was wadded in the straw, child's clothing strange to him and stiff with blood. The men crowded close, feeling his meat and Mischa's.

"Take her, she's going to die anyway. Come and play, come and play."

Singing now, they take her. "Ein Mannlein steht im Walde ganz still und stumm . . ."

He hangs on to Mischa's arm, the children dragged toward the door. He will not release his sister and Blue-Eyes slams the heavy barn door on his arm, the bone cracking, opens the door again and comes back to Hannibal

swinging a stick of firewood, thud against his head, terrific blows falling on him, flashes of light behind his eyes, banging, Mischa calling "Anniba!"

And the blows became First Monitor's stick banging on the bed frame and Hannibal screaming in his sleep, "Mischa! Mischa."

"Shut up! Shut up! Get up you little fuck!" First Monitor ripped the bedclothing off the cot and threw it at him. Outside on the cold ground to the toolshed, prodded with the stick. First Monitor followed him into the shed with a shove. The shed was hung with gardening tools, rope, a few carpenter's tools. First Monitor set his lantern on a keg and raised his stick. He held up his bandaged hand.

"Time to pay for this."

Hannibal seemed to cringe away, circling away from the light, feeling nothing he could name. First Monitor read fear and circled after him, drawn away from the light. First Monitor got a good crack on Hannibal's thigh. The boy was at the lantern now. Hannibal picked up a sickle and blew out the light. He lay down on the floor in the darkness, gripping the sickle in both hands above his head, heard scrambling footfalls past him, swung the sickle hard through the black air, struck nothing, and heard the door close and the rattle of a chain.

"The advantage of beating a mute is he can't tell on you," First Monitor said. He and Second Monitor were looking at a Delahaye parked in the gravel courtyard of the castle, a lovely example of French coachwork, horizon blue, with diplomatic flags on its front fenders, Soviet and GDR. The car was exotic in the way of pre-war French cars, voluptuous to eyes accustomed to square tanks and jeeps. First Monitor wanted to scratch "fuck" in the side of the car with his knife, but the driver was big and watchful.

From the stable Hannibal saw the car arrive. He did not run to it. He watched his uncle go into the castle with a Soviet officer.

Hannibal put his hand flat against Cesar's cheek. The long face turned to him, crunching oats. The Soviet groom was taking good care of him. Hannibal rubbed the horse's neck and put his face close to the turning ear, but no sound came out of his mouth. He kissed the horse between the eyes. At the back of the hayloft, hanging in the space between double walls, were his father's binoculars. He hung them around his neck and crossed the beaten parade ground.

Second Monitor was looking for him from the steps. Hannibal's few possessions were stuffed in a bag.

13

WATCHING FROM HEADMASTER'S window, Robert Lecter saw his driver buy a small sausage and a piece of bread from the cook for a pack of cigarettes. Robert Lecter was actually Count Lecter now, with his brother presumed dead. He was already accustomed to the title, having used it illegitimately for years.

Headmaster did not count the money, but shoved it into a breast pocket, with a glance at Colonel Timka.

"Count, eh, Comrade Lecter, I just want to tell you I saw two of your paintings at the Catherine Palace before the war, and there were some photos published in **Gorn.** I admire your work enormously."

Count Lecter nodded. "Thank you, Headmaster. Hannibal's sister, what do you know?"

"A baby picture is not much help," Headmaster said.

"We're circulating it to the orphanages," Colonel Timka said. He wore the uniform of the Soviet Border Police and his steel-rimmed spectacles winked in concert with his steel dentition. "It takes time. There are so many."

"And I must tell you, Comrade Lecter, the forest is full of . . . remains still unidentified," Headmaster added.

"Hannibal has never said a word?" Count Lecter said.

"Not to me. Physically he is capable of speech—he screams his sister's name in his sleep. Mischa. Mischa." Headmaster paused as he thought how to put it. "Comrade Lecter, I would be . . . careful with Hannibal until you know him better. It might be best if he did not play with other boys until he's settled. Someone always gets hurt."

"He's not a bully?"

"It's the bullies who get injured. Hannibal does not observe the pecking order. They're always bigger and he hurts them very quickly and sometimes severely. Hannibal can be dangerous to persons larger than himself. He's fine with the little ones. Lets them tease him a little. Some of them think he's deaf as well as mute and say in front of him that he's crazy. He gives them his treats, on the rare occasions there are any treats."

Colonel Timka looked at his watch. "We need to go. Shall I meet you in the car, Comrade Lecter?"

Colonel Timka waited until Count Lecter was out of the room. He held out his hand. Headmaster sighed and handed over the money.

With a wink of his spectacles and a flash of his teeth, Colonel Timka licked his thumb and began to count.

14

A SHOWER OF RAIN settled the dust as they covered the last miles to the chateau, wet gravel pinging underneath the muddy Delahaye, and the smell of herbs and turned earth blew through the car. Then the rain stopped and the evening light had an orange cast.

The chateau was more graceful than grand in this strange orange light. The mullions in its many windows were curved like spiderwebs weighted with dew. To Hannibal, casting for omens, the curving loggia of the chateau unwound from the entrance like Huyghens' volute.

Four draft horses, steaming after the rain, were hitched to a defunct German tank protruding from the foyer. Big horses like Cesar. Hannibal was glad to see them, hoped they were his totem. The tank was jacked up on rollers. Little by little the horses pulled it out of the entryway as though they were extracting a tooth, the driver leading the horses, their ears moving when he spoke to them.

"The Germans blew out the doorway with their cannon and backed the tank inside to get away from the airplanes," the count told Hannibal as the car came to a stop. He had become accustomed to speaking to the boy without a reply. "They left it here in the retreat. We couldn't move it, so we decorated the damned thing with window boxes and walked around it for five years. Now I can sell my 'subversive' pictures again and we can pay to get it hauled away. Come, Hannibal."

A houseman had watched for the car and he and the housekeeper came to meet the count with umbrellas if they should need them. A mastiff came with them.

Hannibal liked his uncle for making the introductions in the driveway, courteously facing the staff, instead of rushing toward the house and talking over his shoulder.

"This is my nephew, Hannibal. He's ours now and we're glad to have him. Madame Brigitte, my housekeeper. And Pascal, who's in charge of making things work."

Madame Brigitte was once a good-looking

upstairs maid. She was a quick study and she read Hannibal by his bearing.

The mastiff greeted the count with enthusiasm and reserved judgment on Hannibal. The dog blew some air out of her cheeks. Hannibal opened his hand to her and, sniffing, she looked up at him from under her brows.

"We'll need to find him some clothes," the count told Madame Brigitte. "Look in my old school trunks in the attic to start and we'll improve him as we go along."

"And the little girl, sir?"

"Not yet, Brigitte," he said, and closed the subject with a shake of his head.

Images as Hannibal approached the house: gleam of the wet cobblestones in the courtyard, the gloss of the horses' coats after the shower, gloss of a handsome crow drinking from the rainspout at the corner of the roof; the movement of a curtain in a high window: the gloss of Lady Murasaki's hair, then her silhouette.

Lady Murasaki opened the casement. The evening light touched her face and Hannibal, out of the wastes of nightmare, took his first step on the bridge of dreams . . .

To move from barracks into a private home is sweet relief. The furniture throughout the chateau was odd and welcoming, a mix of periods retrieved from the attic by Count Lecter and Lady Murasaki after the looting Nazis were driven out. During the occupation, all the major furniture left France for Germany on a train.

Hermann Goering and the Führer himself had long coveted the work of Robert Lecter and other major artists in France. After the Nazi takeover, one of Goering's first acts was to arrest Robert Lecter as a "subversive Slavic artist," and seize as many of the "decadent" paintings as he could find in order to "protect the public" from them. The paintings were sequestered in Goering's and Hitler's private collections.

When the count was freed from prison by the advancing Allies, he and Lady Murasaki put things back as well as they could and the staff worked for subsistence until Count Lecter was back at his easel.

Robert Lecter saw his nephew settled in his room. Generous in size and light, the bedroom had been prepared for Hannibal with hangings and posters to enliven the stone. A kendo mask and crossed bamboo swords were mounted high on the wall. Had he been speaking, Hannibal would have asked after Madame.

15

HANNIBAL WAS LEFT alone for less than a minute before he heard a knock at the door.

Lady Murasaki's attendant, Chiyoh, stood there, a Japanese girl of about Hannibal's age, with hair bobbed at her ears. Chiyoh appraised him for an instant, then a veil slid across her eyes like the nictitating goggles of a hawk.

"Lady Murasaki sends greetings and welcome," she said. "If you will come with me . . ." Dutiful and severe, Chiyoh led him to the bathhouse in the former wine-pressing room in a dependency of the chateau.

To please his wife, Count Lecter had converted the winepress into a Japanese bath, the pressing vat now filled with water heated by a Rube Goldberg water heater fashioned from a copper cognac distillery. The room smelled of wood smoke and rosemary. Silver candelabra, buried in the garden during the war, were set about the vat. Chiyoh did not light the candles. An electric bulb would do for Hannibal until his position was clarified.

Chiyoh handed him towels and a robe and pointed to a shower in the corner. "Bathe there first, scrub vigorously before submerging yourself," she said. "Chef will have an omelet for you after your bath, and then you must rest." She gave him a grimace that might have been a smile, threw an orange into the bathwater and waited outside the bathhouse for his clothing. When he handed it out the door, she took the items gingerly between two fingers, draped them over a stick in her other hand and disappeared with them.

It was evening when Hannibal came awake all at once, the way he woke in barracks. Only his eyes moved until he saw where he was. He felt clean in his clean bed. Through the casement glowed the last of the long French twilight. A cotton kimono was on the chair beside him. He put it on. The stone floor of the corridor was pleasantly cool underfoot, the stone stairs worn hollow like those of Lecter Castle. Outside, under the violet sky, he could hear noises from the kitchen, preparations for dinner.

The mastiff saw him and thumped her tail twice without getting up.

From the bathhouse came the sound of a Japanese lute. Hannibal went to the music. A dusty window glowed with candlelight from within. Hannibal looked in. Chiyoh sat beside the bath plucking the strings of a long and elegant koto. She had lit the candles this time. The water heater chuckled. The fire beneath it crackled and the sparks flew upward. Lady Murasaki was in the water. In the water was Lady Murasaki, like the water flowers on the moat where the swans swam and did not sing. Hannibal watched, silent as the swans, and spread his arms like wings.

He backed from the window and returned through the gloaming to his room, a curious heaviness on him, and found his bed again.

Enough coals remain in the master bedroom to glow on the ceiling. Count Lecter, in the semi-darkness, quickens to Lady Murasaki's touch and to her voice.

"Missing you, I felt as I did when you were in prison," she said. "I remembered the poem of an ancestor, Ono no Komachi, from a thousand years ago."

"Ummm."

"She was very passionate."

"I'm anxious to know what she said."

"A poem: **Hito ni awan tsuki no naki yo wa/omoiokite/mune hashiribi ni/kokoro yaki ori.** Can you hear the music in it?"

Robert Lecter's Western ear could not hear the music in it but, knowing where the music lay, he was enthusiastic: "Oh my, yes. Tell me the meaning."

"No way to see him/on this moonless night/I lie awake longing, burning/breasts racing fire, heart in flames."

"My God, Sheba."

She took exquisite care to spare him exertion.

In the hall of the chateau, the tall clock tells the lateness of the hour, soft bongs down the stone corridors. The mastiff bitch in her kennel stirs, and with thirteen short howls she makes her answer to the clock. Hannibal in his own clean bed turns over in his sleep. And dreams.

In the barn, the air is cold, the children's clothes are pulled down to their waists as

Blue-Eyes and Web-Hand feel the flesh of their upper arms. The others behind them nicker and mill like hyenas who have to wait. Here is the one who always proffers his bowl. Mischa is coughing and hot, turning her face from their breath. Blue-Eyes grips the chains around their necks. Blood and feathers from a birdskin he gnawed are stuck to Blue-Eyes' face.

Bowl-Man's distorted voice: "Take her, she's going to dieee anyway. He'll stay freeeeeesh a little longer."

Blue-Eyes to Mischa, a ghastly cozening, "Come and play, come and play!"

Blue-Eyes starts to sing and Web-Hand joins in:

Ein Mannlein steht im Walde ganz still und
    stumm,
Es hat von lauter Purpur ein Mantlein um

Bowl-Man brings his bowl. Web-Hand picks up the axe, Blue-Eyes seizing Mischa and Hannibal screaming flies at him, gets his teeth into Blue-Eyes' cheek, Mischa suspended in the air by her arms, twisting to look back at him.

"Mischa, Mischa!"

The cries ringing down the stone corridors and Count Lecter and Lady Murasaki burst into Hannibal's room. He has ripped the pillow with his teeth and feathers are flying, Hannibal growls and screams, thrashing, fighting, gritting his teeth. Count Lecter puts his weight on him and confines the boy's arms in the blanket, gets his knees on the blanket. "Easy, easy."

Fearing for Hannibal's tongue, Lady Murasaki whips off the belt of her robe, holds his nose until he has to gasp, and gets the belt between his teeth.

He shivers and is still, like a bird dies. Her robe has come open and she holds him against her, holds between her breasts his face wet with tears of rage, feathers stuck to his cheeks.

But it is the count she asks, "Are you all right?"

16

HANNIBAL ROSE EARLY and washed his face at the bowl and pitcher on his nightstand. A little feather floated on the water. He had only a vague and jumbled memory of the night.

Behind him he heard paper sliding over the stone floor, an envelope pushed under his door. A sprig of pussy willow was attached to the note. Hannibal held the note card to his face in his cupped hands before he read it.

Hannibal,

I will be most pleased if you call on me in my drawing room at the Hour of the Goat. (That is 10 a.m. in France.)

Murasaki Shikibu

Hannibal Lecter, thirteen, his hair slicked down with water, stood outside the closed door of the drawing room. He heard the lute. It was not the same song he had heard from the bath. He knocked.

"Come."

He entered a combination workroom and salon, with a frame for needlework near the window and an easel for calligraphy.

Lady Murasaki was seated at a low tea table. Her hair was up, held by ebony hairpins. The sleeves of her kimono whispered as she arranged flowers.

Good manners from every culture mesh, having a common aim. Lady Murasaki acknowledged him with a slow and graceful inclination of her head.

Hannibal inclined from the waist as his father had taught him. He saw a skein of blue incense smoke cross the window like a distant flight of birds, and the blue vein faint in Lady Murasaki's forearm as she held a flower, the sun pink through her ear. Chiyoh's lute sounded softly from behind a screen.

Lady Murasaki invited him to sit opposite her. Her voice was a pleasant alto with a few random notes not found in the Western scale. To Hannibal, her speech sounded like accidental music in a wind chime.

"If you do not want French or English or Italian, we could use some Japanese words, like **kieuseru.** It means 'disappear.'" She placed a stem, raised her eyes from the flowers and looked into him. "My world of Hiroshima was gone in a flash. Your world was torn from you too. Now you and I have the world we make—together. In this moment. In this room."

She picked up other flowers from the mat beside her and placed them on the table beside the vase. Hannibal could hear the leaves rustling together, and the ripple of her sleeve as she offered him flowers.

"Hannibal, where would you put these to best effect? Wherever you like."

Hannibal looked at the blossoms.

"When you were small, your father sent us your drawings. You have a promising eye. If you prefer to draw the arrangement, use the pad beside you."

Hannibal considered. He picked up two flowers and the knife. He saw the arch of the windows, the curve of the fireplace where the tea vessel hung over the fire. He cut the stems of the flowers off shorter and placed them in the vase, creating a vector harmonious to the arrangement and to the room. He put the cut stems on the table.

Lady Murasaki seemed pleased. "Ahhh. We

would call that **moribana,** the slanting style."
She put the silky weight of a peony in his hand.
"But where might you put this? Or would you
use it at all?"

In the fireplace, the water in the tea vessel
seethed and came to a boil. Hannibal heard it,
heard the water boiling, looked at the surface of
the boiling water and his face changed and the
room went away.

**Mischa's bathtub on the stove in the hunting
lodge, horned skull of the little deer banging
against the tub in the roiling water as though
it tried to butt its way out. Bones rattling in
the tumbling water.**

Back at himself, back in Lady Murasaki's room,
and the head of the peony, bloody now, tumbled onto the tabletop, the knife clattering beside it. Hannibal mastered himself, got to his
feet holding his bleeding hand behind him. He
bowed to Lady Murasaki and started to leave
the room.

"Hannibal."

He opened the door.

"Hannibal." She was up and close to him
quickly. She held out her hand to him, held his
eyes with hers, did not touch him, beckoned
with her fingers. She took his bloody hand and

her touch registered in his eyes, a small change in the size of his pupils.

"You will need stitches. Serge can drive us to town."

Hannibal shook his head and pointed with his chin at the needlework frame. Lady Murasaki looked into his face until she was sure.

"Chiyoh, boil a needle and thread."

At the window, in the good light, Chiyoh brought Lady Murasaki a needle and thread wrapped around an ebony hairpin, steaming from the boiling tea water. Lady Murasaki held his hand steady and sewed up his finger, six neat stitches. Drops of blood fell onto the white silk of her kimono. Hannibal looked at her steadily as she worked. He showed no reaction to the pain. He appeared to be thinking of something else.

He looked at the thread pulled tight, unwound from the hairpin. The arc of the needle's eye was a function of the diameter of the hairpin, he thought. Pages of Huyghens scattered on the snow, stuck together with brains.

Chiyoh applied an aloe leaf and Lady Murasaki bandaged his hand. When she returned his hand to him, Hannibal went to the tea table, picked up the peony and trimmed the stem. He added the peony to the vase, completing an elegant arrangement. He faced Lady Murasaki and Chiyoh.

Across his face a movement like the shiver of water and he tried to say "Thank you." She rewarded the effort with the smallest and best of smiles, but she did not let him try for long.

"Would you come with me, Hannibal? And could you help me bring the flowers?"

Together they climbed the attic stairs.

The attic door had once served elsewhere in the house; a face was carved in it, a Greek comic mask. Lady Murasaki, carrying a candle lamp, led the way far down the vast attic, past a three-hundred-year collection of attic items, trunks, Christmas decorations, lawn ornaments, wicker furniture, Kabuki and Noh Theater costumes and a row of life-size marionettes for festivals hanging from a bar.

Faint light came around the blackout shade of a dormer window far from the door. Her candle lit a small altar, a God shelf opposite the window. On the altar were pictures of her ancestors and of Hannibal's. About the photographs was a flight of origami paper cranes, many cranes. Here was a picture of Hannibal's parents on their wedding day. Hannibal looked at his mother and father closely in the candlelight. His mother looked very happy. The only flame was on his candle—her clothes were not on fire.

Hannibal felt a presence looming beside him and above him and he peered into the dark. As Lady Murasaki raised the blind over the dormer window, the morning light rose over Hannibal, and over the dark presence beside him, rose over armored feet, a war fan held in gauntlets, a breastplate and at last the iron mask and horned helmet of a samurai commander. The armor was seated on the raised platform. The samurai's weapons, the long and short swords, a tanto dagger and a war axe, were on a stand before the armor.

"Let's put the flowers here, Hannibal," Lady Murasaki said, clearing a place on the altar before the photos of his parents.

"This is where I pray for you, and I strongly recommend you pray for yourself, that you consult the spirits of your family for wisdom and strength."

Out of courtesy he bowed his head at the altar for a moment, but the pull of the armor was swarming him, he felt it all up his side. He went to the rack to touch the weapons. Lady Murasaki stopped him with an upraised hand.

"This armor stood in the embassy in Paris when my father was ambassador to France before the war. We hid it from the Germans. I only touch it once a year. On my great-great-great-grandfather's birthday I am honored to clean his armor and his weapons and oil them with camellia oil and oil of cloves, a lovely scent."

She removed the stopper from a vial and offered him a sniff.

There was a scroll on the dais before the armor. It was unrolled only enough to show the first panel, the samurai wearing the armor at a levee of his retainers. As Lady Murasaki arranged the items on the God shelf, Hannibal unrolled the scroll to the next panel, where the figure in armor is presiding at a samurai head presentation, each of the enemy heads tagged with the name of the deceased, the tag attached to the hair, or in the case of baldness, tied to the ear.

Lady Murasaki took the scroll from him gently and rolled it up again to show only her ancestor in his armor.

"This is after the battle for Osaka Castle," she said. "There are other, more suitable scrolls that will interest you. Hannibal, it would please your uncle and me very much if you became the kind of man your father was, that your uncle is."

Hannibal looked at the armor, a questioning glance.

She read the question in his face. "Like him too? In some ways, but with more compassion"— she glanced at the armor as though it could hear and smiled at Hannibal—"but I wouldn't say that in front of him in Japanese."

She came closer, the candle lamp in her hand. "Hannibal, you can leave the land of nightmare. You can be anything that you can imagine. Come onto the bridge of dreams. Will you come with me?"

She was very different from his mother. She was not his mother, but he felt her in his chest. His intense regard may have unsettled her; she chose to break the mood.

"The bridge of dreams leads everywhere, but first it passes through the doctor's office, and the schoolroom," she said. "Will you come?"

Hannibal followed her, but first he took the bloodstained peony, lost among the flowers, and placed it on the dais before the armor.

17

DR. J. RUFIN PRACTICED in a townhouse with a tiny garden. The discreet sign beside the gate bore his name and his titles: DOCTEUR EN MÉDECINE, PH.D., PSYCHIATRE.

Count Lecter and Lady Murasaki sat in straight chairs in the waiting room amid Dr. Rufin's patients, some of whom had difficulty sitting still.

The doctor's inner office was heavy Victorian, with two armchairs on opposite sides of the fireplace, a chaise longue with a fringed throw and, nearer the windows, an examining table and stainless-steel sterilizer.

Dr. Rufin, bearded and middle aged, and Hannibal sat in the armchairs, the doctor speaking to him in a low and pleasant voice.

"Hannibal, as you watch the metronome

swinging, swinging, and listen to the sound of my voice, you will enter a state we call wakeful sleep. I won't ask you to speak, but I want you to try to make a vocal sound to indicate yes or no. You have a sense of peace, of drifting."

Between them on a table, the pendulum of a ticking metronome wagged back and forth. A clock painted with zodiac signs and cherubs ticked on the mantle. As Dr. Rufin talked, Hannibal counted the beats of the metronome against those of the clock. They went in and out of phase. Hannibal wondered if, counting the intervals in and out of phase, and measuring the wagging pendulum of the metronome, he could calculate the length of the unseen pendulum inside the clock. He decided yes, Dr. Rufin talking all the while.

"A sound with your mouth, Hannibal, any sound will do."

Hannibal, his eyes fixed dutifully on the metronome, made a low-pitched farting sound by flubbering air between his tongue and lower lip.

"That's very good," Dr. Rufin said. "You remain calm in the state of wakeful sleep. And what sound might we use for no? No, Hannibal. No."

Hannibal made a high farting sound by taking his lower lip between his teeth and expelling air from his cheek past his upper gum.

"This is communicating, Hannibal, and you can do it. Do you think we can work forward now, you and I together?"

Hannibal's affirmative was loud enough to be audible in the waiting room, where patients exchanged anxious looks. Count Lecter went so far as to cross his legs and clear his throat and Lady Murasaki's lovely eyes rolled slowly toward the ceiling.

A squirrelly-looking man said, "That wasn't me."

"Hannibal, I know that your sleep is often disturbed," Dr. Rufin said. "Remaining calm now in the state of wakeful sleep, can you tell me some of the things you see in dreams?"

Hannibal, counting ticks, gave Dr. Rufin a reflective flubber.

The clock used the Roman IV on its face, rather than IIII, for symmetry with the VIII on the other side. Hannibal wondered if that meant it had Roman striking—two chimes, one meaning "five" and another meaning "one."

The doctor handed him a pad. "Could you write down perhaps some of the things you see? You call out your sister's name, do you see your sister?"

Hannibal nodded.

In Lecter Castle some of the clocks had Roman striking and some did not, but all those that did have Roman striking had the IV rather than IIII. When Mr. Jakov opened a clock and explained the escapement, he told about Knibb and his early clocks with Roman striking—it would be good to visit in his mind the Hall of Clocks to examine the escapement. He considered going there right now, but it would be a long shout for Dr. Rufin.

"Hannibal. Hannibal. When you think about the last time you saw your sister, would you write down what you see? Would you write down what you imagine you see?"

Hannibal wrote without looking at the pad, counting both the beats of the metronome and those of the clock at the same time.

Looking at the pad Dr. Rufin appeared encouraged. "You see her baby teeth? Only her baby teeth? Where do you see them, Hannibal?"

Hannibal reached out and stopped the pendulum, regarded its length, and the position of the weight against a scale on the metronome. He wrote on the pad: **In a stool pit, Doctor. May I open the back of the clock?**

Hannibal waited outside with the other patients.

"It was you, it wasn't me," the squirrelly patient offered. "You might as well admit it. Do you have any gum?"

"I tried to ask him further about his sister, but he closed down," Dr. Rufin said. The count stood behind Lady Murasaki's chair in the examining room.

"To be frank, he is perfectly opaque to me. I have examined him and physically he is sound. I find scars on his scalp but no evidence of a depressed fracture. But I would guess the hemispheres of his brain may be acting independently, as they do in some cases of head trauma, when communication between the hemispheres is compromised. He follows several trains of thought at once, without distraction from any, and one of the trains is always for his own amusement.

"The scar on his neck is the mark of a chain frozen to the skin. I have seen others like it, just after the war when the camps were opened. He will not say what happened to his sister. I think he knows, whether he realizes it or not, and here is the danger: The mind remembers what it can afford to remember and at its own speed. He will remember when he can stand it.

"I would not push him, and it's futile to try to

hypnotize him. If he remembers too soon, he could freeze inside forever to get away from the pain. You will keep him in your home?"

"Yes," they both said quickly.

Rufin nodded. "Involve him in your family as much as you can. As he emerges, he will become more attached to you than you can imagine."

18

THE HIGH FRENCH SUMMER, a pollen haze on the surface of the Essonne and ducks in the reeds. Hannibal still did not speak, but he had dreamless sleep, and the appetite of a growing thirteen-year-old.

His uncle Robert Lecter was warmer and less guarded than Hannibal's father had been. He had a kind of artist's recklessness in him that had lasted and combined with the recklessness of age.

There was a gallery on the roof where they could walk. Pollen had gathered in drifts in the valleys of the roof, gilding the moss, and parachute spiders rode by on the wind. They could see the silver curve of the river through the trees.

The count was tall and birdlike. His skin was

grey in the good light on the roof. His hands on the railing were thin, but they looked like Hannibal's father's hands.

"Our family, we are somewhat unusual people, Hannibal," he said. "We learn it early, I expect you already know. You'll become more comfortable with it in years to come, if it bothers you now. You have lost your family and your home, but you have me and you have Sheba. Is she not a delight? Her father brought her to an exhibition of mine at the Tokyo Metropolitan twenty-five years ago. I had never seen so beautiful a child. Fifteen years later, when he became Ambassador to France, she came too. I could not believe my luck and showed up at the embassy at once, announcing my intention to convert to Shinto. He said my religion was not among his primary concerns. He has never approved of me but he likes my pictures. Pictures! Come.

"This is my studio." It was a big whitewashed room on the top floor of the chateau. Canvases in progress stood on easels and more were propped against the walls. A chaise longue sat on a low platform and, beside it on a coat stand, was a kimono. A draped canvas stood on an easel nearby.

They passed into an adjoining room, where a

big easel stood with a pad of blank newsprint, charcoal and some tubes of color.

"I have made a space here for you, your own studio," the count said. "You can find relief here, Hannibal. When you feel that you may explode, draw instead! Paint! Big arm motions, lots of color. Don't try to aim it or finesse it when you draw. You will get enough finesse from Sheba." He looked beyond the trees to the river. "I'll see you at lunch. Ask Madame Brigitte to find you a hat. We'll row in the late afternoon, after your lessons."

After the count left him, Hannibal did not at once go to his easel; he wandered about the studio looking at the count's works in progress. He put his hand on the chaise, touched the kimono on its peg and held it to his face. He stood before the draped easel and raised the cloth. The count was painting Lady Murasaki nude on the chaise. The picture came into Hannibal's wide eyes, points of light danced in his pupils, fireflies glowed in his night.

Fall approached and Lady Murasaki organized lawn suppers where they could view the harvest moon and hear the fall insects. They waited for the moonrise, Chiyoh playing the lute in the dark when the crickets faltered. With only the rustle of silk and a fragrance to guide him, Hannibal always knew exactly where Lady Murasaki was.

The French crickets were no match for the superb bell cricket of Japan, the suzumushi, the count explained to him, but they would do. The count had sent to Japan a number of times before the war to try to obtain suzumushi crickets for Lady Murasaki but none had survived the trip and he never told her.

On still evenings, when the air was damp after a rain, they played the Aroma Identification Game, Hannibal burning a variety of barks and incense on a mica chip for Chiyoh to identify. Lady Murasaki played the koto on these occasions so Chiyoh could concentrate, her teacher sometimes providing musical hints from a repertoire Hannibal could not follow.

He was sent to monitor classes in the village school, and was an object of curiosity because he could not recite. On his second day a lout from an upper form spit in the hair of a small first-grader and Hannibal broke the spitter's coccyx and his nose. He was sent home, his expression never changing throughout.

He attended Chiyoh's lessons at home instead. Chiyoh had been engaged for years to the son of a diplomatic family in Japan and now, at thirteen, she was learning from Lady Murasaki the skills she would need.

The instruction was very different from that of Mr. Jakov, but the subjects had a peculiar beauty, like Mr. Jakov's mathematics, and Hannibal found them fascinating.

Standing near the good light from the windows in her salon, Lady Murasaki taught calligraphy, painting on sheets of the daily newspaper, and could achieve remarkably delicate effects with a large brush. Here was the symbol for eternity, a triangular shape pleasing to contemplate. Beneath this graceful symbol, the headline on the newspaper sheet read DOCTORS INDICTED AT NUREMBERG.

"This exercise is called Eternity in Eight Strokes," she said. "Try it."

At the end of class, Lady Murasaki and Chiyoh each folded an origami crane, which they would later put on the altar in the attic.

Hannibal picked up a piece of origami paper to make a crane. Chiyoh's questioning glance at Lady Murasaki made him feel like an outsider for a moment. Lady Murasaki handed him a scissors. (Later she would correct Chiyoh for the lapse, which could not be permitted in a diplomatic setting.)

"Chiyoh has a cousin in Hiroshima named Sadako," Lady Murasaki explained. "She is dying of radiation poisoning. Sadako believes that if she folds one thousand paper cranes she will survive. Her strength is limited, and we help her each day by making paper cranes. Whether the cranes are curative or not, as we make them she is in our thoughts, along with others everywhere poisoned by the war. You would fold cranes for us, Hannibal, and we would fold them for you. Let us make cranes together for Sadako."

19

ON THURSDAYS the village had a good market under umbrellas around the fountain and statue of Marshal Foch. There was a briny vinegar on the wind from the pickle merchant and the fish and shellfish on beds of seaweed brought the smell of the ocean.

A few radios played rival tunes. The organ grinder and his monkey, released after breakfast from their frequent accommodation in the jail, ground out "Sous les Ponts de Paris" relentlessly until someone gave them a glass of wine and a piece of peanut brittle, respectively. The organ grinder drank all the wine at once and confiscated half the peanut brittle for himself, the monkey noting with his wise little eyes which pocket his master put the candy in. Two gendarmes gave the musician the usual futile admonitions and found the pastry stall.

Lady Murasaki's objective was Legumes Bulot, the premier vegetable booth, to obtain fiddlehead ferns. Fiddleheads were a great favorite of the count, and they sold out early.

Hannibal trailed behind her carrying a basket. He paused to watch as a cheese merchant oiled a length of piano wire and used it to cut a great wheel of Grana. The merchant gave him a bite and asked him to recommend it to Madame.

Lady Murasaki did not see any fiddleheads on display, and before she had the chance to ask, Bulot of the Vegetables brought a basket of the coiled ferns from under his counter. "Madame, these are so superlative I would not allow the sun to touch them. Awaiting your arrival, I covered them with this cloth, dampened not with water, but with actual garden dew."

Across the aisle from the greengrocer, Paul Momund sat in his bloody apron at a butcher-block table cleaning fowl, throwing the offal into a bucket, and dividing gizzards and livers between two bowls. The butcher was a big, beefy man with a tattoo on his forearm—a cherry with the legend **Voici la Mienne, où est la Tienne?** The red of the cherry had faded paler than the blood on his hands. Paul the Butcher's brother, more suited to dealing with the public, worked the counter under the banner of **Momund's Fine Meats.**

Paul's brother brought him a goose to draw. Paul had a drink from the bottle of marc beside him and wiped his face with his bloody hand, leaving blood and feathers on his cheeks.

"Take it easy, Paul," his brother said. "We have a long day."

"Why don't you pluck the fucking thing? I think you'd rather pluck than fuck," Paul the Butcher said, to his own intense amusement.

Hannibal was looking at a pig's head in a display case when he heard Paul's voice.

"Hey, Japonnaise!"

And the voice of Bulot of the Vegetables: "Please, Monsieur! That is unacceptable."

And Paul again: "Hey, Japonnaise, tell me, is it true that your pussy runs crossways? With a little puff of straight hairs like an explosion?"

Hannibal saw Paul then, his face smeared with blood and feathers, **like the Blue-Eyed One, like the Blue-Eyed One gnawing a birdskin.**

Paul turned to his brother now. "I'll tell you, I had one in Marseilles one time that could take your whole—"

The leg of lamb smashing into Paul's face drove him over backward in a spill of bird intestines, Hannibal on top of him, the leg of lamb rising and slamming down until it slipped from

Hannibal's hand, the boy reaching behind him for the poultry knife on the table, not finding it, finding a handful of chicken innards and smashing them into Paul's face, the butcher pounding at him with his great bloody hands. Paul's brother kicked Hannibal in the back of the head, picked up a veal hammer from the counter, Lady Murasaki flying into the butcher stall, shoved away and then a cry, **"Kiai!"**

Lady Murasaki held a large butcher knife against the butcher's brother's throat, exactly where he would stick a pig, and she said, "Be perfectly still, Monsieurs." They froze for a long moment, the police whistles coming, Paul's great hands around Hannibal's throat and his brother's eye twitching on the side where the steel touched his neck, Hannibal feeling, feeling on the tabletop behind him. The two gendarmes, slipping on the offal, pulled Paul the Butcher and Hannibal apart, a gendarme prying the boy off the butcher, lifting him off the ground and setting him on the other side of the booth.

Hannibal's voice was rusty with disuse, but the butcher understood him. He said "Beast" very calmly. It sounded like taxonomy rather than insult.

The police station faced the square, a sergeant behind the counter.

The Commandant of Gendarmes was in civvies today, a rumpled tropical suit. He was about fifty and tired from the war. In his office he offered Lady Murasaki and Hannibal chairs and sat down himself. His desk was bare except for a Cinzano ashtray and a bottle of the stomach remedy Clanzoflat. He offered Lady Murasaki a cigarette. She declined.

The two gendarmes from the market knocked and came in. They stood against the wall, examining Lady Murasaki out of the sides of their eyes.

"Did anyone here strike at you or resist you?" the commandant asked the policemen.

"No, Commandant."

He beckoned for the rest of their testimony.

The older gendarme consulted his notebook. "Bulot of the Vegetables stated that the butcher became deranged and was trying to get the knife, yelling that he would kill everyone, including all the nuns at the church."

The commandant rolled his eyes to the ceiling, searching for patience.

"The butcher was Vichy, and is much hated as you probably know," he said. "I will deal with him. I am sorry for the insult you suffered, Lady Murasaki. Young man, if you see this lady offended again I want you to come to me. Do you understand?"

Hannibal nodded.

"I will not have anyone attacked in this village, unless I attack them myself." The commandant rose and stood behind the boy. "Excuse us, Madame. Hannibal, come with me."

Lady Murasaki looked up at the policeman. He shook his head slightly.

The commandant led Hannibal to the back of the police station, where there were two cells, one occupied by a sleeping drunk, the other recently vacated by the organ grinder and his monkey, whose bowl of water remained on the floor.

"Stand in there."

Hannibal stood in the middle of the cell. The commandant shut the cell door with a clang that made the drunk stir and mutter.

"Look at the floor. Do you see how the boards are stained and shrunken? They are pickled with tears. Try the door. Do it. You see it will not open from that side. Temper is a useful but dangerous gift. Use judgment and you will never occupy a cell like this. I never give but one pass. This is yours. But don't do it again. Flog no one else with meat."

The commandant walked Lady Murasaki and

Hannibal to their car. When Hannibal was inside, Lady Murasaki had a moment with the policeman.

"Commandant, I don't want my husband to know. Dr. Rufin could tell you why."

He nodded. "If the count learns of it at all and asks me, I will say it was a brawl among drunks and the boy happened to be in the middle. I'm sorry if the count is not well. In other ways he is the most fortunate of men."

It was possible that the count, in his working isolation at the chateau, might never have heard of the incident. But in the evening, as he smoked a cigar, the driver Serge returned from the village with the evening papers and drew him aside.

The Friday market was in Villiers, ten miles away. The count, grey and sleepless, climbed out of his car as Paul the Butcher was carrying the carcass of a lamb into his booth. The count's cane caught Paul across the upper lip and the count flew at him, slashing with the cane.

"Piece of filth, you would insult my wife!!"

Paul dropped the meat and shoved the count

hard, the count's thin frame flying back against a counter and the count came on again, slashing with his cane, and then he stopped, a look of surprise on his face. He raised his hands halfway to his waistcoat and fell facedown on the floor of the butcher's stall.

20

DISGUSTED WITH the whining and bleating of the hymns and the droning nonsense of the funeral, Hannibal Lecter, thirteen and the last of his line, stood beside Lady Murasaki and Chiyoh at the church door absently shaking hands as the mourners filed out, the women uncovering their heads as they left the church in the post-war prejudice against head scarves.

Lady Murasaki listened, making gracious and correct responses.

Hannibal's sense of her fatigue took him out of himself and he found that he was talking so she would not have to talk, his new-found voice degenerating quickly to a croak. If Lady Murasaki was surprised to hear him she did not show it, but took his hand and squeezed it tight as she extended her other hand to the next mourner in line.

A gaggle of Paris press and the news services were there to cover the demise of a major artist who avoided them during his lifetime. Lady Murasaki had nothing to say to them.

In the afternoon of this endless day, the count's lawyer came to the chateau along with an official of the Bureau of Taxation. Lady Murasaki gave them tea.

"Madame, I hesitate to intrude upon your grief," the tax official said, "but I want to assure you that you will have plenty of time to make other arrangements before the chateau is auctioned for death duties. I wish we could accept your own sureties for the death tax, but as your resident status in France will now come into question, that is impossible."

Night came at last. Hannibal walked Lady Murasaki to her very chamber door, and Chiyoh had made up a pallet to sleep in the room with her.

He lay awake in his room for a long time and when sleep came, with it came dreams.

The Blue-Eyed One's face smeared with blood and feathers morphing into the face of Paul the Butcher, and back again.

Hannibal woke in the dark and it did not

stop, the faces like holograms on the ceiling. Now that he could speak, he did not scream.

He rose and went quietly up the stairs to the count's studio. Hannibal lit the candelabra on either side of the easel. The portraits on the walls, finished and half-finished had gained presence with their maker gone. Hannibal felt them straining toward the spirit of the count as though they might find him breath.

His uncle's cleaned brushes stood in a canister, his chalks and charcoals in their grooved trays. The painting of Lady Murasaki was gone, and she had taken her kimono from the hook as well.

Hannibal began to draw with big arm motions, as the count had counseled, trying to let it go, making great diagonal strokes across newsprint, slashes of color. It did not work. Toward dawn he stopped forcing; he quit pushing, and simply watched what his hand revealed to him.

21

HANNIBAL SAT on a stump in a small glade beside the river, plucking the lute and watching a spider spin. The spider was a splendid yellow and black orb weaver, working away. The web vibrated as the spider worked. The spider seemed excited by the lute, running to various parts of its web to check for captives as Hannibal plucked the strings. He could approximate the Japanese song, but he still hit clinkers. He thought of Lady Murasaki's pleasant alto voice speaking English, with its occasional accidental notes not on the Western scale. He plucked closer to the web and further away. A slow-flying beetle crashed into the web and the spider rushed to bind it.

The air was still and warm, the river perfectly smooth. Near the banks water bugs ran across the surface and dragonflies darted over the reeds. Paul the Butcher paddled his small boat with one hand, and let it drift near the willows overhanging the bank. The crickets chirped in Paul's bait basket, attracting a red-eyed fly, which fled from Paul's big hand as he grabbed a cricket and put it on his hook. He cast under the willows and at once his quill float plunged and his rod came alive.

Paul reeled in his fish and put it with the others on a chain stringer hanging over the side of his boat. Occupied with the fish he only half-heard a thrumming in the air. He sucked fish blood off his thumb and paddled to a small pier on the wooded bank where his truck was parked. He used the rude bench on the pier to clean his biggest fish and put it in a canvas bag with some ice. The others were still alive on the stringer in the water. They pulled the chain under the pier in an attempt to hide.

A twanging in the air, a broken tune from somewhere far from France. Paul looked at his truck as though it might be a mechanical noise. He walked up the bank, still carrying his filleting knife, and examined his truck, checked the radio aerial and looked at his tires. He made sure his doors were locked. Again came the twanging, a progression of notes now.

Paul followed the sound, rounding some bushes into the little glade, where he found Hannibal seated on the stump playing the Japanese lute, its case propped against a motorbike. Beside him was a drawing pad. Paul went back at once to his truck and checked the gas filler pipe for grains of sugar. Hannibal did not look up from his playing until the butcher returned and stood before him.

"Paul Momund, fine meats," Hannibal said. He was experiencing a sharpness of vision, with edges of refracted red like ice on a window or the edge of a lens.

"You've started talking, you little mute bastard. If you pissed in my heater I'll twist your fucking head off. There's no **flic** to help you here."

"Nor to help you either." Hannibal plucked several notes. "What you have done is unforgivable." Hannibal put down the lute and took up his sketch pad. Looking up at Paul, he used his little finger as a smudge to make a small adjustment on the pad.

He turned the page and rose, extending a blank page to Paul. "You owe a certain lady a written apology." Paul smelled rank to him, sebum and dirty hair.

"Boy, you are crazy to come here."

"Write that you are sorry, you realize that you are despicable, and you will never look at her or address her in the market again."

"Apologize to the Japonnaise?" Paul laughed. "The first thing I'll do is throw you in the river and rinse you off." He put his hand on his knife. "Then maybe I'll slit your pants and give you something where you don't want it." He came toward Hannibal then, the boy backing away toward his motorbike and the lute case.

Hannibal stopped. "You inquired about her pussy, I believe. You speculated that it ran which way?"

"Is she your mother? Jap pussy runs crossways! You should fuck the little Jap and see."

Paul came scuttling fast, his great hands up to crush, and Hannibal in one movement drew the curved sword from the lute case and slashed Paul low across the belly.

"Crossways like that?"

The butcher's scream rang off the trees and the birds flew with a rush. Paul put his hands on himself and they came away covered with thick blood. He looked down at the wound and tried to hold himself together, intestines spilling in his hands, getting away from him. Hannibal stepping to the side and turning with the blow slashed Paul across the kidneys.

"Or more tangential to the spine?"

Swinging the sword to make Xs in Paul now, Paul's eyes wide in shock, the butcher trying to run, caught across the clavicle, an arterial hiss that spatters Hannibal's face. The next two blows sliced him behind the ankles and he went down hamstrung and bellowing like a steer.

Paul the Butcher sits propped against the stump. He cannot raise his arms.

Hannibal looks into his face. "Would you like to see my drawing?"

He offers the pad. The drawing is Paul the Butcher's head on a platter with a name tag attached to the hair. The tag reads **Paul Momund, Fine Meats.** Paul's vision is darkening around the edges. Hannibal swings the sword and for Paul everything is sideways for an instant, before blood pressure is lost and there is the dark.

In his own darkness, Hannibal hears Mischa's voice as the swan was coming, and he says aloud, "Oooh, Anniba!"

Afternoon faded. Hannibal stayed well into the gloaming, his eyes closed, leaning against the stump where stood the butcher's head. He opened his eyes and sat for long minutes. At last he rose and went to the dock. The fish stringer was made of slender chain and the sight of it made him rub the scar around his neck. The fish on the stringer were still alive. He wet his hand before he touched them, turning them loose one by one.

"Go," he said. "Go," and flung the empty chain far across the water.

He turned the crickets loose as well. "Go, go!" he told them. He looked in the canvas bag at the big cleaned fish and felt a twinge of appetite.

"Yum," he said.

22

PAUL THE BUTCHER'S violent death was no tragedy to many of the villagers, whose mayor and several aldermen had been shot by the Nazis as reprisals for Resistance activity during the occupation.

The greater part of Paul himself lay on a zinc table in the embalming room at Pompes Funebres Roget, where he had succeeded Count Lecter on the slab. At dusk a black Citroën Traction Avant pulled up to the funeral home. A gendarme stationed in front hastened to open the car door.

"Good evening, Inspector."

The man who got out was about forty, neat in a suit. He returned the gendarme's smart salute with a friendly nod, turned back to the car and spoke to the driver and another officer in the backseat. "Take the cases to the police station."

The inspector found the funeral home proprietor, Monsieur Roget, and the Commandant of Police in the embalming room, all faucets and hoses and enamel with supplies in cases fronted with glass.

The commandant brightened at the sight of the policeman from Paris.

"Inspector Popil! I'm happy you could come. You won't remember me but . . ."

The inspector considered the commandant. "I do, of course. Commandant Balmain. You delivered De Rais to Nuremberg and sat behind him at the trial."

"I saw you bring the evidence. It's an honor, sir."

"What do we have?"

The funeral director's assistant Laurent pulled back the covering sheet.

Paul the Butcher's body was still clothed, long stripes of red diagonally across him where the clothing was not soaked with blood. He was absent his head.

"Paul Momund, or most of him," the commandant said. "That is his dossier?"

Popil nodded. "Short and ugly. He shipped Jews from Orléans." The inspector considered the body, walked around it, picked up Paul's hand and arm, its rude tattoo brighter now against the pallor. He spoke absently as though to himself. "He has defense wounds on his hands, but the bruises on his knuckles are days old. He fought recently."

"And often," the mortician said.

Assistant Laurent piped up. "Last Saturday he had a bar fight, and knocked teeth from a man and a girl." Laurent jerked his head to illustrate the force of the blows, the pompadour bobbing on his petite skull.

"A list please. His recent opponents," the inspector said. He leaned over the body, sniffing. "You have done nothing to this body, Monsieur Roget?"

"No, Monsieur. The commandant specifically forbade me . . . ."

Inspector Popil beckoned him to the table. Laurent came too. "Is this the odor of anything you use here?"

"I smell cyanide," Mortician Roget said. "He was poisoned first!"

"Cyanide is a burnt-almond smell," Popil said.

"It smells like that toothache remedy," Laurent said, unconsciously rubbing his jaw.

The mortician turned on his assistant. "Cretin! Where do you see his teeth?"

"Yes. Oil of cloves," Inspector Popil said. "Commandant, could we have the pharmacist and his books?"

Under the tutelage of the chef, Hannibal baked the splendid fish in its scales with herbs in a crust of Brittany sea salt and now he took it from the oven. The crust broke at the sharp tap with the back of a chef's knife and peeled away, the scales coming with it, and the kitchen filled with the wonderful aroma.

"Regard, Hannibal," the chef said. "The best morsels of the fish are the cheeks. This is true of many creatures. When carving at the table, you give one cheek to Madame, and the other to the guest of honor. Of course, if you are plating in the kitchen you eat them both yourself."

Serge came in carrying staple groceries from the market. He started unpacking the bags and putting food away.

Behind Serge, Lady Murasaki came quietly into the kitchen.

"I saw Laurent at the Petit Zinc," Serge said. "They haven't found the butcher's damned ugly head yet. He said the body was scented with— get this—oil of cloves, the toothache stuff. He said—"

Hannibal saw Lady Murasaki and cut Serge

off. "You really should eat something, my lady. This will be very, very good."

"And I brought some peach ice cream, fresh peaches," Serge said.

Lady Murasaki looked into Hannibal's eyes for a long moment.

He smiled at her, perfectly calm. "Peach!" he said.

23

MIDNIGHT, LADY MURASAKI lay in her bed. The window was open to a soft breeze that carried the scent of a mimosa blooming in a corner of the courtyard below. She pushed the covers down to feel the moving air on her arms and feet. Her eyes were open, looking up at the dark ceiling, and she could hear the tiny clicks when she blinked her eyes.

Below in the courtyard the old mastiff stirred in her sleep, her nostrils opened and she took in a lot of air. A few folds appeared in the pelt on her forehead, and she relaxed again to pleasant dreams of a chase and blood in her mouth.

Above Lady Murasaki in the dark, the attic floor creaked. Weight on the boards, not the squeak of a mouse. Lady Murasaki took a deep breath and swung her feet onto the cold stone floor of the bedroom. She put on her light kimono, touched her hair, gathered flowers from a vase in the hall and, carrying a candle lamp, mounted the stairs to the attic.

The mask carved on the attic door smiled at her. She straightened, she put her hand on the carved face and pushed. She felt the draft press her robe against her back, a tiny push, and far, far down the dark attic she saw the flicker of a tiny light. Lady Murasaki went toward the light, her candle lamp glowing on the Noh masks watching her, and the hanging row of marionettes gestured in the breath of her passing. Past wicker baskets and stickered trunks of her years with Robert, toward the family altar and the armor where candles burned.

A dark object stood on the altar before the armor. She saw it in silhouette against the candles. She set her candle lamp on a crate near the altar and looked steadily at the head of Paul the Butcher standing in a shallow suiban flower vessel. Paul's face is clean and pale, his lips are intact, but his cheeks are missing and a little blood has leaked from his mouth into the flower vessel, where blood stands like the water beneath a flower arrangement. A tag is attached to Paul's hair. On the tag in a copperplate hand: **Momund, Boucherie de Qualité.**

Paul's head faced the armor, the eyes upturned

to the samurai mask. Lady Murasaki turned her face up too and spoke in Japanese.

"Good evening, Honored Ancestor. Please excuse this inadequate bouquet. With all respect, this is not the type of help I had in mind."

Automatically she picked up a wilted flower and ribbon from the floor and put it in her sleeve, her eyes moving all the while. The long sword was in its place, and the war axe. The short sword was missing from its stand.

She took a step backward, went to the dormer window and opened it. She took a deep breath. Her pulse sounded in her ears. The breeze fluttered her robe and the candles.

A soft rattle from behind the Noh costumes. One of the masks had eyes in it, watching her.

She said in Japanese, "Good evening, Hannibal."

Out of the darkness came the reply in Japanese, "Good evening, my lady."

"May we continue in English, Hannibal? There are matters I prefer to keep private from my ancestor."

"As you wish, my lady. In any case, we have exhausted my Japanese."

He came into the lamplight then, carrying the short sword and a cleaning cloth. She went toward him. The long sword was in its rack before the armor. She could reach it if she had to.

"I would have used the butcher's knife," Hannibal said. "I used Masamune-dono's sword because it seemed so appropriate. I hope you don't mind. Not a nick in the blade, I promise you. The butcher was like butter."

"I am afraid for you."

"Please don't be concerned. I'll dispose of . . . that."

"You did not need to do this for me."

"I did it for myself, because of the worth of your person, Lady Murasaki. No onus on you at all. I think Masamune-dono permitted the use of his sword. It's an amazing instrument, really."

Hannibal returned the short sword to its sheath and with a respectful gesture to the armor, replaced it on its stand.

"You are trembling," he said. "You are in perfect possession of yourself, but you are trembling like a bird. I would not have approached you without flowers. I love you, Lady Murasaki."

Below, outside the courtyard, the two-note cry of a French police siren, sounded only once. The mastiff roused herself and came out to bark.

Lady Murasaki quick to Hannibal, taking his

hands in hers, holding them to her face. She kissed his forehead, and then the intense whisper of her voice: "Quickly! Scrub your hands! Chiyoh has lemons in the maid's room."

Far down in the house the knocker boomed.

24

LADY MURASAKI let Inspector Popil wait through one hundred beats of her heart before she appeared on the staircase. He stood in the center of the high-ceilinged foyer with his assistant and looked up at her on the landing. She saw him alert and still, like a handsome spider standing before the webbed mullions of the windows, and beyond the windows she saw endless night.

Popil's breath came in a bit sharply at the sight of Lady Murasaki. The sound was amplified in the dome of the foyer, and she was listening.

Her descent seemed one motion with no increment of steps. Her hands were in her sleeves.

Serge, red-eyed, stood to the side.

"Lady Murasaki, these gentlemen are from the police."

"Good evening."

"Good evening, ma'am. I'm sorry to disturb you so late. I need to ask questions of your . . . nephew?"

"Nephew. May I see your credentials?" Her hand came out of her sleeve slowly, her hand disrobing. She read all the text in his credentials, and examined the photograph.

"Inspector POP-il?"

"Po-PIL, Madame."

"You wear the Legion of Honor in your photograph, Inspector."

"Yes, Madame."

"Thank you for coming in person."

A fragrance, fresh and faint, reached Popil as she gave him back his identification. She watched his face for its arrival, and saw it there, a minute change in his nostrils and the pupils of his eyes.

"Madame . . . ?"

"Murasaki Shikibu."

"Madame is the Countess Lecter, customarily addressed by her Japanese title as Lady Murasaki," Serge said, brave for him, speaking with a policeman.

"Lady Murasaki, I would like to speak with you in private, and then with your nephew separately."

"With all due respect to your office, I'm afraid

that is not possible, Inspector," Lady Murasaki said.

"Oh, Madame, it is entirely possible," Inspector Popil said.

"You are welcome here in our home, and you are entirely welcome to speak with us together."

Hannibal spoke from the stairs. "Good evening, Inspector."

He turned to Hannibal. "Young man, I want you to come with me."

"Certainly, Inspector."

Lady Murasaki said to Serge, "Would you get my wrap?"

"That will not be necessary, Madame," Popil said. "You won't be coming. I will interview you here tomorrow, Madame. I will not harm your nephew."

"It's fine, my lady," Hannibal said.

Inside her sleeves Lady Murasaki's grip on her wrists relaxed a little in relief.

25

THE EMBALMING ROOM was dark, and silent except for a slow drip in the sink. The inspector stood in the doorway with Hannibal, raindrops on their shoulders and their shoes.

Momund was in there. Hannibal could smell him. He waited for Popil to turn on the light, interested to see what the policeman would consider a dramatic interval.

"Do you think you would recognize Paul Momund if you saw him again?"

"I'll do my best, Inspector."

Popil switched on the light. The mortician had removed Momund's clothing and put it in paper bags as instructed. He had closed the abdomen with coarse stitching over a piece of rubber raincoat, and placed a towel over the severed neck.

"Do you remember the butcher's tattoo?"

Hannibal walked around the body. "Yes. I hadn't read it."

The boy looked at Inspector Popil across the body. He saw in the inspector's eyes the smudged look of intelligence.

"What does it say?" the inspector asked.

"Here's mine, where's yours?"

"Perhaps it should say, **Here's yours, where's mine?** Here is your first kill, where is my head? What do you think?"

"I think that's probably unworthy of you. I would hope so. Do you expect his wounds to bleed in my presence?"

"What did this butcher say to the lady that drove you crazy?"

"It did not drive me crazy, Inspector. His mouth offended everyone who heard it, including me. He was rude."

"What did he say, Hannibal?"

"He asked if it were true that Japanese pussy runs sideways, Inspector. His address was 'Hey, Japonnaise!' "

"Sideways." Inspector Popil traced the line of stitches across Paul Momund's abdomen, nearly touching the skin. "Sideways like this?" The inspector scanned Hannibal's face for something. He did not find it. He did not find anything, so he asked another question.

"How do you feel, seeing him dead?"

Hannibal looked under the towel covering the neck. "Detached," he said.

The polygraph set up in the police station was the first the village policemen had seen, and there was considerable curiosity about it. The operator, who had come from Paris with Inspector Popil, made a number of adjustments, some purely theatrical, as the tubes warmed up and the insulation added a hot-cotton smell to the atmosphere of sweat and cigarettes. Then the inspector, watching Hannibal watching the machine, cleared the room of everyone but the boy, himself and the operator. The polygrapher attached the instrument to Hannibal.

"State your name," the operator said.

"Hannibal Lecter." The boy's voice was rusty.

"What is your age?"

"Thirteen years."

The ink styluses ran smoothly over the polygraph paper.

"How long have you been a resident of France?"

"Six months."

"Were you acquainted with the butcher Paul Momund?"

"We were never introduced."

The styluses did not quiver.

"But you knew who he was."

"Yes."

"Did you have an altercation, that is a fight, with Paul Momund at the market on Thursday?"

"Yes."

"Do you attend school?"

"Yes."

"Does your school require uniforms?"

"No."

"Do you have any guilty knowledge of the death of Paul Momund?"

"Guilty knowledge?"

"Limit your responses to yes or no."

"No."

The peaks and valleys in the ink lines are constant. No increase in blood pressure, no increase in heartbeat, respiration constant and calm.

"You know that the butcher is dead."

"Yes."

The polygrapher appeared to make several adjustments to the knobs of the machine.

"Have you studied mathematics?"

"Yes."

"Have you studied geography?"

"Yes."

"Did you see the dead body of Paul Momund?"

"Yes."

"Did you kill Paul Momund?"

"No."

No distinctive spikes in the inked lines. The operator took off his glasses, a signal to Inspector Popil that ended the examination.

A known burglar from Orléans with a lengthy police record replaced Hannibal in the chair. The burglar waited while Inspector Popil and the polygrapher conferred in the hall outside.

Popil unspooled the paper tape.

"Vanilla."

"The boy responds to nothing," the polygrapher said. "He's a blunted war orphan or he has a monstrous amount of self-control."

"Monstrous," Popil said.

"Do you want to question the burglar first?"

"He does not interest me, but I want you to run him. And I may whack him a few times in front of the boy. Do you follow me?"

On the downslope of the road leading into the village, a motorbike coasted with its lights out, its engine off. The rider wore black coveralls and a black balaclava. Silently the bike rounded a corner at the far side of the deserted square, disappeared briefly behind a postal van parked in front of the post office and moved on, the rider peddling hard, not starting the engine before the upslope out of the village.

Inspector Popil and Hannibal sat in the commandant's office. Inspector Popil read the label on the commandant's bottle of Clanzoflat and considered taking a dose.

Then he put the roll of polygraph tape on the desk and pushed it with his finger. The tape unrolled its line of many small peaks. The peaks looked to him like the foothills of a mountain obscured by cloud. "Did you kill the butcher, Hannibal?"

"May I ask you a question?"

"Yes."

"It's a long way to come from Paris. Do you specialize in the deaths of butchers?"

"My specialty is war crimes, and Paul Momund was suspected in several. War crimes do not end with the war, Hannibal." Popil paused to read the advertising on each facet of the ashtray. "Perhaps I understand your situation better than you think."

"What is my situation, Inspector?"

"You were orphaned in the war. You lived in an institution, living inside yourself, your family dead. And at last, at last your beautiful stepmother made up for all of it." Working for the bond, Popil put his hand on Hannibal's shoulder. "The very scent of her takes away the smell of the camp. And then the butcher spews filth at her. If you killed him, I could understand. Tell me. Together we could explain to a magistrate . . ."

Hannibal moved back in his chair, away from Popil's touch.

"**The very scent of her takes away the smell of the camp?** May I ask if you compose verse, Inspector?"

"Did you kill the butcher?"

"Paul Momund killed himself. He died of stupidity and rudeness."

Inspector Popil had considerable experience and knowledge of the awful, and this was the voice Popil had been listening for; it had a faintly different timbre and was surprising coming from the body of a boy.

This specific wavelength he had not heard before, but he recognized it as Other. It had been some time since he felt the thrill of the hunt, the prehensile quality of the opposing brain. He felt it in his scalp and forearms. He lived for it.

Part of him wished the burglar outside had killed the butcher. Part of him considered how lonely and in need of company Lady Murasaki might be with the boy in an institution.

"The butcher was fishing. He had blood and

scales on his knife, but he had no fish. The chef tells me you brought in a splendid fish for dinner. Where did you get the fish?"

"By fishing, Inspector. We keep a baited line in the water behind the boathouse. I'll show you if you like. Inspector, did you choose war crimes?"

"Yes."

"Because you lost family in the war?"

"Yes."

"May I ask how?"

"Some in combat. Some were shipped east."

"Did you catch who did it?"

"No."

"But they were Vichy—men like the butcher."

"Yes."

"Can we be perfectly honest with each other?"

"Absolutely."

"Are you sorry to see Paul Momund dead?"

On the far side of the square the village barber, M. Rubin, came off a leafy side street for his nightly round of the square with his small terrier. M. Rubin, after talking with his customers all day, continued talking to his dog in the evening. He pulled the dog away from the grassy strip in front of the post office.

"You should have performed your duty on the

lawn of Felipe, where no one was looking," M. Rubin said. "Here you might incur a fine. You have no money. It would fall to me to pay."

In front of the post office was a post box on a pole. The dog strained toward it against the leash and raised his leg.

Seeing a face above the mailbox, Rubin said, "Good evening, Monsieur," and to the dog, "Attend you do not befoul Monsieur!" The dog whined and Rubin noticed there were no legs beneath the mailbox on the other side.

The motorbike sped along the one-lane paved road, nearly overrunning the cast of its dim headlight. Once when a car approached from the other way, the rider ducked into the roadside trees until the car's taillights were out of sight.

In the dark storage shed of the chateau, the headlight of the bike faded out, the motor ticking as it cooled. Lady Murasaki pulled off the black balaclava and by touch she put up her hair.

The beams of police flashlights converged on Paul Momund's head on top of the mailbox. **Boche** was printed across his forehead just below the hairline. Late drinkers and night workers were gathering to see.

Inspector Popil brought Hannibal up close and looked at him by the light glowing off the dead man's face. He could detect no change in the boy's expression.

"The Resistance killed Momund at last," the barber said, and explained to everyone how he had found him, carefully leaving out the transgressions of the dog.

Some in the crowd thought Hannibal shouldn't have to look at it. An older woman, a night nurse going home, said so aloud.

Popil sent him home in a police car. Hannibal arrived at the chateau in the rosy dawn and cut some flowers before he went into the house, arranging them for height in his fist. The poem to accompany them came to him as he was cutting the stems off even. He found Lady Murasaki's brush in the studio still wet and used it to write:

Night heron revealed
By the rising harvest moon—
Which is lovelier?

Hannibal slept easily later in the day. He dreamed of Mischa in the summer before the war, Nanny had her bathtub in the garden at the lodge, letting the sun warm the water, and the cabbage butterflies flew around Mischa in the water. He cut the eggplant for her and she hugged the purple eggplant, warm from the sun.

When he woke there was a note beneath his door along with a wisteria blossom. The note said: **One would choose the heron, if beset by frogs.**

26

CHIYOH PREPARED for her departure to Japan by drilling Hannibal in elementary Japanese, in the hope that he could provide some conversation for Lady Murasaki and relieve her of the tedium of speaking English.

She found him an apt pupil in the Heian tradition of communication by poem and engaged him in practice poem exchanges, confiding that this was a major deficiency in her prospective groom. She made Hannibal swear to look out for Lady Murasaki, using a variety of oaths sworn on objects she thought Westerners might hold sacred. She required pledges as well at the altar in the attic, and a blood oath that involved pricking their fingers with a pin.

They could not hold off the time with wishing. When Lady Murasaki and Hannibal packed for Paris, Chiyoh packed for Japan. Serge and Hannibal heaved Chiyoh's trunk onto the boat train at the Gare de Lyon while Lady Murasaki sat beside her in the train, holding her hand until the last minute. An outsider watching them part might have thought them emotionless as they exchanged a final bow.

Hannibal and Lady Murasaki felt Chiyoh's absence sharply on the way home. Now there were only the two of them.

The Paris apartment vacated before the war by Lady Murasaki's father was very Japanese in its subtle interplay of shadows and lacquer. If the furniture, undraped piece by piece, brought Lady Murasaki memories of her father, she did not reveal them.

She and Hannibal tied back the heavy draperies, letting in the sun. Hannibal looked down upon the Place de Vosges, all light and space and warm red brick, one of the most beautiful squares in Paris despite a garden still scruffy from the war.

There, on the field below, King Henri II jousted under the colors of Diane de Poitiers and fell with fatal splinters in his eye, and even Vesalius at his bedside could not save him.

Hannibal closed one eye and speculated precisely where Henri fell—probably right over there where Inspector Popil now stood, holding a potted plant and looking up at the windows. Hannibal did not wave.

"I think you have a caller, my lady," he said over his shoulder.

Lady Murasaki did not ask who. When the knocking came, she let it go on for a moment before she answered the door.

Popil came in with his plant and a bag of sweets from Fauchon. There was a mild confusion as he attempted to remove his hat while holding parcels in both hands. Lady Murasaki took the hat from him.

"Welcome to Paris, Lady Murasaki. The florist swears to me this plant will do well on your terrace."

"Terrace? I suspect you are investigating me, Inspector—already you have found out I have a terrace."

"Not only that—I have confirmed the presence of a foyer, and I strongly suspect you have a kitchen."

"So you work from room to room?"

"Yes, that is my method, I proceed from room to room."

"Until you arrive where?" She saw some color in his face and let him off. "Shall we put this in the light?"

Hannibal was unpacking the armor when they came upon him. He stood beside the crate, holding the samurai mask. He did not turn his body toward Inspector Popil, but turned his head like an owl to look at the policeman. Seeing Popil's hat in Lady Murasaki's hands, Hannibal estimated the size and weight of his head at 19.5 centimeters and six kilos.

"Do you ever put it on, the mask?" Inspector Popil said.

"I haven't earned it."

"I wonder."

"Do you ever wear your many decorations, Inspector?"

"When ceremonies require them."

"Chocolates from Fauchon. Very thoughtful, Inspector Popil. They will take away the smell of the camp."

"But not the scent of oil of cloves. Lady Murasaki, I need to discuss the matter of your residency."

Popil and Lady Murasaki talked on the terrace. Hannibal watched them through the window, revising his estimate of Popil's hat size to twenty centimeters. In the course of conversation Popil and Lady Murasaki moved the plant a number of times to vary its exposure to the light. They seemed to need something to do.

Hannibal did not continue unpacking the armor, but knelt beside the crate and rested his hand on the rayskin grip of the short sword. He looked out at the policeman through the eyes of the mask.

He could see Lady Murasaki laughing. Inspector Popil must be making some lame attempt at levity and she was laughing out of kindness, Hannibal surmised. When they came back inside, Lady Murasaki left them alone together.

"Hannibal, at the time of his death your uncle was trying to find out what happened to your sister in Lithuania. I can try too. It's hard in the Baltic now—sometimes the Soviets cooperate, more times they don't. But I keep after them."

"Thank you."

"What do you remember?"

"We were living at the lodge. There was an explosion. I can remember being picked up by soldiers and riding on a tank to the village. In between I don't know. I try to remember. I cannot."

"I talked with Dr. Rufin."

No visible reaction to that.

"He would not discuss any specifics of his talks with you."

Nothing to that either.

"But he said you are very concerned about your sister, naturally. He said with time your memory might return. If you remember anything, ever, please tell me."

Hannibal looked at the inspector steadily. "Why would I not?" He wished he could hear a clock. It would be good to hear a clock.

"When we talked after . . . the incident of Paul Momund, I told you I lost relatives in the war. It is very much of an effort for me to think about that. Do you know why?"

"Tell me why, Inspector."

"Because I think I should have saved them, I have a horror of finding something I didn't do, that I could have done. If you have the fear the same way I do, don't let it push away some memory that might be helpful to Mischa. You can tell me anything in the world."

Lady Murasaki came into the room. Popil stood up and changed the subject. "The Lycée is a good school and you earned your way in. If I can help you, I will. I'll drop by the school to see about you from time to time."

"But you would prefer to call here," Hannibal said.

"Where you will be welcome," Lady Murasaki said.

"Good afternoon, Inspector," Hannibal said.

Lady Murasaki let Popil out and she returned angry.

"Inspector Popil likes you, I can see it in his face," Hannibal said.

"What can he see in yours? It is dangerous to bait him."

"You will find him tedious."

"I find you rude. It is quite unlike you. If you wish to be rude to a guest, do it in your own house," Lady Murasaki said.

"Lady Murasaki, I want to stay here with you."

The anger went out of her. "No. We will spend our holidays together, and weekends, but you must board at the school as the rules require. You know my hand is always on your heart." And she put it there.

On his heart. The hand that held Popil's hat was on his heart. The hand that held the knife to Momund's brother's throat. The hand that gripped the butcher's hair and dropped his head into a bag and set it on the mailbox. His heart beat against her palm. Fathomless her face.

27

THE FROGS HAD BEEN preserved in formaldehyde from before the war, and what differentiating color their organs ever had was long ago leached away. There was one for each six students in the malodorous school laboratory. A circle of schoolboys crowded around each plate where the little cadaver rested, the chaff of grubby erasures dusting the table as they sketched. The schoolroom was cold, coal still being in short supply, and some of the boys wore gloves with the fingertips cut out.

Hannibal came and looked at the frog and returned to his desk to work. He made two trips. Professor Bienville had a teacher's suspicion of anyone who chose to sit in the back of the room. He approached Hannibal from the flank, his suspicions justified as he saw the boy sketching a face instead of a frog.

"Hannibal Lecter, why are you not drawing the specimen?"

"I finished it, sir." Hannibal lifted the top sheet and there was the frog, exactly rendered, in the anatomical position and circumscribed like Leonardo's drawing of man. The internals were hatched and shaded.

The professor looked carefully into Hannibal's face. He adjusted his dentures with his tongue and said, "I will take that drawing. There is someone who should see it. You'll have credit for it." The professor turned down the top sheet of Hannibal's tablet and looked at the face. "Who is that?"

"I'm not sure, sir. A face I saw somewhere."

In fact, it was the face of Vladis Grutas, but Hannibal did not know his name. It was a face he had seen in the moon and on the midnight ceiling.

A year of grey light through classroom windows. At least the light was diffuse enough to draw by, and the classrooms changed as the instructors put him up a form, and then another and another.

A holiday from school at last.

In this first fall since the death of the count and the departure of Chiyoh, Lady Murasaki's losses quickened in her. When her husband was alive she had arranged outdoor suppers in the fall in a meadow near the chateau with Count Lecter and Hannibal and Chiyoh, to view the harvest moon and to listen to the fall insects.

Now, on the terrace at her residence in Paris, she read to Hannibal a letter from Chiyoh about her wedding arrangements, and they watched the moon wax toward full, but no crickets could be heard.

Hannibal folded his cot in the living room early in the morning and bicycled across the Seine to the Jardin des Plantes, where he made another of his frequent inquiries at the menagerie. News today, a scribbled note with an address . . .

Ten minutes further south at Place Monge and the Rue Ortolan he found the shop: **Poissons Tropicaux, Petites Oiseaux, & Animaux Exotiques.**

Hannibal took a small portfolio from his saddlebag and went inside.

There were tiers of tanks and cages in the small storefront, twittering and chirping and the whir of hamster wheels. It smelled of grain and warm feathers and fish food.

From a cage beside the cash register, a large

parrot addressed Hannibal in Japanese. An older Japanese man with a pleasant face came from the back of the store, where he was cooking.

"**Gomekudasai,** Monsieur?" Hannibal said.

"**Irasshaimase,** Monsieur," the proprietor said.

"**Irasshaimase,** Monsieur," the parrot said.

"Do you have a suzumushi cricket for sale, Monsieur?"

"**Non, je suis désolée,** Monsieur," the proprietor said.

"**Non, je suis désolée,** Monsieur," the parrot said.

The proprietor frowned at the bird and switched to English to confound the intrusive fowl. "I have a variety of excellent fighting crickets. Fierce fighters, always victorious, famous wherever crickets gather."

"This is a gift for a lady from Japan who pines for the song of the suzumushi at this time of year," Hannibal said. "A plain cricket is unsuitable."

"I would never suggest a French cricket, whose song is pleasing only for its seasonal associations. But I have no suzumushi for sale. Perhaps she would be amused by a parrot with an extensive Japanese vocabulary, whose expressions embrace all walks of life."

"Might you have a personal suzumushi?"

The proprietor looked into the distance for a moment. The law on the importation of insects and their eggs was fuzzy this early in the new Republic. "Would you like to hear it?"

"I would be honored," Hannibal said.

The proprietor disappeared behind a curtain at the rear of the store and returned with a small cricket cage, a cucumber and a knife. He placed the cage on the counter, and under the avid gaze of the parrot, cut off a tiny slice of cucumber and pushed it into the cricket cage. In a moment came the clear sleigh-bell ring of the suzumushi. The proprietor listened with a beatific expression as the song came again.

The parrot imitated the cricket's song as well as it could—loudly and repeatedly. Receiving nothing, it became abusive and raved until Hannibal thought of Uncle Elgar. The proprietor put a cover over the cage.

"Merde," it said from beneath the cloth.

"Do you suppose I might hire the use of a suzumushi, lease one so to speak, on a weekly basis?"

"What sort of fee would you find appropriate?" the proprietor said.

"I had in mind an exchange," Hannibal said. He took from his portfolio a small drawing in pen and ink wash of a beetle on a bent stem.

The proprietor, holding the drawing carefully

by the edges, turned it to the light. He propped it against the cash register. "I could inquire among my colleagues. Could you return after the lunch hour?"

Hannibal wandered, purchased a plum at the street market and ate it. Here was a sporting-goods store with trophy heads in the window, a bighorn sheep, an ibex. Leaning in the corner of the window was an elegant Holland & Holland double rifle. It was wonderfully stocked; the wood looked as though it had grown around the metal and together wood and metal had the sinuous quality of a beautiful snake.

The gun was elegant and it was beautiful in one of the ways that Lady Murasaki was beautiful. The thought was not comfortable to him under the eyes of the trophy heads.

The proprietor was waiting for him with the cricket. "Will you return the cage after October?"

"Is there no chance it might survive the fall?"

"It might last into the winter if you keep it warm. You may bring me the cage at . . . an appropriate time." He gave Hannibal the cucumber. "Don't give it all to the suzumushi at once," he said.

Lady Murasaki came to the terrace from prayers, thoughts of autumn still in her expression.

Dinner at the low table on the terrace in a luminous twilight. They were well into the noodles when, primed with cucumber, the cricket surprised her with its crystal song, singing from concealment in the dark beneath the flowers. Lady Murasaki seemed to think she heard it in her dreams. It sang again, the clear sleigh-bell song of the suzumushi.

Her eyes cleared and she was in the present. She smiled at Hannibal. "I see you and the cricket sings in concert with my heart."

"My heart hops at the sight of you, who taught my heart to sing."

The moon rose to the song of the suzumushi. The terrace seemed to rise with it, drawn into tangible moonlight, lifting them to a place above ghost-ridden earth, a place unhaunted, and being there together was enough.

In time he would say the cricket was borrowed, that he must take it back at the waning of the moon. Best not to keep it too long into the fall.

28

LADY MURASAKI conducted her life with a certain elegance which she achieved by application and taste, and she did it with whatever funds were left to her after the chateau was sold and the death duties paid. She would have given Hannibal anything he asked, but he did not ask.

Robert Lecter had provided for Hannibal's minimal school expenses, but no extras.

The most important element in Hannibal's budget was a letter of his own composition. The letter was signed **Dr. Gamil Jolipoli, Allergist** and it alerted the school that Hannibal had a serious reaction to chalk dust, and should be seated as far as possible from the blackboard.

Since his grades were exceptional, he knew the teachers did not really care what he was doing, as long as the other pupils did not see and follow his bad example.

Freed to sit alone in the very back of the classroom, he was able to manufacture ink and watercolor washes of birds in the style of Musashi Miyamoto, while listening to the lecture with half an ear.

There was a vogue in Paris for things Japanese. The drawings were small, and suited to the limited wall space of Paris apartments, and they could be packed easily in a tourist's suitcase. He signed them with a chop, the symbol called Eternity in Eight Strokes.

There was a market for these drawings in the Quarter, in the small galleries along the Rue Saints-Pères and the Rue Jacob, though some galleries required him to deliver his work after hours, to prevent their clients from knowing the drawings were done by a child.

Late in the summer, while the sunlight still remained in the Luxembourg Gardens after school, he sketched the toy sailboats on the pond while waiting for closing time. Then he walked to Saint-Germain to work the galleries—Lady Murasaki's birthday was approaching and he had his eye on a piece of jade in the Place Furstenberg.

He was able to sell the sailboat sketch to a decorator on the Rue Jacob, but he was holding out his Japanese-type sketches for a larcenous little gallery on the Rue Saints-Pères. The drawings were more impressive matted and framed and he had found a good framer who would extend him credit.

He carried them in a backpack down the Boulevard Saint-Germain. The outdoor tables at the cafés were full and the sidewalk clowns were badgering passersby for the amusement of the crowd at the Café Flore. In the small streets nearer the river, the Rue Saint-Benoit and the Rue de l'Abbaye, the jazz clubs were still shut tight, but the restaurants were open.

Hannibal was trying to forget his lunch at school, an entrée known as "Martyr's Relics," and he examined the bills of fare with keen interest as he passed. Soon he hoped to have the funds for a birthday dinner, and he was looking for sea urchins.

Monsieur Leet of Galerie Leet was shaving for an evening engagement when Hannibal rang his bell. The lights were still on in the gallery, though the curtains were drawn. Leet had a Belgian's impatience with the French and a ravening desire to fleece Americans, whom he believed would buy anything. The gallery featured high-end representational painters, small statuary and antiquities, and was known for marine paintings and seascapes.

"Good evening, Monsieur Lecter," Leet said. "Delighted to see you. I trust you are well. I must ask you to wait while I crate a painting, it has to go tonight to Philadelphia in America."

In Hannibal's experience such a warm welcome usually masked sharp practice. He gave Monsieur Leet the drawings and his price written in a firm hand. "May I look around?"

"Be my guest."

It was pleasant to be away from the school, to be looking at good pictures. After an afternoon of sketching boats on the pond, Hannibal was thinking about water, the problems of depicting water. He thought about Turner's mist and his colors, impossible to emulate, and he went from picture to picture looking at the water, the air over the water. He came upon a small painting on an easel, the Grand Canal in bright sunlight, Santa Maria della Salute in the background.

It was a Guardi from Lecter Castle. Hannibal knew before he knew, a flash from memory on the backs of his eyelids and now the familiar painting before him in this frame. Perhaps it was a copy. He picked it up and looked closely. The mat was stained in a small pattern of brown dots in the upper left corner. When he was a small child he had heard his parents say the stain was "foxing" and he had spent minutes staring at it, trying to make out the image of a fox or a fox's pawprint. The painting was not a copy. The frame felt hot in his hands.

Monsieur Leet came into the room. He frowned. "We don't touch unless we are prepared to buy. Here is a check for you." Leet laughed. "It is too much, but it won't cover the Guardi."

"No, not today. Until next time, Monsieur Leet."

29

INSPECTOR POPIL, IMPATIENT with the genteel tones of the door chime, banged upon the door of Galerie Leet in the Rue Saints-Pères. Admitted by the gallery owner, he got straight to the point.

"Where did you get the Guardi?"

"I bought it from Kopnik, when we divided the business," Leet said. He mopped his face and thought how abominably French Popil looked in his ventless frog jacket. "He said he got it from a Finn, he didn't say the name."

"Show me the invoice," Popil said. "You are required to have on this premises the Arts and Monuments advisory on stolen art. Show me that too."

Leet compared the list of stolen documents to his own catalog. "Look, see here, the looted

Guardi is described differently. Robert Lecter listed the stolen painting as 'View of Santa Maria della Salute,' and I bought this painting as 'View of the Grand Canal.' "

"I have a court order to seize the picture, whatever it's called. I'll give you a receipt for it. Find me this 'Kopnik,' Monsieur Leet, and you could save yourself a lot of unpleasantness."

"Kopnik is dead, Inspector. He was my associate in this firm. We called it Kopnik and Leet. Leet and Kopnik would have had a better ring to it."

"Do you have his records?"

"His attorney might."

"Look for them, Monsieur Leet. Look for them well," Popil said. "I want to know how this painting got from Lecter Castle to Galerie Leet."

"Lecter," Leet said. "Is it the boy who does these drawings?"

"Yes."

"Extraordinary," Leet said.

"Yes, extraordinary," Popil replied. "Wrap the painting for me, please."

Leet appeared at the Quai des Orfèvres in two days carrying papers. Popil arranged for him to be seated in the corridor near the room marked **Audition 2**, where the noisy interrogation of a rape suspect was under way punctuated by thumps and cries. Popil allowed Leet to marinate in this atmosphere for fifteen minutes before admitting him to the private office.

The art dealer handed over a receipt. It showed Kopnik bought the Guardi from one Emppu Makinen for eight thousand English pounds.

"Do you find this convincing?" Popil asked. "I do not."

Leet cleared his throat and looked at the floor. A full twenty seconds passed.

"The public prosecutor is eager to initiate criminal proceedings against you, Monsieur Leet. He is a Calvinist of the severest stripe, did you know that?"

"The painting was—"

Popil held up his hand, shushing Leet. "For the moment, I want you to forget about your problem. Assume I could intervene for you if I chose. I want you to help me. I want you to look at this." He handed Leet a sheaf of legal-length onionskin pages close-typed. "This is the list of items the Arts Commission is bringing to Paris from the Munich Collection Point. All stolen art."

"To display at the Jeu de Paume."

"Yes, claimants can view it there. Second page, halfway down. I circled it."

" 'The Bridge of Sighs,' Bernardo Bellotto, thirty-six by thirty centimeters, oil on board."

"Do you know this painting?" Popil said.

"I have heard of it, of course."

"If it is genuine, it was taken from Lecter Castle. You know it is famously paired with another painting of the Bridge of Sighs."

"By Canaletto, yes, painted the same day."

"Also taken from Lecter Castle, probably stolen at the same time by the same person," Popil said. "How much more money would you make selling the pair together than if you sold them separately?"

"Four times. No rational person would separate them."

"Then they were separated through ignorance or by accident. Two paintings of the Bridge of Sighs. If the person who stole them still has one of them, wouldn't he want to get the other back?" Popil said.

"Very much."

"There will be publicity about this painting when it hangs in the Jeu de Paume. You are going to the display with me and we will see who comes sniffing around it."

30

LADY MURASAKI'S invitation got her into the Jeu de Paume Museum ahead of the big crowd that buzzed in the Tuileries, impatient to see more than five hundred stolen artworks brought from the Munich Collection Point by the Allied Commission on Monuments, Fine Arts, and Archives in an attempt to find their rightful owners.

A few of the pieces were making their third trip between France and Germany, having been stolen first by Napoleon in Germany and brought back to France, then stolen by the Germans and taken home, then brought back to France once more by the Allies.

Lady Murasaki found in the ground floor of the Jeu de Paume an amazing jumble of Western images. Bloody religion pictures filled one end of the hall, a meathouse of hanging Christs.

For relief she turned to the "Meat Lunch," a cheerful painting of a sumptuous buffet, unattended except for a springer spaniel who was about to help herself to the ham. Beyond it were big canvases attributed to "School of Rubens," featuring rosy women of vast acreage surrounded by plump babies with wings.

And that is where Inspector Popil first caught sight of Lady Murasaki in her counterfeit Chanel, slender and elegant against the pink nudes of Rubens.

Popil soon spotted Hannibal coming up the stairs from the floor below. The inspector did not show himself, but watched.

Ah, now they see each other, the beautiful Japanese lady and her ward. Popil was interested to see their greeting; they stopped a few feet from each other and, while they did not bow, they each acknowledged the other's presence with a smile. Then they came together in a hug. She kissed Hannibal's forehead and touched his cheek, and at once they were in conversation.

Hanging over their warm greeting was a good copy of Caravaggio's "Judith Beheading Holofernes." Popil might have been amused, before the war. Now the back of his neck prickled.

Popil caught Hannibal's eye and nodded

toward a small office near the entrance, where Leet was waiting.

"Munich Collection Point says the painting was seized from a smuggler at the Polish border a year and a half ago," Popil said.

"Did he roll over? Did he tell his source?" Leet said.

Popil shook his head. "The smuggler was strangled in the U.S. Military Prison at Munich by a German trusty. The trusty disappeared that night, into the Dragunovic ratline, we think. It was a dead end.

"The painting is hanging in position eighty-eight near the corner. Monsieur Leet says it looks real. Hannibal, you can tell if it is the painting from your home?"

"Yes."

"If it is your painting, Hannibal, touch your chin. If you are approached, you are just so happy to see it, you have only passing curiosity about who stole it. You are greedy, you want to get it back and sell it as soon as possible, but you want the mate to it as well.

"Be difficult, Hannibal, selfish and spoiled," Popil said, with unbecoming relish. "Do you think you can manage that? Have some friction with your guardian. The person will want a way to contact you, not the other way around. He'll feel safer if the two of you are at odds. Insist on a way to contact him. Leet and I will go out, give us a couple of minutes before you come into the show.

"Come," Popil said to Leet beside him. "We're on legitimate business, man, you don't have to slink."

Hannibal and Lady Murasaki looking, looking along a row of small paintings.

There, at eye level, "The Bridge of Sighs." The sight of it affected Hannibal more than finding the Guardi; with this picture he saw his mother's face.

Other people were streaming in now, lists of artworks in their hands, documentation of ownership in sheaves beneath their arms. Among them was a tall man in a suit so English the jacket appeared to have ailerons.

Holding his list in front of his face, he stood close enough to Hannibal to listen.

"This painting was one of two in my mother's sewing room," Hannibal said. "When we left the castle for the last time, she handed it to me and told me to take it to Cook. She told me not to smudge the back."

Hannibal took the painting off the wall and turned it over. Sparks snapped in his eyes. There, on the back of the painting, was the chalk outline of a baby's hand, mostly worn away, just the thumb and forefinger remaining. The tracing was protected with a sheet of glassine.

Hannibal looked at it for a long time. In this heady moment he thought the finger and thumb moved, a fragment of a wave.

With an effort he remembered Popil's instructions. **If it is your painting, touch your chin.**

He took a deep breath at last and gave the signal.

"This is Mischa's hand," he told Lady Murasaki. "When I was eight they were whitewashing upstairs. This painting and its partner were moved to a divan in my mother's room and draped with a sheet. Mischa and I got under the sheet with the paintings; it was our tent, we were nomads in the desert. I took a chalk from my pocket and traced around her hand to keep away the evil eye. My parents were angry, but the painting wasn't hurt, and finally they were amused, I think."

A man in a homburg hat was coming, hurrying, identification swinging from a string around his neck.

The Monuments man will take a tone with you, quickly be at odds with him, Popil had instructed.

"Please don't do that. Please don't touch," the official said.

"I wouldn't touch it if it didn't belong to me," Hannibal said.

"Until you prove ownership don't touch it or I'll have you escorted from the building. Let me get someone from Registry."

As soon as the official left them, the man in the English suit was at their elbow. "I'm Alec Trebelaux," he said. "I can be of some assistance to you."

Inspector Popil and Leet watched from twenty meters away.

"Do you know him?" Popil said.

"No," Leet said.

Trebelaux invited Hannibal and Lady Murasaki into the shelter of a recessed casement window. He was in his fifties, his bald head deeply suntanned, as were his hands. In the good light of the window, flakes were visible in his eyebrows. Hannibal had never seen him before.

Most men are happy to see Lady Murasaki. Trebelaux was not and she sensed it at once, though his manner was unctuous.

"I'm delighted to meet you, Madame. Is there a question of guardianship?"

"Madame is my valued advisor," Hannibal said. "You deal with me."

Be greedy, Popil said. **Lady Murasaki will be the voice of moderation.**

"There is a question of guardianship, Monsieur," Lady Murasaki said.

"But it's my painting," Hannibal said.

"You'll have to present your claim at a hearing before the commissioners, and they are booked solid for a year and a half. The painting will be impounded until then."

"I am in school, Monsieur Trebelaux, I had counted on being able to—"

"I can help you," Trebelaux said.

"Tell me how, Monsieur."

"I have a hearing scheduled on another matter in three weeks."

"You are a dealer, Monsieur?" Lady Murasaki asked.

"I would be a collector if I could, Madame. But to buy, I must sell. It's a pleasure to have beautiful things in my hands if only for a little while. Your family's collection at Lecter Castle was small but exquisite."

"You knew the collection?" Lady Murasaki said.

"The Lecter Castle losses were listed with the MFAA by your late—by Robert Lecter, I believe."

"And you could present my case at your hearing?" Hannibal said.

"I would claim it for you under the Hague

Convention of 1907; let me explain it to you—"

"Yes, under Article Forty-six, we have talked about it," Hannibal said, glancing at Lady Murasaki and licking his lips to appear avaricious.

"But we talked about a lot of options, Hannibal," Lady Murasaki said.

"What if I do not want to sell, Monsieur Trebelaux?" Hannibal said.

"You would have to wait your turn before the commission. You may be an adult by then."

"This painting is one of a pair, my husband explained to me," Lady Murasaki said. "They are worth much more together. You wouldn't happen to know where the other one is, the Canaletto?"

"No, Madame."

"It would be very much worth your while to find it, Monsieur Trebelaux." She met Trebelaux's eyes. "Can you tell me how I can reach you?" she said, with the faintest emphasis on "I."

He gave the name of a small hotel near the Gare de l'Este, shook Hannibal's hand without looking at him, and disappeared into the crowd.

Hannibal registered as a claimant, and he and Lady Murasaki wandered through the great jumble of art. Seeing the tracing of Mischa's hand left him numb, except for his face where he could feel her touch, patting his cheek.

He stopped in front of a tapestry called "The Sacrifice of Isaac" and looked at it for a long time. "Our upstairs corridors were hung with tapestries," he said. "I could just stand on my tiptoes and reach the bottom edges." He turned up the corner of the fabric and looked at the back. "I've always preferred this side of a tapestry. The threads and strings that make the picture."

"Like tangled thoughts," Lady Murasaki said.

He dropped the corner of the tapestry and Abraham quivered, holding his son's throat taut, the angel extending a hand to stop the knife.

"Do you think God intended to eat Isaac, and that's why he told Abraham to kill him?" Hannibal said.

"No, Hannibal. Of course not. The angel intervenes in time."

"Not always," Hannibal said.

When Trebelaux saw them leave the building, he wet his handkerchief in the men's room and returned to the picture. He looked around quickly. No museum officials were facing him. With a little thrill he took down the painting and, raising the glassine sheet, with his wet handkerchief he scrubbed the outline of Mischa's hand off the back. It could have happened from careless handling when the painting went into escrow. Just as well to get the sentimental value out of the way.

31

THE PLAINCLOTHES OFFICER Rene Aden waited outside Trebelaux's hotel until he saw the light go out in the third-floor walk-up. Then he went to the train station for a fast snack and was lucky to return to his post in time to see Trebelaux come out of the hotel again carrying a gym bag.

Trebelaux took a taxi from the line outside the Gare de l'Este and crossed the Seine to a steam bath in the Rue de Babylone and went inside. Aden parked his unmarked car in a fire zone, counted fifty and went into the lobby area. The air was thick and smelled of liniment. Men in bathrobes were reading newspapers in several languages.

Aden did not want to take off his clothes and pursue Trebelaux into the steam. He was a man of some resolution but his father had died of trench foot and he did not want to take off his shoes in this place. He took a newspaper on its wooden holder from a rack and sat down in a chair.

Trebelaux clopped in clogs too short for him through successive rooms of men slumped on the tile benches, giving themselves up to the heat.

The private saunas could be rented by the fifteen-minute interval. He went into the second one. His entry had already been paid. The air was thick and he wiped his glasses on his towel.

"What kept you," Leet said out of the steam. "I'm about to dissolve."

"The clerk didn't give me the message until I'd already gone to bed," Trebelaux said.

"The police were watching you today at the Jeu de Paume; they know the Guardi you sold me is hot."

"Who put them onto me? You?"

"Hardly. They think you know who has the paintings from Lecter Castle. Do you?"

"No. Maybe my client does."

"If you get the other 'Bridge of Sighs,' I can move both of them," Leet said.

"Where could you sell them?"

"That's my business. A major buyer in America. Let's say an institution. Do you know anything, or am I sweating for nothing?"

"I'll get back to you," Trebelaux said.

On the following afternoon, Trebelaux bought a ticket for Luxembourg at the Gare de l'Este. Officer Aden watched him board the train with his suitcase. The porter seemed dissatisfied with his tip.

Aden made a quick call to the Quai des Orfèvres and swung aboard the train at the last moment, cupping his badge in his hand for the conductor.

Night fell as the train approached its stop at Meaux. Trebelaux took his shaving kit to the bathroom. He hopped off the train just as it began to roll, abandoning his suitcase.

A car was waiting for him a block from the station.

"Why here?" Trebelaux said as he got in beside the driver. "I could have come to your place in Fontainebleau."

"We have business here," said the man behind the wheel. "Good business." Trebelaux knew him as Christophe Kleber.

Kleber drove to a café near the station, where he ate a hearty dinner, lifting his bowl to drink the vichyssoise. Trebelaux toyed with a salad Nicoise and wrote his initials on the edge of the plate with string beans.

"The police seized the Guardi," Trebelaux said as Kleber's veal paillard arrived.

"So you told Hercule. You shouldn't say those things on the telephone. What is the question?"

"They're telling Leet it was looted in the East. Was it?"

"Of course not. Who's asking the question?"

"A police inspector with a list from Arts and Monuments. He said it was stolen. Was it?"

"Did you look at the stamp?"

"A stamp from the Commissariat of Enlightenment, what is that worth?" Trebelaux said.

"Did the policeman say who it belonged to in the East? If it's a Jew it doesn't matter, the Allies are not sending back art taken from Jews. The Jews are dead. The Soviets just keep it."

"It's not a policeman, it's a police **inspector**," said Trebelaux.

"Spoken like a Swiss. What's his name?"

"Popil, something Popil."

"Ah," Kleber said, mopping his mouth with his napkin. "I thought so. No difficulty then. He has been on my payroll for years. It's just a shakedown. What did Leet tell him?"

"Nothing yet, but Leet sounds nervous. For now he'll lay it on Kopnik, his dead colleague," Trebelaux said.

"Leet knows nothing, not an inkling of where you got the picture?"

"Leet thinks I got it in Lausanne, as we agreed. He's squealing for his money back. I said I would check with my client."

"I own Popil, I'll take care of it, forget the whole thing. I have something much more important to talk with you about. Could you possibly travel to America?"

"I don't take things through customs."

"Customs is not your problem, only the negotiations while you're there. You have to see the stuff before it goes, then you see it again over there, across a table in a bank meeting room. You could go by air, take a week."

"What sort of stuff?"

"Small antiquities. Some icons, a salt cellar. We'll take a look, you tell me what you think."

"About the other?"

"You are safe as houses," Kleber said.

Kleber was his name only in France. His birth name was Petras Kolnas and he knew Inspector Popil's name, but not from his payroll.

32

THE CANAL BOAT **Christabel** was tied up with only a spring line at a quay on the Marne River east of Paris, and after Trebelaux came aboard the boat was under way at once. It was a black Dutch-built double-ender with low deck-houses to pass under the bridges and a container garden on deck with flowering bushes.

The boat's owner, a slight man with pale blue eyes and a pleasant expression, was at the gangway to welcome Trebelaux and invite him below. "I'm glad to meet you," the man said and extended his hand. The hair on the owner's hand grew backward, toward the wrist, making his hand feel creepy to the Swiss. "Follow Monsieur Milko. I have the things laid out below."

The owner lingered on deck with Kolnas. They strolled for a moment among the terracotta planters, and stopped beside the single ugly object in the neat garden, a fifty-gallon oil drum with holes cut in it big enough to admit a fish, the top cut out with a torch and tied back on loosely with wire. A tarp was spread on the deck under it. The owner of the boat patted the steel drum hard enough to make it ring.

"Come," he said.

On the lower deck he opened a tall cabinet. It contained a variety of arms: a Dragunov sniper rifle, an American Thompson submachine gun, a couple of German Schmeissers, five Panzer-faust anti-tank weapons for use against other boats, a variety of handguns. The owner se-lected a trident fish spear with the barbs filed off the tines. He handed it to Kolnas.

"I'm not going to cut him a lot," the owner said in pleasant tones. "Eva's not here to clean it up. You do it on deck after we find out what he's told. Puncture him good so he won't float the barrel."

"Milko can—" Kolnas began.

"He was your idea, it's your ass, you do it. Don't you cut meat every day? Milko will bring him up dead and help you load him in the bar-rel when you've stuck him enough. Keep his keys and go through his room. We'll do the dealer Leet if we have to. No loose ends. No more art for a while," said the boat owner, whose name in France was Victor Gustavson.

Victor Gustavson is a very successful businessman, dealing in ex-SS morphine and new prostitutes, mostly women. The name is an alias for Vladis Grutas.

Leet remained alive, but without any of the paintings. They were held in a government vault for years while the court was stalemated on whether the Croatian agreement on reparations could be applied to Lithuania, and Trebelaux stared sightless from his barrel on the bottom of the Marne, no longer bald, hirsute now with green hair algae and eelgrass that wave in the current like the locks of his youth.

No other painting from Lecter Castle would surface for years.

Through Inspector Popil's good offices, Hannibal Lecter was allowed to visit the paintings in custody from time to time over the following years. Maddening to sit in the dumb silence of the vault under the eye of a guard, in earshot of the man's adenoidal breathing.

Hannibal looks at the painting he took from his mother's hands and knows the past was not the past at all; the beast that panted its hot stench on his and Mischa's skins continues to breathe, is breathing now. He turns the "Bridge of Sighs" to the wall and stares at the back of the painting for minutes at a time—Mischa's hand erased, it is only a blank square now where he projects his seething dreams.

He is growing and changing, or perhaps emerging as what he has ever been.

II

When I said that Mercy stood
Within the borders of the wood,
I meant the lenient beast with claws
And bloody swift-dispatching jaws.

——LAWRENCE SPINGARN

33

ON CENTER STAGE in the Paris Opera, Dr. Faust's time was running out in his deal with the Devil. Hannibal Lecter and Lady Murasaki watched from an intimate box at stage left as Faust's pleas to avoid the flames soared to the fireproof ceiling of Garnier's great theater.

Hannibal at eighteen was rooting for Mephistopheles and contemptuous of Faust, but he only half-listened to the climax. He was watching and breathing Lady Murasaki, in full fig for the opera. Winks of light came from the opposite boxes as gentlemen turned their opera glasses away from the stage to look at her as well.

Against the stage lights she was in silhouette, just as Hannibal first saw her at the chateau when he was a boy. The images came to him in order: **gloss of a handsome crow drinking**

from the rainspout, gloss of Lady Murasaki's hair. First her silhouette, then she opened a casement and the light touched her face.

Hannibal had come a long way on the bridge of dreams. He had grown to fill the late count's evening clothes, while in appearance Lady Murasaki remained exactly the same.

Her hand closed on the material of her skirt and he heard the rustle of the cloth above the music. Knowing she could feel his gaze, he looked away from her, looked around the box.

The box had character. Behind the seats, screened from the opposing boxes, was a wicked little goat-footed chaise where lovers might retire while the orchestra provided cadence from down below—in the previous season, an older gentleman had succumbed to heart failure on the chaise during the final measures of "Flight of the Bumblebee," as Hannibal had occasion to know from ambulance service.

Hannibal and Lady Murasaki were not alone in the box.

In the front pair of seats sat the Commissioner of Police for the Prefecture of Paris and his wife, leaving little doubt as to where Lady Murasaki got the tickets. From Inspector Popil, of course. How pleasant that Popil himself could not attend—probably detained by a murder investigation, hopefully a time-consuming and dangerous one, out-of-doors in bad weather perhaps, with the threat of fatal lightning.

The lights came up and tenor Beniamino Gigli got the standing ovation he deserved, and from a tough house. The police commissioner and his wife turned in the box and shook hands all around, everyone's palms still numb from applauding.

The commissioner's wife had a bright and curious eye. She took in Hannibal, fitted to perfection in the count's dinner clothes, and she could not resist a question. "Young man, my husband tells me you were the youngest person ever admitted to medical school in France."

"The records are not complete, Madame. Probably there were surgeon's apprentices . . ."

"Is it true that you read through your textbooks once and then return them to the bookstore within the week to get all your money back?"

Hannibal smiled. "Oh no, Madame. That is not entirely accurate," he said. **Wonder where that information came from? The same place as the tickets.** Hannibal leaned close to the lady. Trying for an exit line, he rolled his eyes at the commissioner and bent over the lady's hand, to whisper loudly, "That sounds like a crime to me."

The commissioner was in a good humor, having seen Faust suffer for his sins. "I'll turn a blind eye, young man, if you confess to my wife at once."

"The truth is, Madame, I don't get all my money back. The bookstore holds out a two-hundred-franc restocking fee for their trouble."

Away then and down the great staircase of the opera, beneath the torchieres, Hannibal and Lady Murasaki descending faster than Faust to get away from the crowd, Pils' painted ceilings moving over them, wings everywhere in paint and stone. There were taxis now in the Place de l'Opera. A vendor's charcoal brazier laced the air with a whiff of Faust's nightmare. Hannibal flagged a taxi.

"I'm surprised you told Inspector Popil about my books," he said inside the car.

"He found it out himself," Lady Murasaki said. "He told the commissioner, the commissioner told his wife. She needs to flirt. You are not naturally obtuse, Hannibal."

She is uneasy in closed places with me now; she expresses it as irritation.

"Sorry."

She looked at him quickly as the taxi passed a streetlight. "Your animosity clouds your judgment. Inspector Popil keeps up with you because you intrigue him."

"No, my lady, you intrigue him. I expect he pesters you with his verse . . ."

Lady Murasaki did not satisfy Hannibal's curiosity. "He knows you are first in the class," she said. "He's proud of that. His interest is largely benign."

"Largely benign is not a happy diagnosis."

The trees were budding in the Place de Vosges, fragrant in the spring night. Hannibal dismissed the cab, feeling Lady Murasaki's quick glance even in the darkness of the loggia. Hannibal was not a child, he did not stay over anymore.

"I have an hour and I want to walk," he said.

34

"YOU HAVE TIME for tea," Lady Murasaki said.

She took him at once to the terrace, clearly preferring to be outdoors with him. He did not know how he felt about that. He had changed and she had not. A puff of breeze and the oil lamp flame stretched high. When she poured green tea he could see the pulse in her wrist, and the faint fragrance from her sleeve entered him like a thought of his own.

"A letter from Chiyoh," she said. "She has ended her engagement. Diplomacy no longer suits her."

"Is she happy?"

"I think so. It was a good match in the old way of thinking. How can I disapprove—she writes that she is doing what I did—following her heart."

"Following it where?"

"A young man at Kyoto University, the School of Engineering."

"I would like to see her happy."

"I would like to see you happy. Are you sleeping, Hannibal?"

"When there's time. I take a nap on a gurney when I can't sleep in my room."

"You know what I mean."

"Do I dream? Yes. Do you not revisit Hiroshima in your dreams?"

"I don't invite my dreams."

"I need to remember, any way I can."

At the door she gave him a bento box with a snack for overnight and packets of chamomile tea. "For sleep," she said.

He kissed Lady Murasaki's hand, not the little nod of French politesse, but kissed the back of her hand so that he could taste it.

He repeated the haiku he had written to her so long ago, on the night of the butcher.

**"Night heron revealed
By the rising harvest moon—
Which is lovelier?"**

"This is not the harvest," she said, smiling, putting her hand on his heart as she had done since he was thirteen years old. And then she took her hand away, and the place on his chest felt cold.

"Do you really return your books?"

"Yes."

"Then you can remember everything in the books."

"Everything important."

"Then you can remember it is important not to tease Inspector Popil. Unprovoked he is harmless to you. And to me."

She has put on irritation like a winter kimono. Seeing that, can I use it to keep from thinking about her in the bath at the chateau so long ago, herfaceandbreastslikewaterflowers? Like the pink and cream lilies on the moat? Can I? I can not.

He went out into the night, uncomfortable in his stride for the first block or two, and emerged from the narrow streets of the Marais to cross the Pont Louis Phillippe with the Seine sliding under the bridge and the bridge touched by the moon.

Seen from the east, Notre Dame was like a great spider with its flying-buttress legs and the many eyes of its round windows. Hannibal could see the stone spider-cathedral scuttling around town in the darkness, grabbing the odd train from the Gare d'Orsay like a worm for its delectation or, better, spotting a nutritious police inspector coming out of his headquarters on the Quai des Orfèvres, an easy pounce away.

He crossed the footbridge to the Ile de la Cite and rounded the cathedral. Sounds of a choir practice came from Notre Dame.

Hannibal paused beneath the arches of the center entrance, looking at the Last Judgment in relief on the arches and lintels above the door. He was considering it for a display in his memory palace, to record a complex dissection of the throat: There on the upper lintel St. Michael held a pair of scales as though he himself were conducting an autopsy. St. Michael's scales were not unlike the hyoid bone, and he was over-arched by the Saints of the Mastoid Process. The lower lintel, where the damned were being marched away in chains, would be the clavicle, and the succession of arches would serve as the structural layers of the throat, to a catechism easy to remember, **Sternohyoid omohyoid thyrohyoid/juuugular, Amen.**

No, it wouldn't do. The problem was the lighting. Displays in a memory palace must be well lit, with generous spaces between them. This dirty stone was too much of one color as well. Hannibal had missed a test question once because the answer was dark, and in his mind he had placed it against a dark background. The complex dissection of the cervical triangle scheduled for the coming week would require clear, well-spaced displays.

The last choristers trailed out of the cathedral, carrying their vestments over their arms. Hannibal went inside. Notre Dame was dark but for the votive candles. He went to St. Joan of Arc, in marble near a southside exit. Before her, tiers of candles flared in the draft from the door. Hannibal leaned against a pillar in the darkness and looked through the flames at her face. **Fire on his mother's clothes.** The candle flames reflected redly in his eyes.

The candlelight played on St. Joan and gave random expressions to her face like chance tunes in a wind chime. Memory, memory. Hannibal wondered if St. Joan, with her memories, might prefer a votive other than fire. He knew his mother would.

Footsteps of the sexton coming, his jangling keys echoed off the near walls first, then again from the high ceiling, his footsteps made a double-tap too as they sounded from the floor and echoed down from the vast upper dark.

The sexton saw Hannibal's eyes first, shining red beyond the firelight, and a primal caution stirred in him. The back of the sexton's neck prickled and he made a cross with his keys. Ah, it was only a man, and a young one at that. The sexton waved his keys before him like a censer. "It's time," he said and gestured with his chin.

"Yes, it's time, and past time," Hannibal replied and went out the side door into the night.

35

ACROSS THE SEINE on the Pont au Double and down the Rue de la Bûcherie, where he heard a saxophone and laughter from a basement jazz club. A couple in the doorway smoking, a whiff of kif about them. The girl raised on her tiptoes to kiss the young man's cheek and Hannibal felt the kiss distinctly on his face. Scraps of music mixed with the music running in his head, keeping time, time. Time.

Along the Rue Dante and across the wide Boulevard Saint-Germain, feeling moonlight on his head, and behind the Cluny to the Rue de l'Ecole de Médecine and the night entrance to the medical school, where a dim lamp burned. Hannibal unlocked the door and let himself in.

Alone in the building, he changed into a

white coat and picked up the clipboard with his list of tasks. Hannibal's mentor and supervisor at the medical school was Professor Dumas, a gifted anatomist who chose to teach instead of practice on the living. Dumas was a brilliant, abstracted man and lacked the glint of a surgeon. He required each of his students to write a letter to the anonymous cadaver he would dissect, thanking this specific donor for the privilege of studying his or her body, and including assurances that the body would be treated with respect, and draped at all times in any area not under immediate study.

For tomorrow's lectures, Hannibal was to prepare two displays: a reflection of the rib cage, exposing the pericardium intact, and a delicate cranial dissection.

Night in the gross-anatomy laboratory. The large room with its high windows and big vent fan was cool enough so that the draped cadavers, preserved with formalin, remained on the twenty tables overnight. In summer they would be returned to the cadaver tank at the end of the workday. Pitiful little bodies underneath the sheets, the unclaimed, the starvelings found huddled in alleys, still hugging themselves in death until rigor passed and then, in the formalin bath of the cadaver tank with their fellows, they let themselves go at last. Frail and birdlike, they were shriveled like the birds frozen and fallen to the snow, that starving men skin with their teeth.

With forty million dead in the war it seemed odd to Hannibal that the medical students would have to use cadavers long preserved in tanks, the color leached out of them by the formalin.

Occasionally the school was lucky enough to get a criminal corpse from the gallows or the firing squad at the fort of Montrouge or Fresnes, or the guillotine at La Santé. Faced with the cranial dissection, Hannibal was lucky to have the head of a La Santé graduate watching him from the sink now, countenance caked with blood and straw.

While the school's autopsy saw awaited a new motor, back-ordered for months, Hannibal had modified an American electric drill, brazing a small rotary blade to the drill bit to aid in dissection. It had a current converter the size of a bread box that made a humming sound nearly as loud as the saw.

Hannibal had finished with the chest dissection when the electricity failed, as it often did, and the lights went out. He worked at the sink by the light of a kerosene lamp, flushing away the blood and straw from his subject's face and waiting for the electricity to come on again.

When the lights came up, he wasted no time reflecting the scalp and removing the top of the cranium in a coronal dissection to expose the brain. He injected the major blood vessels with colored gel, piercing the dura mater covering the brain as little as possible. It was more difficult, but the professor, inclined to the theatrical, would want to remove the dura mater himself before the class, whipping the curtain off the brain, so Hannibal left it largely intact.

He rested his gloved hand lightly on the brain. Obsessed with memory, and the blank places in his own mind, he wished that by touch he could read a dead man's dreams, that by force of will he could explore his own.

The laboratory at night was a good place to think, the quiet broken only by the clink of instruments and, rarely, the groan of a subject in an early stage of dissection, when organs might still contain some air.

Hannibal performed a meticulous partial dissection of the left side of the face, then sketched the head, both the dissected side of the face and the untouched side as well, for the anatomical illustrations that were part of his scholarship.

Now he wanted to permanently store in his mind the muscular, neural and venous structures of the face. Sitting with his gloved hand on the head of his subject, Hannibal went to the center of his own mind and into the foyer of his memory palace. He elected for music in the corridors, a Bach string quartet, and passed quickly through the Hall of Mathematics, through Chemistry, to a room he'd adopted recently from the Carnavalet Museum and renamed the Hall of the Cranium. It took only a few minutes to store everything, associating anatomical details with the set arrangement of displays in the Carnavalet, being careful not to put the venous blues of the face against blues in the tapestries.

When he had finished in the Hall of the Cranium, he paused for a moment in the Hall of Mathematics, near the entrance. It was one of the oldest parts of the palace in his mind. He wanted to treat himself to the feeling he got at the age of seven when he understood the proof Mr. Jakov showed him. All of Mr. Jakov's tutorial sessions at the castle were stored there, but none of their talks from the hunting lodge.

Everything from the hunting lodge was outside the memory palace, still on the grounds, but in the dark sheds of his dreams, scorched black like the hunting lodge, and to get there he would have to go outside. He would have to cross the snow where the ripped pages of

Huyghens' **Treatise on Light** blew across Mr. Jakov's brains and blood, scattered and frozen to the snow.

In these palace corridors he could choose music or not, but in the sheds he could not control the sound, and a particular sound there could kill him.

He emerged from the memory palace back into his mind, came back behind his eyes and to his eighteen-year-old body, which sat beside the table in the anatomy laboratory, his hand upon a brain.

He sketched for another hour. In his finished sketch, the veins and nerves of the dissected half of the face exactly reflected the subject on the table. The unmarked side of the face did not resemble the subject at all. It was a face from the sheds. It was the face of Vladis Grutas, though Hannibal only thought of him as Blue-Eyes.

Up the five flights of narrow stairs to his room above the medical school, and sleep.

The garret's ceiling sloped, and the low side was neat, harmonious, Japanese, with a low bed. His desk was on the high side of the room. The walls around and over his desk were wild with images, drawings of dissections, anatomical illustrations in progress. In each case the organs and vessels were exactly rendered, but the faces of the subjects were faces he saw in dreams. Over all, a long-fanged gibbon skull watched from a shelf.

He could scrub away the smell of formalin, and the chemical smell of the lab did not reach this high in the drafty old building. He did not carry grotesque images of the dead and half-dissected into his sleep, nor the criminals, cleaved or hanged, he sometimes picked up from the jails. There was only one image, one sound, that could drive him out of sleep. And he never knew when it was coming.

Moonset. The moonlight diffused by the wavy, bubbled window glass creeps across Hannibal's face and inches silent up the wall. It touches Mischa's hand in the drawing above his bed, moves over the partial faces in the anatomical drawings, moves over the faces from his dreams, and comes at last to the gibbon skull, first shining white on the great fangs and then the brow above the deep eye sockets. From the dark inside its skull, the gibbon watches Hannibal asleep. Hannibal's face is childlike. He makes a noise and turns on his side, pulling his arm away from an unseen grip.

Standing with Mischa in the barn beside the lodge, holding her close, Mischa coughing. Bowl-Man feels the flesh of their arms and speaks, but no sound comes out of his mouth, only his vile breath visible in the freezing air. Mischa buries her face against Hannibal's chest to get away from Bowl-Man's breath. Blue-Eyes is saying something, and now they are singing, cozening. Seeing the axe and bowl. Flying at Blue-Eyes, taste of blood and beard stubble, they are taking Mischa away. They have the axe and the bowl. Breaking free and running after them, feet lifting tooo slooooow to the door, Blue-Eyed One and Bowl-Man holding Mischa by her wrists above the ground, she twisting her head to look back desperately at him across the bloody snow and calling—

Hannibal came awake, choking, holding on to the end of the dream, clamping his eyes tight shut and tried to force himself past the point where he awoke. He bit the corner of the pillowcase and made himself go over the dream. What did the men call each other? What were their names? When did he lose the sound? He couldn't remember when it went away. He wanted to know what they called each other. He had to finish the dream. He went into his memory palace and tried to cross the grounds to the dark sheds, past Mr. Jakov's brains on the snow, but he could not. He could endure to see his mother's clothes on fire, his parents and Berndt and Mr. Jakov dead in the yard. He could see the looters moving below him and Mischa in the hunting lodge. But he could not go past Mischa suspended in the air, turning her head to look at him. He could remember nothing after that, he could only recall much later, he was riding on a tank, found by the soldiers with the chain locked around his neck. He wanted to remember. He had to remember. **Teethinastoolpit**. The flash did not come often; it made him sit up. He looked at the gibbon in the moonlight. **Teeth much smaller than that. Baby teeth. Not terrible. Like mine can be. I have to hear the voices carried on their stinking breath, I know what their words smell like. I have to remember their names. I have to find them. And I will. How can I interrogate myself?**

36

PROFESSOR DUMAS WROTE a mild, round hand, unnatural in a physician. His note said: **Hannibal, would you please see what you can do in the matter of Louis Ferrat at La Santé?**

The professor had attached a newspaper clipping about Ferrat's sentencing with a few details about him: Ferrat, from Lyon, had been a minor Vichy functionary, a petty collaborator during the German occupation, but then was arrested by the Germans for forging and selling ration coupons. After the war he was accused of complicity in war crimes, but released for insufficient evidence. A French court convicted him of killing two women in 1949–1950 for personal reasons. He was scheduled to die in three days.

La Santé Prison is in the 14th arrondissement,

not far from the medical school. Hannibal reached it in a fifteen-minute walk.

Workmen with a load of pipe were repairing the drains in the courtyard, the site of guillotine executions since the public was barred from attending in 1939. The guards at the gate knew Hannibal by sight and passed him in. As he signed the visitors' log he saw the signature of Inspector Popil high on the page.

The sound of hammering came from a large bare room off the main corridor. As he passed by, Hannibal caught sight of a face he recognized. The state executioner, Anatole Tourneau himself, traditionally known as "Monsieur Paris," had brought the guillotine from its garage on the Rue de la Tombe-Issoire to set it up inside the prison. He was twiddling the little wheels of the blade carrier, the **mouton,** which prevent the blade from jamming on its way down.

Monsieur Paris was a perfectionist. To his credit, he always used a cover at the top of the uprights so the subject did not have to see the blade.

Louis Ferrat was in the condemned cell, separated by a corridor from the other cells on a second-floor tier in the first building of La Santé. The din of the crowded prison reached his cell as a wash of murmurings and cries and clangs, but he could hear the blows of Monsieur

Paris' mallet as the assembly proceeded on the floor below.

Louis Ferrat was a slender man, with dark hair, newly cropped off his neck and the back of his head. The hair on top was left long, to provide Monsieur Paris' assistant a better grip than Louis' small ears would provide.

Ferrat sat on his cot in combination underwear, rubbing between his thumb and fingers a cross on a chain about his neck. His shirt and pants were carefully arranged on a chair, as though a person had been seated there and evaporated out of the clothing. The shoes were side by side beneath the pants cuffs. The clothing reclined in the chair in the anatomical position. Ferrat heard Hannibal but he did not look up.

"Monsieur Louis Ferrat, good afternoon," Hannibal said.

"Monsieur Ferrat has stepped away from his cell," Ferrat said. "I represent him. What do you want?"

Hannibal took in the clothing without moving his eyes. "I want to ask him to make a gift of his body to the medical school, for science. It will be treated with great respect."

"You'll take his body anyway. Drag it away."

"I can't and I wouldn't take his body without his permission. Or ever drag it."

"Ah, here is my client now," Ferrat said. He turned away from Hannibal and conferred quietly with the clothing as though it had just walked into the cell and seated itself in the chair. Ferrat returned to the bars.

"He wants to know why should he give it to you?"

"Fifteen thousand francs for his relatives."

Ferrat turned to the clothing and then back to Hannibal. "Monsieur Ferrat says, **Fuck my relatives. They hold out their hand and I'll shit in it.**" Ferrat dropped his voice. "Forgive the language—he is distraught, and the gravity of the matter requires me to quote him exactly."

"I understand perfectly," Hannibal said. "Do you think he'd like to contribute the fee to a cause his family despises, would that be a satisfaction to him, Monsieur . . . ?"

"You may call me Louis—Monsieur Ferrat and I share the same first name. No. I believe he is adamant. Monsieur Ferrat lives somewhat apart from himself. He says he has very little influence on himself."

"I see. He is not alone in that."

"I hardly see how you understand anything, you're not much more than a chi—not much more than a schoolboy yourself."

"You might help me then. Each student at the medical school writes a personal letter of appreciation to the donor with whom he is involved. Knowing Monsieur Ferrat as you do, could you help me compose a letter of appreciation? Just in case he should decide favorably?"

Ferrat rubbed his face. His fingers appeared to have an extra set of knuckles where they had been broken and badly set years ago.

"Who would ever read it, other than Monsieur Ferrat himself?"

"It would be posted at the school, if he wishes. All the faculty would see it, prominent and influential people. He could submit it to **Le Canard Enchaîné** for publication."

"What sort of thing would you want to say?"

"I'd describe him as selfless, cite his contribution to science, to the French people, to medical advances that will help the oncoming generation of children."

"Never mind children. Leave children out."

Hannibal quickly wrote a salutation on his notepad. "Do you think this is sufficiently honorific?" He held it up high enough for Louis Ferrat to have to look up at it, the better to gauge the length of his neck.

Not a very long neck. Unless Monsieur Paris got a good grip on his hair, there wouldn't be much left below the hyoid bone, useless for a frontal cervical triangle display.

"We mustn't neglect his patriotism," Ferrat

said. "When Le Grand Charles broadcast from London, who responded? It was Ferrat at the barricades! Vive la France!"

Hannibal watched as patriotic fervor swelled the artery in the traitor Ferrat's forehead and caused the jugular and carotid to stand out in his neck—**an eminently injectable head.**

"Yes, vive la France!" Hannibal said, redoubling his efforts: "Our letter should emphasize that, though they call him Vichy, he was actually a hero of the Resistance, then?"

"Certainly."

"He saved downed airmen, I would imagine?"

"On a number of occasions."

"Performed the customary acts of sabotage?"

"Often, and without regard for his own safety."

"Tried to protect the Jews?"

Quarter-second hitch. "Heedless of risk to himself."

"Was tortured perhaps, he suffered broken fingers for the sake of France?"

"He could still use them to salute proudly when Le Grand Charles returned," Ferrat said.

Hannibal finished scribbling. "I've just listed the highlights here, do you think you could show it to him?"

Ferrat looked over the sheet of notebook paper, touching each point with his forefinger, nodding, murmuring to himself. "You might put in a few testimonials from his friends in the Resistance, I could supply those. A moment please." Ferrat turned his back to Hannibal and leaned close to his clothing. He turned back with a decision.

"My client's response is: **Merde. Tell the young fucker I'll see the dope and rub it on my gums first before I sign.** Pardon, but that is verbatim literatim." Ferrat became confidential, leaning close to the bars. "Others on the tier told him he could get enough laudanum— enough laudanum to be indifferent to the knife. 'To dream and not to scream' is how I'd couch it in a courtroom setting. The St. Pierre medical school is giving laudanum in exchange for . . . permission. Do you give laudanum?"

"I will be back to see you, with an answer for him."

"I wouldn't wait too long," Ferrat said. "St. Pierre will be coming round." He raised his voice and gripped the neck of his combination underwear as he might clutch his waistcoat during an oration. "I'm empowered to negotiate on his behalf with St. Pierre as well." Close to the bars and quiet now: "Three days and poor Ferrat will be dead, and I'll be in mourning and out a client. You are a medical person. Do you think it's going to hurt? Hurt Monsieur Ferrat when they . . ."

"Absolutely not. The uncomfortable part is now. Beforehand. As for the thing itself, no. Not even for an instant." Hannibal had started away, when Ferrat called to him and he went back to the bars.

"The students wouldn't laugh at him, at his parts."

"Certainly not. A subject is always draped, except for the exact field of study."

"Even if he were . . . somewhat unique?"

"In what way?"

"Even if he had, well, infantile parts?"

"A common circumstance, and never, ever, an occasion for humor," Hannibal said. **There's a candidate for the anatomy museum, where donors are not credited.**

The pounding of the executioner's mallet registered as a twitch in the corner of Louis Ferrat's eye as he sat on his bunk, his hand on the sleeve of his companion, the clothes. Hannibal saw him imagining the assembly in his mind, the uprights lifted into place, the blade with its edge protected by a slit piece of garden hose, beneath it the receptacle.

With a start, seeing it in his mind, Hannibal realized what the receptacle was. It was a

baby's bathtub. Like a falling blade Hannibal's mind cut off the thought and, in the silence after, Louis' anguish was as familiar to him as the veins in the man's face, as the arteries in his own.

"I'll get him the laudanum," Hannibal said. Failing laudanum, he could buy a ball of opium in a doorway.

"Give me the consent form. Collect it when you bring the dope."

Hannibal looked at Louis Ferrat, reading his face as intently as he had studied his neck, smelling the fear on him, and said, "Louis, something for your client to consider. All the wars, all the suffering and pain that happened in the centuries before his birth, before his life, how much did all that bother him?"

"Not at all."

"Then why should anything after his life bother him? It is untroubled sleep. The difference is he will not wake to this."

37

THE ORIGINAL WOOD BLOCK engravings for Vesalius' great atlas of anatomy, **De Fabrica,** were destroyed in Munich in World War II. For Dr. Dumas the engravings were holy relics and in his grief and anger he became inspired to compile a new atlas of anatomy. It would be the best to date in the line of atlases that succeeded Vesalius' in the four hundred years since **De Fabrica.**

Dumas found that drawings were superior to photography in illustrating the anatomy, and essential in elucidating cloudy X-rays. Dr. Dumas was a superior anatomist, but he was not an artist. To his great good fortune, he saw Hannibal Lecter's schoolboy drawing of a frog, followed his progress and secured for him a medical scholarship.

Early evening in the laboratory. During the day, Professor Dumas had dissected the inner ear in his daily lecture, and left it to Hannibal, who now drew the cochlear bones on chalkboard at 5x enlargement.

The night bell rang. Hannibal was expecting a delivery from the Fresnes firing squad. He collected a gurney and pushed it down the long corridor to the night entrance. One wheel of the gurney clicked on the stone floor and he made a mental note to fix it.

Standing beside the body was Inspector Popil. Two ambulance attendants transferred the limp and leaking burden from their litter to the gurney and drove away.

Lady Murasaki had once remarked, to Hannibal's annoyance, that Popil looked like the handsome actor Louis Jourdan.

"Good evening, Inspector."

"I'll have a word with you," Inspector Popil said, looking nothing whatever like Louis Jourdan.

"Do you mind if I work while we talk?"

"No."

"Come, then." Hannibal rolled the gurney down the corridor, clicking louder now. A wheel bearing probably.

Popil held open the swinging doors of the laboratory.

As Hannibal had expected, the massive chest wounds occasioned by the Fresnes rifles had drained the body very well. It was ready for the cadaver tank. That procedure could have waited, but Hannibal was curious to see if Popil in the cadaver tank room might look even less like Louis Jourdan, and if the surroundings might affect his peachy complexion.

It was a raw concrete space adjacent to the laboratory, reached through double doors with rubber seals. A round tank of formalin twelve feet in diameter was set into the floor and covered with a zinc lid. The lid had a series of doors in it on piano hinges. In one corner of the room an incinerator burned the waste of the day, an assortment of ears on this occasion.

A chain hoist stood above the tank. The cadavers, tagged and numbered, each in a chain harness, were tethered to a bar around the circumference of the tank. A large fan with dusty blades was set into the wall. Hannibal started the fan and opened the heavy metal doors of the tank. He tagged the body and put it into a harness and with the hoist swung the body over the tank and lowered it into the formalin.

"Did you come from Fresnes with him?" Hannibal said as the bubbles came up.

"Yes."

"You attended the execution?"

"Yes."

"Why, Inspector?"

"I arrested him. If I brought him to that place, I attend."

"A matter of conscience, Inspector?"

"The death is a consequence of what I do. I believe in consequences. Did you promise Louis Ferrat laudanum?"

"Laudanum legally obtained."

"But not legally prescribed."

"It's a common practice with the condemned, in exchange for permission, I'm sure you know that."

"Yes. Don't give it to him."

"Ferrat is one of yours? You prefer him sober?"

"Yes."

"You want him to feel the full consequence, Inspector? Will you ask Monsieur Paris to take the cover off the guillotine so he can see the blade, sober, with his vision unclouded?"

"My reasons are my own. What you will not do is give him laudanum. If I find him under the influence of laudanum you will never hold a medical license in France: Look at that with your vision unclouded."

Hannibal saw that the room didn't bother Popil. He watched the inspector's duty come up in him.

Popil turned away from him to speak. "It

would be a shame, because you show promise. I congratulate you on your remarkable grades," Popil said. "You have pleased . . . your family would be—and is—very proud. Good night."

"Good night, Inspector. Thank you for the opera tickets."

38

EVENING IN PARIS, soft rain and the cobbles shining. Shopkeepers, closing for the night, directed the flow of the rainwater in the gutters to suit them with rolled scraps of carpet.

The tiny windshield wiper on the medical school van was powered by manifold vacuum and Hannibal had to lift off the gas from time to time to clear the windshield on the short drive to La Santé Prison.

He backed through the gate into the courtyard, rain falling cold on the back of his neck as he stuck his head out the van window to see, the guard in the sentry box not coming out to direct him.

Inside the main corridor of La Santé, Monsieur Paris' assistant beckoned him into the room with the machine. The man was wearing an oilskin apron and had an oilskin cover on his new derby for the occasion. He had placed the splash shield before his station in front of the blade to better protect his shoes and cuffs.

A long wicker basket lined with zinc stood beside the guillotine, ready for the body to be tipped into it.

"No bagging in here, warden's orders," he said. "You'll have to take the basket and bring it back. Will it go in the van?"

"Yes."

"Had you better measure?"

"No."

"Then you'll take him all together. We'll tuck it under his arm. They're next door."

In a whitewashed room with high barred windows Louis Ferrat lay bound on a gurney in the harsh light of overhead bulbs.

The plank tipping board, the **bascule,** from the guillotine was under him. An IV was in his arm.

Inspector Popil stood over Louis Ferrat, talking quietly to him, shading Ferrat's eyes from the glare with his hand. The prison doctor inserted a hypodermic into the IV and injected a small amount of clear fluid.

When Hannibal came into the room Popil did not look up.

"**Remember,** Louis," Popil said. "I need for you to remember."

Louis' rolling eye caught Hannibal at once.

Popil saw Hannibal then and held up a hand for him to keep back. Popil bent close to Louis Ferrat's sweating face. "Tell me."

"I put Cendrine's body in two bags. I weighted them with plowshares, and the rhymes were coming—"

"Not Cendrine, Louis. **Remember.** Who told Klaus Barbie where the children were hidden, so he could ship them East? I want you to remember."

"I asked Cendrine, I said, 'Just touch it'—but she laughed at me and the rhymes started coming—"

"No! Not Cendrine," Popil said. "Who told the Nazis about the children?"

"I can't stand to think about it."

"You only have to stand it once more. This will help you remember."

The doctor pushed a little more drug into Louis' vein, rubbing his arm to move the drug along.

"Louis, you must remember. Klaus Barbie shipped the children to Auschwitz. Who told him where the children were hidden? Did you tell him?"

Louis' face was grey. "The Gestapo caught me

forging ration cards," he said. "When they broke my fingers, I gave them Pardou—Pardou knew where the orphans were hidden. He got so much a head for them and kept his fingers. He's mayor of Trent-la-Forêt now. I saw it, but I didn't help. They looked out of the back of the truck at me."

"Pardou." Popil nodded. "Thank you, Louis."

Popil started to turn from him when Louis said, "Inspector?"

"Yes, Louis?"

"When the Nazis threw the children into the trucks, where were the police?"

Popil closed his eyes for a moment, then nodded to a guard, who opened the door into the guillotine room. Hannibal could see a priest and Monsieur Paris standing beside the machine. The executioner's assistant removed the chain and crucifix from around Louis' neck and put it in his hand, bound by his side. Louis looked at Hannibal. He lifted his head and opened his mouth. Hannibal went to his side and Popil did not try to stop him.

"The money, Louis?"

"St.-Sulpice. Not the poor box, the box for souls in Purgatory. Where's the dope?"

"I promise." Hannibal had a vial of dilute tincture of opium in the pocket of his jacket. The guard and executioner's assistant officially looked away. Popil did not look away. Hannibal held it to Louis' lips and he drank it down. Louis nodded toward his hand and opened his mouth again. Hannibal put the crucifix and chain in Louis' mouth before they turned him over on the plank that would carry him under the blade.

Hannibal watched the burden of Louis' heart roll away. The gurney bumped over the threshold of the guillotine room and the guard closed the door.

"He wanted his crucifix to remain with his head instead of his heart," Popil said. "You knew what he wanted, didn't you? What else do you and Louis have in common?"

"Our curiosity about where the police were when the Nazis threw the children into the trucks. We have that in common."

Popil might have swung at him then. The moment passed. Popil shut his notebook and left the room.

Hannibal approached the doctor at once.

"Doctor, what is that drug?"

"A combination of thiopental sodium and two other hypnotics. The Sûreté has it for interrogations. It releases repressed memory sometimes. In the condemned."

"We need to allow for it in our blood work in the lab. May I have the sample?"

The doctor handed over the vial. "The formula and the dosage are on the label."

From the next room came a heavy thud.

"I'd wait a few minutes if I were you," the doctor said. "Let Louis settle down."

39

HANNIBAL LAY ON the low bed in his garret room. His candles flickered on the faces he has drawn from his dreams, and shadows played over the gibbon skull. He stared into the gibbon's empty sockets and put his lower lip behind his teeth as if to match the gibbon's fangs. Beside him was a windup phonograph with a lily-shaped trumpet. He had a needle in his arm, attached to a hypodermic filled with the cocktail of hypnotics used in the interrogation of Louis Ferrat.

"Mischa, Mischa. I'm coming." **Fire on his mother's clothes, the votive candles flaring before St. Joan. The sexton said, "It's time."**

He started the turntable and lowered the thick needle arm onto the record of children's songs.

The record was scratchy, the sound tinny and thin, but it pierced him.

Sagt, wer mag das Mannlein sein
Das da steht im Walde allein

He pushed the plunger of the needle a quarter of an inch and felt the drug burn in his vein. He rubbed his arm to move it along. Hannibal stared steadily by candlelight at the faces sketched from his dreams, and tried to make their mouths move. Perhaps they would sing at first, and then say their names. Hannibal sang himself, to start them singing.

He could not make the faces move any more than he could flesh the gibbon. But it was the gibbon who smiled behind his fangs, lipless, his mandible curving in a grin, **and the Blue-Eyed One smiled then, the bemused expression burnt in Hannibal's mind. And then the smell of wood smoke in the lodge, the tiered smoke in the cold room, the cadaverine breath of the men crowded around him and Mischa on the hearth. They took them out to the barn then. Pieces of children's clothing in the barn, stained and strange to him. He could not hear the men talking, could not hear what they called each other, but then the distorted voice of Bowl-Man saying, "Take** her, she's going to die anyway. He'll stay freeeeeaaassh a little longer." Fighting and biting and coming now the thing he could not stand to see, Mischa held up by the arms, feet clear of the bloody snow, twisting, LOOKING BACK AT HIM.

"ANNIBA!!" her voice—

Hannibal sat up in the bed. His arm in bending pushed the plunger of the hypodermic all the way down.

And then the barn swam around him.

"ANNIBA!!"

Hannibal pulling free running to the door after them, the barn door slamming on his arm, bones cracking, Blue-Eyes turning back to raise the firewood stick, swinging at his head, from the yard the sound of the axe and now the welcome dark.

Hannibal heaved on his garret bed, his vision going in and out of focus, the faces swimming on the wall.

Past it. Past the thing he could not look at, the thing he could not hear and live. Waking in the lodge with blood dried on the side of his head and pain shooting from his upper arm, chained to the upstairs banister and the rug pulled over him. Thunder—no, those were artillery bursts in the trees, the men huddled in front of the fireplace with the cook's leather pouch, pulling off their dog tags and throwing them into the pouch along with their papers, dumping the papers from their wallets, and pulling on Red Cross armbands. And then the scream and brilliant flash of a phosphorus shell bursting against the hull of the dead tank outside and the lodge is burning, burning. The criminals rushing out into the night, to their half-track truck, and at the door the Cooker stops. Holding the satchel up beside his face to protect it from the heat, he takes a padlock key from his pocket and tosses it up to Hannibal as the next shell came and they never heard the shell scream, just the house heaving, the balcony where Hannibal lay tipping, him sliding against the banister and the staircase coming down on top of the Cooker. Hannibal hearing his hair crisp in a tongue of flame and then he is outside, the half-track roaring away through the forest, the rug around him smoldering at its edge, shellbursts shaking the ground, and splinters howling past him. Putting out the smoldering blanket with snow, and trudging, trudging, his arm hanging.

———

Dawn grey on the roofs of Paris. In the garret room the phonograph has slowed and stopped, and the candles gutter low. Hannibal's eyes open. The faces on the walls are still. They are chalk sketches once again, flat sheets moving in a draft. The gibbon has resumed his usual expression. Day is coming. Everywhere the light is rising. New light is everywhere.

40

UNDER A LOW GREY SKY in Vilnius, Lithuania, a Skoda police sedan turned off the busy Sventaragio and into a narrow street near the university, honking the pedestrians out of the way, making them curse into their collars. It pulled to a stop in front of a new Russian-built hive of flats, raw-looking in the block of decrepit apartment buildings. A tall man in Soviet police uniform got out of the car and, running his finger down a line of buttons, pushed a buzzer marked **Dortlich.**

The buzzer rang in a third-floor flat where an old man lay in bed, medicines crowded on a table beside him. Above the bed was a Swiss pendulum clock. A string hung from the clock to the pillow. This was a tough old man, but in the night, when the dread came on him, he could pull the string in the dark and hear the clock chime the hour, hear that he was not dead yet. The minute hand moved jerk by jerk. He fancied the pendulum was deciding, eeny meeny, the moment of his death.

The old man mistook the buzzer for his own rasping breath. He heard his maid's voice raised in the hall outside and then she stuck her head in the door, bristling beneath her mobcap.

"Your son, sir."

Officer Dortlich brushed past her and came into the room.

"Hello, Father."

"I'm not dead yet. It's too soon to loot." The old man found it odd how the anger only flashed in his head now and no longer reached his heart.

"I brought you some chocolates."

"Give them to Bergid on your way out. Don't rape her. Goodbye, Officer Dortlich."

"It's late to be carrying on like this. You are dying. I came to see if there is something I can do for you, other than provide this flat."

"You could change your name. How many times did you change sides?"

"Enough to stay alive."

Dortlich wore the forest green piping of the Soviet Border Guards. He took off a glove and went to his father's bedside. He tried to take the old man's hand, his finger feeling for the pulse, but his father pushed Dortlich's scarred hand away. The sight of Dortlich's hand brought a shine of water to his father's eyes. With an effort the old man reached up and touched the medals swinging off Dortlich's chest as he leaned over the bed. The decorations included Excellent MVD Policeman, the Institute for Advanced Training in Managing Prison Camps and Jails, and Excellent Soviet Pontoon Bridge Builder. The last decoration was a stretch; Dortlich had built some pontoon bridges, but for the Nazis in a labor battalion. Still, it was a handsome enameled piece and, if questioned about it, he could talk the talk. "Did they throw these to you out of a pasteboard box?"

"I did not come for your blessing, I came to see if you needed anything and to say goodbye."

"It was bad enough to see you in Russian uniform."

"The Twenty-seventh Rifles," Dortlich said.

"Worse to see you in Nazi uniform; that killed your mother."

"There were a lot of us. Not just me. I have a life. You have a bed to die in instead of a ditch. You have coal. That's all I have to give you. The trains for Siberia are jammed. The people trample each other and shit in their hats. Enjoy your clean sheets."

"Grutas was worse than you, and you knew it." He had to pause to wheeze. "Why did you follow him? You looted with criminals and hooligans, you robbed houses and you stripped the dead."

Dortlich replied as though he had not heard his father. "When I was little and I got burned you sat beside the bed and carved the top for me. You gave it to me and when I could hold the whip you showed me how to spin it. It is a beautiful top, with all the animals on it. I still have it. Thank you for the top." He put the chocolates near the foot of the bed where the old man could not shove them off on the floor.

"Go back to your police station, pull out my file and mark it **No Known Family,**" Dortlich's father said.

Dortlich took a piece of paper from his pocket. "If you want me to send you home when you die, sign this and leave it for me. Bergid will help you and witness your signature."

In the car, Dortlich rode in silence until they were moving with the traffic on the Radvilaites.

Sergeant Svenka at the wheel offered Dortlich a cigarette and said, "Hard to see him?"

"Glad it's not me," Dortlich said. "His fucking maid—I should go there when Bergid's at church. Church—she's risking jail to go. She thinks I don't know. My father will be dead in a month. I will ship him to his birth town in Sweden. We should have maybe three cubic meters of space underneath the body, good space three meters long."

Lieutenant Dortlich did not have a private office yet, but he had a desk in the common room of the police station, where prestige meant proximity to the stove. Now, in spring, the stove was cold and papers were piled on it. The paperwork that covered Dortlich's desk was fifty percent bureaucratic nonsense, and half of that could be safely thrown away.

There was very little communication laterally with police departments and MVD in neighboring Latvia and Poland. Police in the Soviet satellite countries were organized around the Central Soviet in Moscow like a wheel with spokes and no rim.

Here was the stuff he had to look at: by official telegraph the list of foreigners holding a visa for Lithuania. Dortlich compared it to the lengthy wanted list and list of the politically suspect. The eighth visa holder from the top was Hannibal Lecter, brand-new member of the youth league of the French Communist Party.

Dortlich drove his own two-cycle Wartburg to the State Telephone Office, where he did business about once a month. He waited outside until he saw Svenka enter to begin his shift. Soon, with Svenka in control of the switchboard, Dortlich was alone in a telephone cabin with a crackling and spitting trunk line to France. He put a signal-strength meter on the telephone and watched the needle in case of an eavesdropper.

In the basement of a restaurant near Fontainebleau, France, a telephone rang in the dark. It rang for five minutes before it was answered.

"Speak."

"Somebody needs to answer faster, me sitting here with my ass hanging out. We need an arrangement in Sweden, for friends to receive a body," Dortlich said. "And the Lecter child is coming back. On a student visa through the Youth for the Rebirth of Communism."

"Who?"

"Think about it. We discussed it the last time we had dinner together," Dortlich said. He glanced at his list. "Purpose of his visit: to **catalog for the people the library at Lecter Castle.** That's a joke—the Russians wiped their ass with the books. We may need to do something on your end. You know who to tell."

41

NORTHWEST OF VILNIUS near the Neris River are the ruins of an old power plant, the first in the region. In happier times it supplied a modest amount of electricity to the city, and to several lumber mills and a machine shop along the river. It ran in all weathers, as it could be supplied with Polish coal by a narrow-gauge rail spur or by river barge.

The Luftwaffe bombed it flat in the first five days of the German invasion. With the advent of the new Soviet transmission lines, it had never been rebuilt.

The road to the power plant was blocked by a chain padlocked to concrete posts. The lock was rusty on the outside, but well-greased within. A sign in Russian, Lithuanian and Polish said: UNEXPLODED ORDNANCE, ENTRY FORBIDDEN.

Dortlich got out of the truck and dropped the chain to the ground. Sergeant Svenka drove across it. The gravel was covered in patches by spreading weeds that brushed beneath the truck with a gasping sound.

Svenka said, "This is where all the crew—"

"Yes," Dortlich said, cutting him off.

"Do you think there are really mines?"

"No. And if I'm wrong keep it to yourself," Dortlich said. It was not his nature to confide, and his need for Svenka's help made him irritable.

A Lend-Lease Nissen hut, scorched on one side, stood near the cracked and blackened foundation of the power plant.

"Pull up over there by the mound of brush. Get the chain out of the back," Dortlich said.

Dortlich tied the chain to the tow bar on the truck, shaking the knot to settle the links. He rooted in the brush to find the end of a timber pallet and fastening the chain to it, he waved the truck forward until the pallet piled with brush moved enough to reveal the metal doors of a bomb shelter.

"After the last air raid, the Germans dropped paratroopers to control the crossings of the Neris," Dortlich said. "The power-station crew had taken shelter in here. A paratrooper knocked on the door and when they opened it he threw in a phosphorus grenade. It was difficult to clean. Takes a minute to get used to it." As Dortlich talked he took off three padlocks securing the door.

He swung it open and the puff of stale air that hit Svenka's face had a scorched smell. Dortlich turned on his electric lantern and went down the steep metal steps. Svenka took a deep breath and followed him. The inside was whitewashed and there were rows of rough wooden shelves. On them were art. Icons wrapped in rags, and row after row of numbered aluminum-tube map cases, their threaded caps sealed with wax. In the back of the shelter were stacked empty picture frames, some with the tacks pulled out, some with the frayed edges of paintings that had been cut hastily out of the frames.

"Bring everything on that shelf, and the ones standing on end there," Dortlich said. He gathered several bundles in oilcloth and led Svenka to the Nissen hut. Inside on sawhorses was a fine oak coffin carved with the symbol of the Klaipeda Ocean and River Workers Association. The coffin had a decorative rub rail around it and the bottom half was a darker color like the waterline and hull of a boat, a handsome piece of design.

"My father's soul ship," Dortlich said. "Bring me that box of cotton waste. The important thing is for it not to rattle."

"If it rattles they'll think it's his bones," Svenka said.

Dortlich slapped Svenka across the mouth. "Show some respect. Get me the screwdriver."

42

HANNIBAL LECTER LOWERED the dirty window of the train, watching, watching as the train wound through tall second growths of linden and pine on both sides of the tracks and then, as he passed at a distance of less than a mile, he saw the towers of Lecter Castle. Two miles further, the train came to a screeching and wheezing halt at the Dubrunst watering station. Some soldiers and a few laborers climbed off to urinate on the roadbed. A sharp word from the conductor made them turn their backs to the passenger cars. Hannibal climbed off with them, his pack on his back. When the conductor went back into the train, Hannibal stepped into the woods. He tore a page of newspaper as he went, in case the second trainman saw him from the top of the tank. He waited in the woods through the chuff, chuff of the steam locomotive laboring away. Now he was alone in the quiet woods. He was tired and gritty.

When Hannibal was six Berndt had carried him up the winding stairs beside the water tank and let him peer over the mossy edge into water that reflected a circle of the sky. There was a ladder down the inside too. Berndt used to swim in the tank with a girl from the village at every opportunity. Berndt was dead, back there, deep in the forest. The girl was probably dead too.

Hannibal took a quick bath in the tank and did his laundry. He thought about Lady Murasaki in the water, thought about swimming with her in the tank.

He hiked back along the railroad, stepping off into the woods once when he heard a handcart coming down the tracks. Two brawny Magyars pumped the handles with their shirts tied around their waists.

A mile from the castle a new Soviet power line crossed the rails. Bulldozers had cleared its path through the woods. Hannibal could feel the static as he passed under the heavy electrical lines and the hair stood up on his arms. He walked far enough from the lines and the rails for the compass on his father's binoculars to settle down. So there were two ways to the hunting lodge, if it was still there. This power line ran dead straight out of sight. If it continued in that direction it would pass within a few kilometers of the hunting lodge.

He took a U.S. surplus C-ration from his pack, threw the yellowed cigarettes away, and ate the potted meat while he considered. **The stairs collapsing on the Cooker, the timbers coming down.**

The lodge might not be there at all. If the lodge was there and anything remained at the lodge it was because looters could not move heavy wreckage. To do what the looters could not do, he needed strength. To the castle, then.

Just before nightfall Hannibal approached Lecter Castle through the woods. As he looked at his home, his feelings remained curiously flat; it is not healing to see your childhood home, but it helps you measure whether you are broken, and how and why, assuming you want to know.

Hannibal saw the castle black against the fading light in the west, flat like the cutout pasteboard castle where Mischa's paper dolls used to live. Her pasteboard castle loomed larger in him than this stone one. Paper dolls curl when they burn. **Fire on his mother's clothes.**

From the trees behind the stable he could hear

the clatter of supper and the orphans singing "The Internationale." A fox barked in the woods behind him.

A man in muddy boots left the stable with a spade and pail and walked across the kitchen garden. He sat down on the Ravenstone to take off his boots and went inside to the kitchen.

Cook was sitting on the Ravenstone, Berndt said. Shot for being a Jew, and he spit on the Hiwi that shot him. Berndt never said the Hiwi's name. "Better you don't know when I settle it after the war," he said, squeezing his hands together.

Full dark now. The electricity was working in at least part of Lecter Castle. When the light came on up in Headmaster's office, Hannibal raised his field glasses. He could see through the window that his mother's Italian ceiling had been covered with Stalinist whitewash to cover the painted figures from the bourgeois religion-myth. Soon Headmaster himself appeared in the window with a glass in his hand. He was heavier, stooped. First Monitor came up behind him and put a hand on his shoulder. Headmaster turned away from the window and in a few moments the light went out.

Ragged clouds blew across the moon, their shadows scaling the battlements and slipping over the roof. Hannibal waited another half-hour. Then, moving with a cloud shadow, he crossed to the stable. He could hear the big horse snoring in the dark.

Cesar woke and cleared his throat, and his ears turned back to listen as Hannibal came into the stall. Hannibal blew in the horse's nose and rubbed his neck.

"Wake up, Cesar," he said in the horse's ear. Cesar's ear twitched across Hannibal's face. Hannibal had to put his finger under his nose to keep from sneezing. He cupped his hand over his flashlight and looked over the horse. Cesar was brushed and his hooves looked good. He would be thirteen now, born when Hannibal was five. "You've only put on about a hundred kilos," Hannibal said. Cesar gave him a friendly bump with his nose and Hannibal had to catch himself against the side of the stall. Hannibal put a bridle and padded collar and a two-strap pulling harness on the horse and tied up the traces. He hung a nosebag and grain on the harness, Cesar turning his head in an attempt to put on the nosebag at once.

Hannibal went to the shed where he had been locked as a child and took a coil of rope, tools and a lantern. No lights showed in the castle. Hannibal led the horse off the gravel and across soft ground, toward the forest and the horns of the moon.

There was no alarm from the castle. Watching from the crenellated top of the west tower, Sergeant Svenka picked up the handset of the field radio he had lugged up two hundred steps.

43

AT THE EDGE of the woods a big tree had been felled across the trail, and a sign said in Russian DANGER, UNEXPLODED ORDNANCE.

Hannibal had to lead the horse around the fallen tree and into the forest of his childhood. Pale moonlight through the forest canopy made patches of grey on the overgrown trail. Cesar was cautious about his footing in the dark. They were well into the woods before Hannibal lit a lantern. He walked ahead, the horse's plate-sized hooves treading the edge of the lantern light. Beside the forest path the ball of a human femur stuck out of the ground like a mushroom.

Sometimes he talked to the horse. "How many times did you bring us up this trail in the cart, Cesar? Mischa and me and Nanny and Mr. Jakov?"

Three hours breasting the weeds brought them to the edge of the clearing.

The lodge was there, all right. It did not look diminished to him. The lodge was not flat like the castle; it loomed as it did in his dreams. Hannibal stopped at the edge of the woods and stared. Here the paper dolls still curled in the fire. The hunting lodge was half-burned, with part of the roof fallen in; stone walls had prevented its total collapse. The clearing was grown up in weeds waist high and bushes taller than a man.

The burned-out tank in front of the lodge was overgrown with vines, a flowering vine hanging from its cannon, and the tail of the crashed Stuka stood up out of the high grass like a sail. There were no paths in the grass. The beanpoles from the garden stuck up above the high weeds.

There, in the kitchen garden, Nanny put Mischa's bathtub, and when the sun had warmed the water, Mischa sat in the tub and waved her hands at the white cabbage butterflies around her. Once he cut the stem of an eggplant and gave it to her in the tub because she loved the color, the purple in the sun, and she hugged the warm eggplant.

The grass before the door was not trampled.

Leaves were piled on the steps and in front of the door. Hannibal watched the lodge while the moon moved the width of a finger.

Time, it was time. Hannibal came out of the cover of the trees leading the big horse in the moonlight. He went to the pump, primed it with a cup of water from the waterskin and pumped until the squealing suckers pulled cold water from the ground. He smelled and tasted the water and gave some to Cesar, who drank more than a gallon and had two handfuls of grain from the nosebag. The squealing of the pump carried into the woods. An owl hooted and Cesar turned his ears toward the sound.

A hundred meters into the trees, Dortlich heard the squealing pump and took advantage of its noise to move forward. He could push quietly through the high-grown ferns, but his footsteps crunched on the forest mast. He froze when silence fell in the clearing, and then he heard the bird cry somewhere between him and the lodge, then it flew, shutting out patches of sky as it passed over him, wings stretched impossibly wide as it sailed through the tangle of branches without a sound.

Dortlich felt a chill and turned his collar up. He sat down among the ferns to wait.

Hannibal looked at the lodge and the lodge looked back. All the glass was blown out. The dark windows watched him like the sockets of the gibbon skull. Its slopes and angles changed by the collapse, its apparent height changed by the high growth around it, the hunting lodge of his childhood became the dark sheds of his dreams. Approaching now across the overgrown garden.

There his mother lay, her dress on fire, and later in the snow he put his head on her chest and her bosom was frozen hard. There was Berndt, and there Mr. Jakov's brains frozen on the snow among the scattered pages. His father facedown near the steps, dead of his own decisions.

There was nothing on the ground anymore.

The front door to the lodge was splintered and hung on one hinge. He climbed the steps and pushed it into the darkness. Inside something small scratched its way to cover. Hannibal held his lantern out beside him and went in.

The room was partly charred, half-open to the sky. The stairs were broken at the landing and roof timbers lay on top of them. The table was crushed. In the corner the small piano lay on its side, the ivory keyboard toothy in his light. A few words of Russian graffiti were on the walls. FUCK THE FIVE-YEAR PLAN and CAPTAIN GRENKO HAS A BIG ASSHOLE. Two small animals jumped out the window.

The room pressed a hush on Hannibal. Defiant, he made a great clatter with his pry bar, raking off the top of the big stove to set his lantern there. The ovens were open and the oven racks were gone, probably taken along with the pots for thieves to use over a campfire.

Working by lantern, Hannibal cleared away as much loose debris from around the staircase as he could move. The rest was pinned down by the big roof timbers, a scorched pile of giant pick-up sticks.

Dawn came in the empty windows as he worked and the eyes of a singed trophy head on the wall caught the red gleam of sunrise.

Hannibal studied the pile of timbers for several minutes, hitched a doubled line around a timber near the middle of the pile and paid out rope as he backed through the door.

Hannibal woke Cesar, who was alternately dozing and cropping grass. He walked the horse around for a few minutes to loosen him up. A heavy dew soaked through his trouser legs and sparkled on the grass and stood like cold sweat on the aluminum skin of the dive bomber. In the daylight he could see a vine had gotten an early start in the greenhouse of the Stuka canopy with big leaves and new tendrils now. The pilot was still inside with his gunner behind him and the vine had grown around and through him, curling between his ribs and through his skull.

Hannibal hitched his rope to the harness traces and walked Cesar forward until the big horse's shoulders and chest felt the load. He clicked in Cesar's ear, a sound from his boyhood. Cesar leaned into the load, his muscles bunched and he moved forward. A crash and thud from inside the lodge. Soot and ash puffed out the window and blew into the woods like fleeing darkness.

Hannibal patted the horse. Impatient for the dust to settle, he tied a handkerchief over his face and went inside, climbing over the collapsed pile of wreckage, coughing, tugging to free his lines and hitch them again. Two more pulls and the heaviest debris was off the deep layer of rubble where the stairs had collapsed. He left Cesar hitched and with pry bar and shovel he dug into the wreckage, throwing broken pieces of furniture, half-burned cushions, a cork thermos chest. He lifted out of the pile a singed boar's head on a plaque.

His mother's voice: Pearls before swine.

The boar's head rattled when he shook it.

Hannibal grasped the boar's tongue and tugged. The tongue came out with its attached stopper. He tilted the head nose-down and his mother's jewelry spilled out onto the stovetop. He did not stop to examine the jewelry, but went back at once to digging.

When he saw Mischa's bathtub, the end of the copper tub with its scrolled handle, he stopped and stood up. The room swam for a moment and he held on to the cold edge of the stove, put his forehead against the cold iron. He went outside and returned with yards of flowering vine. He did not look inside the tub, but coiled the line of flowers on top and set it on the stove, could not stand to see it there, and carried it outside to set it on the tank.

The noise of digging and prying made it easy for Dortlich to advance. He watched from the dark wood, exposing one eye and one barrel of his field glasses, peeping only when he heard the sound of shoveling and prying.

Hannibal's shovel hit and scooped up a skeletal hand and then exposed the skull of the cook. Good tidings in the skeleton smile—its gold teeth showed looters had not reached this far— and then he found, still clutched by arm bones in a sleeve, the cook's leather dispatch case. Hannibal seized it from under the arm, and carried it to the stove. The contents rattled on the iron as he dumped them out: assorted military collar brass, Lithuanian police insignia, Nazi SS lightning brass, Nazi Waffen-SS skull-and-crossbones cap device, Lithuanian aluminum police eagles, Salvation Army collar brass, and last, six stainless-steel dog tags.

The top one was Dortlich's.

Cesar took notice of two classes of things in the hands of men: apples and feedbags were the first, and whips and sticks second. He could not be approached with a stick in hand, a consequence of being driven out of the vegetables by an infuriated cook when he was a colt. If Dortlich had not been carrying a leaded riot baton in his hand when he came out of the trees, Cesar might have ignored him. As it was, the horse snorted and clopped a few steps further away, trailing his rope down the steps of the lodge, and turned to face the man.

Dortlich backed into the trees and disappeared in the woods. He went a hundred meters further from the lodge, among the breast-high ferns wet with dew and out of the view of the empty windows. He took out his pistol and jacked a round into the chamber. A Victorian privy with gingerbread under the eaves was about forty meters behind the lodge, the thyme planted on its narrow path grown wild and tall, and the hedges that screened it from the lodge were grown together across the path. Dortlich could barely squeeze through, branches and leaves in his collar, brushing his neck, but the hedge was supple and did not crackle. He held his baton before his face and pushed through quietly. Baton ready in one hand and pistol in the other, he advanced two steps toward a side window of the lodge when the edge of a shovel caught him across the spine and his legs went numb. He fired a shot into the ground as his legs crumpled under him and the flat of the shovel clanged against the back of his skull and he was conscious of grass against his face before the dark came down.

Birdsong, ortolans flocking and singing in the trees and the morning sunlight yellow on the tall grass, bent over where Hannibal and Cesar had passed.

Hannibal leaned against the burned-out tank with his eyes closed for about five minutes. He turned to the bathtub, and moved the vine with his finger enough to see Mischa's remains. It was oddly comforting to him to see she had all her baby teeth—one awful vision dispelled. He plucked a bay leaf out of the tub and threw it away.

From the jewelry on the stove he chose a brooch he remembered seeing on his mother's breast, a line of diamonds turned into a Möbius tape. He took a ribbon from a cameo and fastened the brooch where Mischa had worn a ribbon in her hair.

On a pleasant east-facing slope above the lodge he dug a grave and lined it with all the wildflowers he could find. He put the tub into the grave and covered it with roof tiles.

He stood at the head of the grave. At the sound of Hannibal's voice, Cesar raised his head from cropping.

"Mischa, we take comfort in knowing there is no God. That you are not enslaved in a Heaven, made to kiss God's ass forever. What you have is better than Paradise. You have blessed oblivion. I miss you every day."

Hannibal filled in the grave and patted down the dirt with his hands. He covered the grave with pine needles, leaves and twigs until it looked like the rest of the forest floor.

In a small clearing at some distance from the grave, Dortlich sat gagged and bound to a tree. Hannibal and Cesar joined him.

Settling himself on the ground, Hannibal examined the contents of Dortlich's pack. A map and car keys, an army can opener, a sandwich in an oilskin pouch, an apple, a change of socks, and a wallet. From the wallet he took an ID card and compared it to the dog tags from the lodge.

"Herr . . . Dortlich. On behalf of myself and my late family, I want to thank you for coming today. It means a great deal to us, and to me personally, having you here. I'm glad to have this chance to talk seriously with you about eating my sister."

He pulled out the gag and Dortlich was talking at once.

"I am a policeman from the town, the horse was reported stolen," Dortlich said. "That's all I want here, just say you'll return the horse and we'll forget it."

Hannibal shook his head. "I remember your face. I have seen it many times. And your hand on us with the webs between your fingers, feeling who was fattest. Do you remember that bathtub bubbling on the stove?"

"No. From the war I only remember being cold."

"Did you plan to eat **me** today, Herr Dortlich? You have your lunch right here." Hannibal examined the contents of the sandwich. "So much mayonnaise, Herr Dortlich!"

"They'll come looking for me very soon," Dortlich said.

"You felt our arms." Hannibal felt Dortlich's arm. "You felt our cheeks, Herr Dortlich," he said, tweaking Dortlich's cheek. "I call you 'Herr' but you aren't German, are you, or Lithuanian, or Russian or anything, are you? You are your own citizen—a citizen of Dortlich. Do you know where the others are? Do you keep in touch?"

"All dead, all dead in the war."

Hannibal smiled at him and untied the bundle of his own handkerchief. It was full of mushrooms. "Morels are one hundred francs a centigram in Paris, and these were growing on a stump!" He got up and went to the horse.

Dortlich writhed in his bonds for the moment when Hannibal's attention was elsewhere.

There was a coil of rope on Cesar's broad back. Hannibal attached the free end to the traces of the harness. The other end was tied in a hangman's noose. Hannibal paid out rope and brought the noose back to Dortlich. He opened Dortlich's sandwich and greased the rope with mayonnaise, and applied a liberal coating of mayonnaise to Dortlich's neck.

Flinching away from his hands, Dortlich said, "One remains alive! In Canada—Grentz—look there for his ID. I would have to testify."

"To what, Herr Dortlich?"

"To what you said. I didn't do it, but I will say I saw it."

Hannibal fixed the noose about Dortlich's neck and looked into his face. "Do I seem upset with you?" He returned to the horse.

"That's the only one, Grentz—he got out on a refugee boat from Bremerhaven—I could give a sworn statement—"

"Good, then you are willing to sing?"

"Yes, I will sing."

"Then let us sing for Mischa, Herr Dortlich. You know this song. Mischa loved it." He turned Cesar's rump to Dortlich. "I don't want you to see this," he said into the horse's ear, and broke into song:

"Ein Mannlein steht im Walde ganz still und stumm . . ." He clicked in Cesar's ear and walked him forward. "Sing for slack, Herr Dortlich. **Es hat von lauter Purpur ein Mant-lein um."**

Dortlich turned his neck from side to side in the greasy noose, watching the rope uncoil in the grass.

"You're not singing, Herr Dortlich."

Dortlich opened his mouth and sang in a tuneless shout, **"Sagt, wer mag das Mannlein sein."**

And then they were singing together, **"Das da

steht im Wald allein . . ." The rope rose out of the grass, some belly in it, and Dortlich screamed, "Porvik! His name was Porvik! We called him Pot Watcher. Killed in the lodge. You found him."

Hannibal stopped the horse and walked back to Dortlich, bent over and looked into his face.

Dortlich said, "Tie him, tie the horse, a bee might sting him."

"Yes, there are a lot of them in the grass." Hannibal consulted the dog tags. "Milko?"

"I don't know, I don't know. I swear."

"And now we come to Grutas."

"I don't know, I don't. Let me go and I will testify against Grentz. We will find him in Canada."

"A few more verses, Herr Dortlich."

Hannibal led the horse forward, dew glistened on the rope, almost level now.

"Das da steht im Walde allein—"

Dortlich's strangled scream, "It's Kolnas! Kolnas deals with him."

Hannibal patted the horse and came back to bend over Dortlich. "Where is Kolnas?"

"Fontainebleau, near the Place Fontainebleau in France. He has a café. I leave messages. It's the only way I can contact him." Dortlich looked Hannibal in the eye. "I swear to God she was dead. She was dead anyway, I swear it."

Staring into Dortlich's face, Hannibal clicked to the horse. The rope tightened and the dew flew off it as the little hairs on the rope stood up. A strangled scream from Dortlich cut off, as Hannibal howled the song into his face.

**"Das da steht im Walde allein,
Mit dem purporroten Mantelein."**

A wet crunch and a pulsing arterial spray. Dortlich's head followed the noose for about six meters and lay looking up at the sky.

Hannibal whistled and the horse stopped, his ears turned backward.

"Dem purporroten Mantelein, indeed."

Hannibal dumped the contents of Dortlich's pack on the ground and took his car keys and ID. He made a crude spit from green sticks and patted his pockets for matches.

While his fire was burning down to useful coals, Hannibal took Dortlich's apple to Cesar. He took all the harness off the horse so he could not get tangled in the brush and walked him down the trail toward the castle. He hugged the horse's neck and then slapped him on the rump. "Go home. Cesar, go home."

Cesar knew the way.

44

GROUND FOG SETTLED in the bare ripped path of the power line and Sergeant Svenka told his driver to slow the truck for fear of hitting a stump. He looked at his map and checked the number on a pylon holding up the heavy transmission line.

"Here."

The tracks of Dortlich's car continued into the distance, but here it had sat and dripped oil on the ground.

The dogs and policemen came off the back of the truck, two big black Alsatians excited about going into the woods, and a serious hound. Sergeant Svenka gave them Dortlich's flannel pajama top to sniff and they were off. Under the overcast sky the trees looked grey with soft-edged shadows and mist hung in the glades.

The dogs were milling about the hunting lodge, the hound casting around the perimeter, dashing into the woods and back, when a trooper called out from back in the trees. When the others did not hear him at once, he blew his whistle.

Dortlich's head stood on a stump and on his head stood a raven. As the troopers approached, the raven flew, taking with it what it could carry.

Sergeant Svenka took a deep breath and set an example for the men, walking up to Dortlich's head. Dortlich's cheeks were missing, excised cleanly, and his teeth were visible at the sides. His mouth was held open by his dog tag, wedged between his teeth.

They found the fire and the spit. Sergeant Svenka felt the ashes to the bottom of the little fire pit. Cold.

"A brochette, cheeks and morels," he said.

45

INSPECTOR POPIL WALKED from police headquarters on the Quai des Orfèvres to the Place de Vosges, carrying a slender portfolio. When he stopped at a bar on the way for a fast espresso, he smelled a calvados on the service bar and wished it were already evening.

Popil walked back and forth on the gravel, looking up at Lady Murasaki's windows. Sheer draperies were closed. Now and then the thin cloth moved in a draft.

The daytime concierge, an older Greek woman, recognized him.

"Madame is expecting me," Popil said. "Has the young man been by?"

The concierge felt a tremor in her concierge antennae and she said the safe thing. "I haven't seen him, sir, but I've had days off." She buzzed Popil in.

Lady Murasaki reclined in her fragrant bath. She had four gardenias floating in the water, and several oranges. Her mother's favorite kimono was embroidered with gardenias. It was cinders now. Remembering, she made a wavelet that rearranged the blossoms. It was her mother who understood when she married Robert Lecter. Her father's occasional letters from Japan still carried a chill. Instead of a pressed flower or fragrant herb, his most recent note contained a blackened twig from Hiroshima.

Was that the doorbell? She smiled, thinking "Hannibal," and reached for her kimono. But he always called or sent a note before he came, and rang before he used his key. No key in the lock now, just the bell again.

She left the bath and wrapped herself hurriedly in the cotton robe. Her eye at the peephole. **Popil.** Popil in the peephole.

Lady Murasaki had enjoyed occasional lunches with Popil. The first one, at Le Pré Catalan in the Bois de Boulogne, was rather stiff, but the others were at Chez Paul near his work and they were easier and more relaxed. He sent dinner invitations as well, always by note, one accompanied by a haiku with excessive seasonal references. She had declined the dinners, also in writing.

She unbolted the door. Her hair was gathered up and she was gloriously barefoot.

"Inspector."

"Forgive me for coming unannounced, I tried to call."

"I heard the telephone."

"From your bath, I think."

"Come in."

Following his eyes, she saw him account at once for the weapons in place before the armor: the tanto dagger, the short sword, the long sword, the war axe.

"Hannibal?"

"He is not here."

Being attractive, Lady Murasaki was a still hunter. She stood with her back to the mantle, her hands in her sleeves, and let the game come to her. Popil's instinct was to move, to flush game.

He stood behind a divan, touched the cloth. "I have to find him. When did you last see him?"

"How many days is it? Five. What is wrong?"

Popil stood near the armor. He rubbed the lacquered surface of a chest. "Do you know where he is?"

"No."

"Did he indicate where he might be going?"

Indicate. Lady Murasaki watched Popil. Now the tips of his ears were flushed. He was moving and asking and touching things. He liked alternate textures, touching something smooth, then something with a nap. She'd seen it at the table too. Rough then smooth. Like the top and bottom of the tongue. She knew she could electrify him with that image and divert blood from his brain.

Popil went around a potted plant. When he peered at her through the foliage, she smiled at him and disrupted his rhythm.

"He is at an outing, I am not sure where."

"Yes, an outing," Popil said. "An outing hunting war criminals, I think."

He looked into her face. "I'm sorry, but I have to show you this." Popil put on the tea table a fuzzy picture, still damp and curling from the Thermo-Fax at the Soviet embassy. It showed Dortlich's head on the stump and police standing around it with two Alsatians and a hound. Another photo of Dortlich was from a Soviet police ID card. "He was found in the forest Hannibal's family owned before the war. I know Hannibal was nearby—he crossed the Polish border the day before."

"Why must it be Hannibal? This man must have many enemies, you said he was a war criminal."

Popil pushed forward the ID photo. "This is how he looked in life." Popil took a sketch from his portfolio, the first of a series. "This is how Hannibal drew him and put the drawing on the wall of his room." Half the face in the sketch was dissected, the other half clearly Dortlich.

"You were not in his room by invitation."

Popil was suddenly angry. "Your pet snake has killed a man. Probably not the first, as you would know better than I. Here are others," he said, putting down sketches. "This was in his room, and this and this and this. That face is from the Nuremberg Trials, I remember it. They are fugitives and now they will kill him if they can."

"And the Soviet police?"

"They are inquiring quietly in France. A Nazi like Dortlich on the People's Police is an embarrassment to the Soviets. They have his file now from Stasi in the GDR."

"If they catch Hannibal—"

"If they catch him in the East, they'll just shoot him. If he gets out, they might let the case wither and die if he keeps his mouth shut."

"Would you let it wither and die?"

"If he strikes in France he'll go to prison. He could lose his head." Popil stopped moving. His shoulders slumped.

Popil put his hands in his pockets.

Lady Murasaki took her hands out of her sleeves.

"You would be deported," he said. "I would be unhappy. I like to see you."

"Do you live by your eyes alone, Inspector?"

"Does Hannibal? You would do anything for him, wouldn't you?"

She started to say something, some qualifier to protect herself, and then she just said "Yes," and waited.

"Help him. Help me. Pascal." She had never said his first name before.

"Send him to me."

46

THE RIVER ESSONNE, smooth and dark, slid past the warehouse and beneath the black houseboat moored to a quay near Vert le Petit. Its low cabins were curtained. Telephone and power lines ran to the boat. The leaves of the container garden were wet and shiny.

The ventilators were open on the deck. A shriek came out of one of them. A woman's face appeared at one of the lower portholes, agonized, cheek pressed against the glass, and then a thick hand pushed the face away and jerked the curtain closed. No one saw.

A light mist made halos around the lights on the quay, but directly overhead a few stars shone through. They were too weak and watery to read.

Up on the road, a guard at the gate shined his

light into the van marked **Café de L'Este** and, recognizing Petras Kolnas, waved him into the barbed-wire parking compound.

Kolnas walked quickly through the warehouse, where a workman was painting out the markings on appliance crates stenciled U.S. POST EXCHANGE, NEUILLY. The warehouse was jammed with boxes and Kolnas weaved through them to come out onto the quay.

A guard sat beside the boat's gangway at a table made from a wooden box. He was eating a sausage with his pocketknife and smoking at the same time. He wiped his hands on his handkerchief to perform a pat-down, then recognized Kolnas and sent him past with a jerk of his head.

Kolnas did not meet often with the others, having a life of his own. He went about his restaurant kitchen with his bowl, sampling everything, and he had gained weight since the war.

Zigmas Milko, lean as ever, let him into the cabin.

Vladis Grutas was on a leather settee getting a pedicure from a woman with a bruise on her cheek. She looked cowed and was too old to sell. Grutas looked up with the pleasant, open expression that was often a sign of temper. The boat captain played cards at a chart table with a boulder-bellied thug named Mueller, late of the SS Dirlewanger Brigade, whose prison tattoos covered the back of his neck and his hands and continued up his sleeves out of sight. When Grutas turned his pale eyes on the players, they folded the cards and left the cabin.

Kolnas did not waste time on greetings.

"Dortlich's dog tag was jammed in his teeth. Good German stainless steel, didn't melt, didn't burn. The boy will have yours too, and mine and Milko's, and Grentz's."

"You told Dortlich to search the lodge four years ago," Milko said.

"Poked around with his picnic fork, lazy bastard," Grutas said. He pushed the woman away with his foot, never looking at her, and she hurried out of the cabin.

"Where is he, this poison little boy who kills Dortlich?" Milko said.

Kolnas shrugged. "A student in Paris. I don't know how he got the visa. He used it going in. No information on him coming out. They don't know where he is."

"What if he goes to the police?" Kolnas said.

"With what?" Grutas said. "Baby memories, child nightmares, old dog tags?"

"Dortlich could have told him how he telephones me to get in touch with you," Kolnas said.

Grutas shrugged. "The boy will try to be a nuisance."

Milko snorted. "A **nuisance?** I would say he was nuisance enough to Dortlich. Killing Dortlich could not have been easy; he probably shot him in the back."

"Ivanov owes me," Grutas said. "Soviet Embassy security will point out little Hannibal, and we will do the rest. So Kolnas will not worry."

Muffled cries and the sound of blows came from elsewhere in the boat. The men paid no attention.

"Taking over from Dortlich will be Svenka," Kolnas said, to show he was not worrying.

"Do we want him?" Milko said.

Kolnas shrugged. "We have to have him. Svenka worked with Dortlich two years. He has our items. He's the only link we have left to the pictures. He sees the deportees, he can mark the decent-looking ones for DPC Bremerhaven. We can get them from there."

Frightened by the Pleven Plan's potential for rearming Germany, Joseph Stalin was purging Eastern Europe with mass deportations. The jammed trains ran weekly, to death in the labor camps in Siberia, and to misery in refugee camps in the West. The desperate deportees provided Grutas with a rich supply of women and boys. He stood behind his merchandise. His morphine was German medical-grade. He supplied AC/DC converters for the black-market appliances, and made any mental adjustments his human merchandise required in order to perform.

Grutas was pensive. "Was this Svenka at the front?" They did not believe anyone innocent of the Eastern Front could be truly practical.

Kolnas shrugged. "He sounds young on the telephone. Dortlich had some arrangements."

"We'll bring everything out now. It's too soon to sell, but we need to get it out. When is he calling again?"

"Friday."

"Tell him to do it now."

"He'll want out. He'll want papers."

"We can get him to Rome. I don't know if we want him here. Promise him whatever, you know?"

"The art is hot," Kolnas said.

"Go back to your restaurant, Kolnas. Keep feeding the **flics** for free and they will keep tearing up your traffic tickets. Bring some profiteroles next time you come down here to bleat."

"He's all right," Grutas told Milko, when Kolnas was gone.

"I hope so," Milko said. "I don't want to run a restaurant."

"Dieter! Where is Dieter?" Grutas pounded on a cabin door on the lower deck, and shoved it open.

Two frightened young women were sitting on their bunks, each chained by a wrist to the pipe frame of the bunk. Dieter, twenty-five, held one of them by a fistful of her hair.

"You bruise their faces, split their lip, the money goes down," Grutas said. "And that one is mine for now."

Dieter released the woman's hair and rummaged in the manifold contents of his pockets for a key. "Eva!"

The older woman came into the cabin and stood close to the wall.

"Clean that one up and Mueller will take her to the house," Dieter said.

Grutas and Milko walked through the warehouse to the car. In a special area bound off by a rope were crates marked HOUSEHOLD. Grutas spotted among the appliances a British refrigerator.

"Milko, do you know why the English drink warm beer? Because they have Lucas refrigerators. Not for my house. I want Kelvinator,

Frigidaire, Magnavox, Curtis-Mathis. I want all made in America." Grutas raised the cover of an upright piano and played a few notes. "This is a whorehouse piano. I don't want it. Kolnas found me a Bosendorfer. The best. Pick it up in Paris, Milko . . . when you do the other thing."

47

KNOWING HE WOULD not come to her until he was scrubbed and groomed, she waited in his room. He had never invited her there, and she did not poke around. She looked at the drawings on the walls, the medical illustrations that filled one half of the room. She stretched out on his bed in the perfect order of the Japanese half beneath the eaves. On a small shelf facing the bed was a framed picture covered by a silk cloth embroidered with night herons. Lying on her side Lady Murasaki reached over and lifted the silk. It covered a beautiful drawing of her naked in the bath at the chateau, in pencil and chalk and tinted with pastel. The drawing was signed with the chop for Eternity in Eight Strokes and the Japanese symbols in the grass style, and not strictly correct, for "water flowers."

She looked at it for a long time, and then she covered it and closed her eyes, a poem of Yosano Akiko running in her head:

**Amid the notes of my koto is another
Deep mysterious tone,
A sound that comes from
Within my own breast.**

Shortly after daylight on the second day, she heard footsteps on the stairs. A key in the lock, and Hannibal stood there, scruffy and tired, his pack hanging from his hand.

Lady Murasaki was standing.

"Hannibal, I need to hear your heart," she said. "Robert's heart went silent. Your heart stopped in my dreams." She went to him and put her ear against his chest. "You smell of smoke and blood."

"You smell of jasmine and green tea. You smell of peace."

"Do you have wounds?"

"No."

Her face was against the scorched dog tags hanging around Hannibal's neck. She took them out of his shirt.

"Did you take these from the dead?"

"What dead would that be?"

"The Soviet police know who you are. Inspector Popil came to see me. If you go directly to him he will help you."

"These men are not dead. They are very much alive."

"Are they in France? Then give them to Inspector Popil."

"Give them to the French police? Why?" He shook his head. "Tomorrow is Sunday—do I have that right?"

"Yes, Sunday."

"Come with me tomorrow. I'll pick you up. I want you to look at a beast with me and tell me he should fear the French police."

"Inspector Popil—"

"When you see Inspector Popil, tell him I have some mail for him." Hannibal's head was nodding.

"Where do you bathe?"

"The hazard shower in the lab," he said. "I'm going down there now."

"Would you like some food?"

"No, thank you."

"Then sleep," she said. "I will go with you tomorrow. And the days after that."

48

HANNIBAL LECTER'S motorcycle was a BMW boxer twin left behind by the retreating German army. It was resprayed flat black and had low handlebars and a pillion seat. Lady Murasaki rode behind him, her headband and boots giving her a touch of Paris Apache. She held on to Hannibal, her hands lightly on his ribs.

Rain had fallen in the night and the pavement now was clean and dry in the sunny morning, grippy when they leaned into the curves on the road through the forest of Fontainebleau, flashing through the stripes of tree shadow and sunlight across the road, the air hanging cool in the dips, then warm in their faces as they crossed the open glades.

The angle of a lean on a motorcycle feels exaggerated on the pillion, and Hannibal felt her behind him trying to correct it for the first few miles, but then she got the feel of it, the last five degrees being on faith, and her weight became one with his as they sped through the forest. They passed a hedge full of honeysuckle and the air was sweet enough to taste on her lips. Hot tar and honeysuckle.

The Café de L'Este is on the west bank of the Seine about a half-mile from the village of Fontainebleau, with a pleasant prospect of woods across the river. The motorcycle went silent, and began to tick as it cooled. Near the entrance to the café terrace is an aviary and the birds in it are ortolans, a sub-rosa specialty of the café. Ordinances against the serving of ortolans came and went. They were listed on the menu as larks. The ortolan is a good singer, and these were enjoying the sunshine.

Hannibal and Lady Murasaki paused to look at them.

"So small, so beautiful," she said, her blood still up from the ride.

Hannibal rested his forehead against the cage. The little birds turned their heads to look at him using one eye at a time. Their songs were the Baltic dialect he heard in the woods at home. "They're just like us," he said. "They can smell the others cooking, and still they try to sing. Come."

Three quarters of the terrace tables were taken, a mixture of country and town in Sunday clothes, eating an early lunch. The waiter found a place for them.

A table of men next to them had ordered ortolans all around. When the little roasted birds arrived, they bent low over their plates and tented their napkins over their heads to keep all the aroma in.

Hannibal sniffed their wine from the next table and determined it was corked. He watched without expression as, oblivious, they drank it anyway.

"Would you like an ice cream sundae?"

"Perfect."

Hannibal went inside the restaurant. He paused before the specials chalked on the blackboard while he read the restaurant license posted near the cash register.

In the corridor was a door marked **Privé.** The corridor was empty. The door was not locked. Hannibal opened it and went down the basement steps. In a partly opened crate was an American dishwasher. He bent to read the shipping label.

Hercule, the restaurant helper, came down the

stairs carrying a basket of soiled napkins. "What are you doing down here, this is private."

Hannibal turned and spoke English. "Well, where is it then? The door says **privy,** doesn't it? I come down here and there's only the basement. The loo, man, the pissoir, the toilet, where is it? Speak English. Do you understand loo? Tell me quickly, I'm caught rather short."

"Privé, privé!" Hercule gestured up the stairs. **"Toilette!"** and at the top waved Hannibal in the right direction.

He arrived back at the table as the sundaes arrived. "Kolnas is using the name 'Kleber.' It's on the license. Monsieur Kleber residing on the Rue Juliana. Ahhh, regard."

Petras Kolnas came onto the terrace with his family, dressed for church.

The conversations around Hannibal took on a swoony sound as he looked at Kolnas, and dark motes swarmed in his vision.

Kolnas' suit was of inky new broadcloth, a Rotary pin in the lapel. His wife and two children were handsome, Germanic-looking. In the sun, the short red hairs and whiskers on Kolnas' face gleamed like hog bristles. Kolnas went to the cash register. He lifted his son onto a barstool.

"Kolnas the Prosperous," Hannibal said. "The Restaurateur. The Gourmand. He's come by to check the till on his way to church. How neat he is."

The headwaiter took the reservation book from beside the telephone and opened it for Kolnas' inspection.

"Remember us in your prayers, Monsieur," the headwaiter said.

Kolnas nodded. Shielding his movement from the diners with his thick body, he took a Webley .455 revolver from his waistband, put it on a curtained shelf beneath the cash register and smoothed down his waistcoat. He selected some shiny coins from the till and wiped them with his handkerchief. He gave one to the boy on the barstool. "This is your offering for church, put it in your pocket."

He bent and gave the other to his little daughter. "Here is your offering, liebchen. Don't put it in your mouth. Put it safe in the pocket!"

Some drinkers at the bar engaged Kolnas and there were customers to greet. He showed his son how to give a firm handshake. His daughter let go of his pants leg and toddled between the tables, adorable in ruffles and a lacy bonnet and baby jewelry, customers smiling at her.

Hannibal took the cherry from the top of his sundae and held it at the edge of the table. The child came to get it, her hand extended, her thumb and forefinger ready to pluck. Hannibal's eyes were bright. His tongue appeared briefly, and then he sang to the child.

"Ein Mannlein steht im Walde ganz still und stumm—do you know that song?"

While she ate the cherry, Hannibal slipped something into her pocket. **"Es hat von lauter Purpur ein Mantlein um."**

Suddenly Kolnas was beside the table. He picked his daughter up. "She doesn't know that song."

"You must know it, you don't sound French to me."

"Neither do you, Monsieur," Kolnas said. "I would not guess that you and your wife are French. We're all French now."

Hannibal and Lady Murasaki watched Kolnas bundle his family into a Traction Avant.

"Lovely children," she said. "A beautiful little girl."

"Yes," Hannibal said. "She's wearing Mischa's bracelet."

High above the altar at the Church of the Redeemer is a particularly bloody representation of Christ on the cross, a seventeenth-century spoil from Sicily. Beneath the hanging Christ, the priest raised the communion cup.

"Drink," he said. "This is my blood, shed for

the remission of your sins." He held up the wafer. "This is my body, broken for you, sacrificed that you might not perish, but have everlasting life. Take, eat, and as oft as ye do this, do it in remembrance of me."

Kolnas, carrying his children in his arms, took the wafer in his mouth, and returned to the pew beside his wife. The line shuffled around and then the collection plate was passed. Kolnas whispered to his son. The child took a coin from his pocket and put it in the plate. Kolnas whispered to his daughter, who sometimes was reluctant to give up her offering.

"Katerina . . ."

The little girl felt in her pocket and put into the plate a scorched dog tag with the name **Petras Kolnas.** Kolnas did not see it until the steward took the dog tag from the plate and returned it, waiting with a patient smile for Kolnas to replace the dog tag with a coin.

49

ON LADY MURASAKI'S terrace a weeping cherry in a planter overhung the table, its lowest tendrils brushing Hannibal's hair as he sat across from her. Above her shoulder floodlit Sacré Coeur hung in the night sky like a drop of the moon.

She was playing Miyagi Michio's "The Sea in Spring" on the long and elegant koto. Her hair was down, the lamplight warm on her skin. She looked steadily at Hannibal as she played.

She was difficult to read, a quality Hannibal found refreshing much of the time. Over the years he had learned to proceed, not with caution, but with care.

The music slowed progressively. The last note rang still. A suzumushi cricket in a cage answered the koto. She put a sliver of cucumber between the bars and the cricket pulled it inside. She seemed to look through Hannibal, beyond him, at a distant mountain, and then he felt her attention envelop him as she spoke the familiar words. "I see you and the cricket sings in concert with my heart."

"My heart hops at the sight of you, who taught my heart to sing," he said.

"Give them to Inspector Popil. Kolnas and the rest of them."

Hannibal finished his sake and put down the cup. "It's Kolnas' children, isn't it? You fold cranes for the children."

"I fold cranes for your soul, Hannibal. You are drawn into the dark."

"Not drawn. When I couldn't speak I was not drawn into silence, silence captured me."

"Out of the silence you came to me, and you spoke to me. I know you, Hannibal, and it is not easy knowledge. You are drawn toward the darkness, but you are also drawn to me."

"On the bridge of dreams."

The lute made a little noise as she put it down. She extended her hand to him. He got to his feet, the cherry trailing across his cheek, and she led him toward the bath. The water was steaming. Candles burned beside the water. She invited him to sit on a tatami. They were facing knee to knee, their faces a foot apart.

"Hannibal, come home with me to Japan. You could practice at a clinic in my father's country house. There is much to do. We would be there together." She leaned close to him. She kissed his forehead. "In Hiroshima green plants push up through ashes to the light." She touched his face. "If you are scorched earth, I will be warm rain."

Lady Murasaki took an orange from a bowl beside the bath. She cut into it with her fingernails and pressed her fragrant hand to Hannibal's lips.

"One real touch is better than the bridge of dreams." She snuffed the candle beside them with a sake cup, leaving the cup inverted on the candle, her hand on the candle longer than it had to be.

She pushed the orange with her finger and it rolled along the tiles into the bath. She put her hand behind Hannibal's head and kissed him on the mouth, a blossoming bud of a kiss, fast opening.

Her forehead pressed against his mouth, she unbuttoned his shirt. He held her at arm's length and looked into her lovely face, her shining. They were close and they were far, like a lamp between two mirrors.

Her robe fell away. Eyes, breasts, points of light at her hips, symmetry on symmetry, his breath growing short.

"Hannibal, promise me."

He pulled her to him very tight, his eyes squeezed tight shut. Her lips, her breath on his neck, the hollow of his throat, **his collarbone. His clavicle. St. Michael's scales.**

He could see the orange bobbing in the bath. For an instant it was the skull of the little deer in the boiling tub, butting, butting in the knocking of his heart, as though in death it were still desperate to get out. The damned in chains beneath his chest marched off across his diaphragm to hell beneath the scales. Sternohyoid omohyoid thyrohyoid/juuuguular, ahhhhhmen.

Now was the time and she knew it. "Hannibal, promise me."

A beat, and he said, "I already promised Mischa."

She sat still beside the bath until she heard the front door close. She put on her robe and carefully tied the belt. She took the candles from the bath and put them before the photographs on her altar. They glowed on the faces of the present dead, and on the watching armor, and in the mask of Date Masamune she saw the dead to come.

50

DR. DUMAS PUT HIS laboratory coat on a hanger and buttoned the top button with his plump pink hands. He was pink cheeked too, with crispy blond hair, and the crispness of his clothes lasted throughout the day. There was a sort of unearthly cheer about him that lasted through the day as well. A few students remained in the lab, cleaning their dissection stations.

"Hannibal, tomorrow morning in the theater I will need a subject with the thoracic cavity open, the ribs reflected and the major pulmonary vessels injected, as well as the major cardiac arteries. I suspect from his color that Number Eighty-eight died of a coronary occlusion. That would be useful to see," he said cheerfully. "Do the left anterior descending and circumflex in yellow. If there's a blockage, shoot from both sides. I left you notes. It's a lot of work. I'll have Graves stay and help you if you like."

"I'll work alone, Professor Dumas."

"I thought so. Good news—Albin Michel has the first engravings back. We can see them to-morrow! I can't wait."

Weeks ago Hannibal had delivered his sketches to the publisher on the Rue Huyghens. Seeing the name of the street made him think of Mr. Jakov, and Christiaan Huyghens' **Treatise on Light.** He sat in the Luxembourg Gardens for an hour after that, watching the toy sailboats on the pond, mentally unspooling a volute from the half-circle of the flower bed. The drawings in the new anatomy text would be credited Lecter-Jakov.

The last student left the laboratory. The building was empty now and dark, except for Hannibal's bright work lights in the anatomy lab. After he turned off the electric saw the only sounds were the wind's faint moan in chimneys, the insect click of the instruments and the bub-bling retorts where the colored injection dyes were warming.

Hannibal considered his subject, a stocky middle-aged man, draped except for his opened thorax, ribs spread like the ribs of a boat. Here were areas Dr. Dumas would want to expose in the course of his lecture, making the last incision himself and lifting out a lung. For his illustration Hannibal needed to see the posterior aspect of the lung, out of sight in the cadaver. Hannibal went down the corridor to the anatomy museum for a reference, turning on lights as he went.

Zigmas Milko, sitting in a truck across the street, could look into the medical school's tall windows and track Hannibal's progress down the hall. Milko had a short crowbar up the sleeve of his jacket, the pistol and silencer in the pockets.

He got a good look when Hannibal turned up the museum lights. The pockets of Hannibal's lab coat were flat. He did not appear to be armed. He left the museum carrying a jar, and the lights went out progressively as he returned to the anatomy lab. Now only the lab was lighted, the frosted windows and the skylight glowing.

Milko did not think this would require much of a lurk, but just in case he decided to smoke a cigarette first—if the spotter from the embassy had left him any cigarettes before slinking away. You'd think the mooching prick had never seen a decent smoke. Did he take the entire packet? Dammit, at least fifteen of the Lucky Strikes. Do this thing now, get some American cigarettes later at the **bal musette.** Unwind, rub against the bar girls with the silencer tube in the front trouser pocket, look into their faces when they felt it hard against them, pick up Grutas' piano in the morning.

This boy killed Dortlich. Milko recalled that Dortlich, with a crowbar up his sleeve, had once chipped his own tooth when he tried to light a cigarette. "**Scheisskopf,** you should have come out with the rest of us," he said to Dortlich, wherever he was, Hell probably.

Milko carried the black ladder, along with a lunch bucket for cover, across the street and into the shelter of the hedges beside the medical school. He put his foot on the bottom rung and muttered, "Fuck the farm." It had been his mantra in action since he ran away from home at twelve.

Hannibal completed the blue, venous injections and sketched his work in colored pencil at a drawing board beside the body, referring now and then to the lung preserved in a jar of alcohol. Some papers clipped to the board fluttered slightly in a draft and settled again. Hannibal looked up from his work, looked down the corridor in the direction of the draft, then finished coloring a vein.

Milko closed the window of the anatomy museum behind him, slipped off his boots and, in his socks, crept between the glass cases. He moved along the row of the digestive system, and paused near an enormous pair of clubbed feet in a jar. There was just enough light to move. Wouldn't want to shoot in here, splash this crap everywhere. He turned up his collar against the draft on the back of his neck. Bit by bit he edged his face into the corridor, looking across the bridge of his nose so his ear was not exposed.

Above the sketchboard, Hannibal's nostrils opened wide and the work light reflected redly in his eyes.

Looking down the corridor and through the laboratory door, Milko could see Hannibal's back as he worked around the corpse with his big hypodermic of dye. It was a bit far to shoot, as the silencer blocked the pistol's sights. Didn't want to wing him and have to chase him around, knocking things over. God knows what would splash on you, some of these nasty fluids.

Milko made the slight adjustment of the heart that we make before we kill.

Hannibal went out of sight and Milko could

only see his hand on the drawing board, sketching, sketching, making a small erasure.

Abruptly, Hannibal put down his pen, came to the corridor and turned on the light. Milko ducked back into the museum, then the light went off again. Milko peered around the door frame. Hannibal was working over the draped body.

Milko heard the autopsy saw. When he looked again Hannibal was out of sight. **Drawing again. Fuck this. Walk in there and shoot him. Tell him say hello to Dortlich when he gets to Hell.** Down the corridor on long strides in his socks, silent on the stone floor, watching the hand on the drawing board, Milko raised the pistol and stepped through the door and saw the hand and sleeve, the lab coat piled on the chair—**where is the rest of him**—and Hannibal stepped close behind Milko and sank the hypodermic full of alcohol into the side of Milko's neck, catching him as his legs gave way and his eyes rolled up, easing him to the floor.

First things first. Hannibal put the corpse's hand back in place and tacked it on with a few fast stitches in the skin. "Sorry," he said to his subject. "I'll include thanks in your note."

Burning, coughing, cold on Milko's face now as he came to consciousness, the room swimming and then settling down. He started to lick his lips, and spit. Water pouring over his face.

Hannibal set his pitcher of cold water on the edge of the cadaver tank and sat down in a conversational attitude. Milko wore the chain cadaver harness. He was submerged up to his neck in formalin solution in the tank. The other occupants crowded close around him, regarded him with eyes gone cloudy in embalming fluid, and he shrugged their shriveled hands away.

Hannibal examined Milko's wallet. He took from his own pocket a dog tag and placed it beside Milko's ID card on the rim of the tank.

"Zigmas Milko. Good evening."

Milko coughed and wheezed. "We talked about it. I brought you money. A settlement. We want you to have the money. I brought it. Let me take you to it."

"That sounds like a superior plan. You killed so many, Milko. So many more than these. Do you feel them in the tank around you? There by your foot, that's a child from a fire. Older than my sister, and partly cooked."

"I don't know what you want."

Hannibal pulled on a rubber glove. "To hear what you have to say about eating my sister."

"I did not."

Hannibal pressed Milko under the surface of the embalming fluid. After a long moment, he seized the chain tether and pulled him up again, poured water in his face, flushing his eyes.

"Don't say that again," Hannibal said.

"We all felt badly, so badly," Milko said as soon as he could talk. "Freezing hands and rotting feet. Whatever we did, we did it to live. Grutas was quick, she never—we kept you alive, we—"

"Where is Grutas?"

"If I tell you, will you let me take you to the money? It's a lot, in dollars. There is a lot more money too, we could blackmail them with what I know, with your evidence."

"Where is Grentz?"

"Canada."

"Correct. The truth for once. Where is Grutas?"

"He has a house near Milly-le-Forêt."

"What is his name now?"

"He does business as Satrug, Inc."

"Did he sell my pictures?"

"Once, to buy a lot of morphine, no more. We can get them back."

"Have you tried the food at Kolnas' restaurant? The sundaes aren't bad."

"I have the money in the truck."

"Last words? A valedictory?"

Milko opened his mouth to speak and Hannibal put the heavy cover down with a clang. Less than an inch of air remained between the cover and the surface of the embalming fluid. He left the room, Milko bumping against the lid like a lobster in a pot. He closed the door behind him, rubber seals squealing against the paint.

Inspector Popil stood beside his worktable, looking at his sketch.

Hannibal reached for the cord and switched on the big vent fan and it started with a clatter.

Popil looked up at the sound of the fan. Hannibal did not know what else he had heard. Milko's gun was between the cadaver's feet, underneath the sheet.

"Inspector Popil." Hannibal picked up a syringe of dye and made an injection. "If you'll excuse me just a moment, I need to use this before it hardens again."

"You killed Dortlich in your family's woods."

Hannibal's face did not change. He wiped the tip of the needle.

"His face was eaten," Popil said.

"I would suspect the ravens. Those woods are rife with them. They were at the dog's dish whenever he turned his back."

"Ravens who made a shish kabob."

"Did you mention that to Lady Murasaki?"

"No. Cannibalism—it happened on the Eastern Front, and more than once when you were a child." Popil turned his back on Hannibal, watching him in the glass front of a cabinet. "But you know that, don't you? You were there. And you were in Lithuania four days ago. You went in on a legitimate visa and you came out another way. How?" Popil did not wait for an answer. "I'll tell you how, you bought papers through a con at Fresnes, and that is a felony."

In the tank room the heavy lid rose slightly and Milko's fingers appeared under the edge. He pursed his lips against the lid, sucking for the quarter-inch of air, a wavelet over his face choked him, he pressed his face to the crack at the edge of the lid and sucked in a choking breath.

In the anatomy lab, looking at Popil's back, Hannibal leaned some weight onto his subject's lung, producing a satisfactory gasp and gurgle. "Sorry," he said. "They do that." He turned up the Bunsen burner underneath a retort to magnify the bubbling.

"That drawing is not the face of your subject. It is the face of Vladis Grutas. Like the ones in your room. Did you kill Grutas too?"

"Absolutely not."

"Have you found him?"

"If I found him, I give you my word I would bring him to your attention."

"Don't fool with me! Do you know that he sawed off the rabbi's head in Kaunas? That he shot the Gypsy children in the woods? Do you know he walked away from Nuremberg when a witness got acid down her throat? Every few years I pick up the stench of him and then he's gone. If he knows you are hunting him, he'll kill you. Did he murder your family?"

"He killed my sister and ate her."

"You saw it?"

"Yes."

"You would testify."

"Of course."

Popil looked at Hannibal for a long moment. "If you kill in France, Hannibal, I will see your head in a bucket. Lady Murasaki will be deported. Do you love Lady Murasaki?"

"Yes. Do you?"

"There are photographs of him in the Nuremberg archives. If the Soviets will circulate them, if they can find him, the Sureté is holding someone we might trade for him. If we can get him, I will need your deposition. Is there any other evidence?"

"Teeth marks on the bones."

"If you are not in my office tomorrow, I'll have you arrested."

"Good night, Inspector."

In the tank room, Milko's spadelike farmer's hand slips back into the tank, the lid closes down tight, and to a shriveled face before him he mouths his valediction: **Fuck the farm.**

Night in the anatomy laboratory, Hannibal working alone. He was nearly finished with his sketch, working beside the body. On the counter was a fat rubber glove filled with fluid and tied at the wrist. The glove was suspended over a beaker of powder. A timer ticked beside it.

Hannibal covered the sketch pad with a clear overlay. He draped the cadaver and rolled it into the lecture theater. From the anatomy museum he brought Milko's boots and put them beside Milko's clothing on a gurney near the incinerator, with the contents of his pockets, a jackknife, keys and a wallet. The wallet contained money and the rim of a condom Milko rolled on to deceive women in semi-darkness. Hannibal removed the money. He opened the incinerator. Milko's head stood in the flames. He looked like the Stuka pilot burning. Hannibal threw in his boots and one of them kicked the head over backward out of sight.

51

A WAR SURPLUS five-ton truck with new canvas was parked across the street from the anatomy lab, blocking half of the sidewalk. Surprisingly there was no ticket yet on the windshield. Hannibal tried Milko's keys on the driver's door. It opened. An envelope of papers was over the sun visor on the driver's side. He looked through them quickly.

A ramp in the bed of the truck let him load his motorcycle at the curb. He drove the truck to Porte de Montempoivre near the Bois de Vincennes and put it in a truck park near the railroad. He locked the plates in the cab beneath the seat.

Hannibal Lecter sat on his motorcycle in a hillside orchard, breakfasting on some excellent African figs he had found in the Rue de Buci market, along with a bite of Westphalian ham. . He could see the road below the hill and, a quarter mile further along, the entrance to Vladis Grutas' home.

Bees were loud in the orchard and several buzzed around his figs until he covered them with his handkerchief. Garcia Lorca, now enjoying a revival in Paris, said the heart was an orchard. Hannibal was thinking about the figure and thinking, as young men do, about the shapes of peaches and pears, when a carpenter's truck passed below him and pulled up to Grutas' gate.

Hannibal raised his father's field glasses.

The house of Vladis Grutas is a Bauhaus mansion built in 1938 on farmland with a view of the Essonne River. It was neglected in the war and, lacking eaves, suffered dark water stains down its white walls. The whole façade and one of the sides had been repainted blinding white and scaffolding was going up on the walls yet unpainted. It had served the Germans as a staff headquarters during the occupation and the Germans had added protection.

The glass and concrete cube of the house

was protected by high chain link and barbed wire around the perimeter. The entrance was guarded by a concrete gatehouse that looked like a pillbox. A slit window across the front of the gatehouse was softened by a window box of flowers. Through the window a machine gun could traverse the road, its barrel brushing the blossoms aside.

Two men came out of the gatehouse, one blond and the other dark-haired and covered with tattoos. They used a mirror on a long handle to search beneath the truck. The carpenters had to climb down and show their national identity cards. There was some waving of hands and shrugging. The guards passed the truck inside.

Hannibal rode his motorcycle into a copse of trees and parked it in the brush. He grounded out the motorcycle's ignition with a bit of hidden wire behind the points and put a note on the saddle saying he had gone for parts. He walked a half-hour to the high road and hitchhiked back to Paris.

The loading dock of the Gabrielle Instrument Co. is on the Rue de Paradis between a seller of lighting fixtures and a crystal repair shop. In the last task of their workday, the warehousemen loaded a Bosendorfer baby grand piano into Milko's truck, along with a piano stool crated separately. Hannibal signed the invoice **Zigmas Milko,** saying the name silently as he wrote.

The instrument company's own trucks were coming in at the end of the day. Hannibal watched as a woman driver got out of one of them. She was not bad looking in her coveralls, with a lot of French flounce. She went inside the building and came out minutes later in slacks and a blouse, carrying the coveralls folded under her arm. She put them in the saddlebag of a small motorbike. She felt Hannibal's eyes on her, and turned her gamine face to him. She took out a cigarette and he lit it.

"**Merci,** Monsieur . . . Zippo." The woman was very street French, animated, with a lot of eye movement, and she exaggerated the gestures of smoking.

The busybodies sweeping the loading dock strained to hear what they were saying, but could only hear her laugh. She looked into Hannibal's face as they talked and little by little the coquetry stopped. She seemed fascinated with him, almost mesmerized. They walked together down the street toward a bar.

Mueller had the gatehouse duty with a German named Gassmann, who had recently finished a tour in the Foreign Legion. Mueller was trying to sell him a tattoo when Milko's truck approached up the drive.

"Call the clap doctor, Milko's back from Paris," Mueller said.

Gassmann had the better eyes. "That's not Milko."

They went outside.

"Where is Milko?" Mueller asked the woman at the wheel.

"How would I know? He paid me to bring you this piano. He said he would be along in a couple of days. Get my moto out of the back with your big muscles."

"Who paid you?"

"Monsieur Zippo."

"You mean Milko."

"Right, Milko."

A caterer's truck stopped behind the five-ton and waited, the caterer fuming, drumming his fingers on the wheel.

Gassmann raised the flap over the tailgate of the five-ton. He saw a piano in a crate and a smaller crate plastered with a sign: POUR LA CAVE and FOR THE WINE CELLAR—STORE IN A COOL PLACE. The motorbike was lashed to the side rails of the truck. A plank ramp was in the truck, but it was easier to lift the little motorbike down.

Mueller came to help Gassmann with the bike. He looked at the woman.

"Do you want a drink?"

"Not here," she said, swinging a leg over the bike.

"Your moto sounds like a fart," Mueller called after her as she rode away.

"You're winning her over with suave conversation," the other German said.

The piano tuner was a skeletal man with dark places between his teeth and a fixed rictus smile like that of Lawrence Welk. When he had finished tuning the black Bosendorfer, he changed into his ancient white tie and tailcoat and came out to play cocktail piano as Grutas' guests arrived. The piano sounded brittle against the tile floor and glass expanses of the house. The shelves of a glass-and-steel bookcase near the piano buzzed along with B-flat until he moved the books around and then it buzzed at B. He had used a kitchen chair when tuning, but he did not want to sit on it to play.

"Where am I to sit? Where is the piano bench?" he asked the maid, who asked Mueller. Mueller found him a chair of the correct height, but it had arms. "I'll have to play with my elbows spread," the tuner said.

"Shut the fuck up and play American," Mueller said. "Cocktail American he wants, with the singing along."

The cocktail buffet served thirty guests, curious flotsam of the war. Ivanov from the Soviet embassy was there, too well tailored for a servant of the state. He was talking with an American first sergeant who kept the books at the U.S. Post Exchange in Neuilly. The sergeant was in mufti, a sack suit in windowpane check of a color that brought out the spider angioma on the side of his nose. The bishop down from Versailles was accompanied by the acolyte who did his nails.

Under the pitiless tube lighting, the bishop's black suit had a greenish roast-beef sheen, Grutas observed as he kissed the bishop's ring. They talked briefly about mutual acquaintances in Argentina. There was a strong strain of Vichy in the room.

The piano player favored the crowd with his skeletal smile and approximated some Cole Porter songs. English was his fourth language and he was forced sometimes to improvise. **"Night and day, you are the sun. Only you beneese the moon, you are the one."**

The basement was almost dark. A single bulb burned near the stairs. Faintly the music sounded from the floor above.

One wall of the basement was covered with a wine rack. Near it were a number of crates, some of them opened with shavings spilling out. A new stainless-steel sink lay on the floor beside a Rock-Ola Luxury Light-Up jukebox with the latest platters and rolls of nickels to put in it. Beside the wine wall was a crate labeled POUR LA CAVE and STORE IN A COOL PLACE. A faint creak came from the crate.

The pianist added some fortissimo to drown himself out at uncertain verses: **"Whether me or you depart, no matter darling I'm apart, I think of you Night and Dayyyyy."**

Grutas moved through his guests shaking hands. With a small motion of his head he summoned Ivanov into his library. It was stark modern, a trestle-table desk, steel and glass shelves and a sculpture after Picasso by Anthony Quinn entitled "Logic Is a Woman's Behind." Ivanov considered the carving.

"You like sculpture?" Grutas said.

"My father was a curator at St. Petersburg, when it was St. Petersburg."

"You can touch it if you like," Grutas said.

"Thank you. The appliances for Moscow?"

"Sixty refrigerators on the train in Helsinki at this moment. Kelvinator. And what do you have for me?" Grutas could not help snapping his fingers.

Because of the snap, Ivanov made Grutas wait while he perused the stone buttocks. "There is no file on the boy at the embassy," he said at last. "He got a visa for Lithuania by proposing to do an article for **L'Humanité.** It was supposed to be on how well the collectivization worked when the farmlands were seized from his family and how delighted the farmers are to move to the city and build a sewage plant. An aristocrat endorsing the revolution."

Grutas snorted through his nose.

Ivanov put a photograph on the desk and pushed it across to Grutas. It showed Lady Murasaki and Hannibal outside her apartment building.

"When was this taken?"

"Yesterday morning. Milko was with my man when he took it. The Lecter boy is a student, he works at night, sleeps over the medical school. My man showed Milko everything—I don't want to know anything else."

"When did he last see Milko?"

Ivanov looked up sharply. "Yesterday. Something's wrong?"

Grutas shrugged it off. "Probably not. Who is the woman?"

"His stepmother, or something like that. She's beautiful," Ivanov said, touching the stone buttocks.

"Has she got an ass like that one?"

"I don't think so."

"The French police came around?"

"An inspector named Popil."

Grutas pursed his lips and for a moment he seemed to forget Ivanov was in the room.

Mueller and Gassmann looked over the crowd. They were taking coats and watching that none of the guests stole anything. In the coatroom Mueller pulled Gassmann's bow tie away from his collar on its rubber band, turned it a half-turn, and let it pop back.

"Can you wind it up like a little propeller and fly like a fairy?" Mueller said.

"Turn it again and you'll think it's the door-knob to Hell," Gassmann said. "Look at you. Tuck in your blouse. Were you never in the service?"

They had to help the caterer pack up. Carrying a folding banquet table down to the basement, they did not see concealed beneath the stairs a fat rubber glove suspended over a dish of powder, with a fuse leading into a three-kilo tin that once held lard. A chemical reaction slows as the temperature cools. Grutas' basement was five degrees cooler than the medical school.

52

THE MAID WAS laying out Grutas' silk pajamas on the bed when he called for more towels.

The maid did not like to take towels into Grutas' bathroom, but she was always summoned to do it. She had to go in there but she did not have to look. Grutas' bathroom was all white tile and stainless steel, with a big freestanding tub and a steam room with frosted glass doors and a shower off the steam room.

Grutas reclined in his tub. The woman captive he had brought from the boat was shaving his chest using a prison safety razor, the blade locked in with a key. The side of her face was swollen. The maid did not want to meet her eyes.

Like a sense-deprivation chamber, the shower was all white, and big enough for four. Its curious acoustics bounced every crumb of sound. Hannibal could hear his hair crunch between his head and the tile as he lay on the white floor of the shower. Covered by a couple of white towels he was nearly invisible from the steam room through the frosted shower door. Under the towels he could hear his own breathing. It was like being rolled in the rug with Mischa. Instead of her warm hair near his face, he had the smell of the pistol, machine oil and brass cartridges and cordite.

He could hear Grutas' voice, and he had not yet seen his face except through field glasses. The tone of voice had not changed—the mirthless teasing that precedes the blow.

"Warm up my terry robe," Grutas told the maid. "I want some steam after. Turn it on." She slid back the steam room door and opened the valve. In the all-white steam chamber the only color was the red bezels of the timer and the thermometer. They had the look of a ship's gauges, with numbers big enough to read in the steam. The timer's minute hand was already moving around the dial toward the red marker hand.

Grutas had his hands behind his head. Tattooed under his arm was the Nazi lightning SS insignia. He twitched his muscle and made the lightning jump. "Boom! **Donnerwetter!**" He laughed when the woman captive flinched away. "Noooo, I won't hit you more. I like you now. I'm going to fix your teeth with some teeth you can put in a glass beside the bed, out of the way."

Hannibal came through the glass doors in a cloud of steam, the gun up and pointed at Grutas' heart. In his other hand he had a bottle of reagent alcohol.

Grutas' skin squeaked as he pushed himself up in the tub and the woman shied from him before she knew Hannibal was behind her.

"I'm glad you're here," Grutas said. He looked at the bottle, hoping Hannibal was drunk. "I've always felt I owed you something."

"I discussed that with Milko."

"And?"

"He arrived at a solution."

"The money of course! I sent it with him, and he gave it to you? Good!"

Hannibal spoke to the woman without looking down at her. "Wet your towel in the tub. Go over to the corner and sit down, and put the towel over your face. Go on. Wet it in the tub."

The woman doused the towel and backed into the corner with it.

"Kill him," she said.

"I've waited so long to see your face," Hannibal said. "I put your face on every bully I ever hurt. I thought you would be bigger."

The maid came into the bedroom with the robe. Through the open bathroom door she could see the barrel and the silencer of the extended gun. She backed out of the room, her slippers silent on the carpet.

Grutas was looking at the gun too. It was Milko's gun. It had a breech lock on the receiver for use with the silencer. If little Lecter was not familiar with it, he would be limited to one shot. Then he'd have to fumble with the pistol.

"Did you see the things I have in this house, Hannibal? Opportunities from the war! You are accustomed to nice things, and you can have them. We are alike! We are the New Men, Hannibal. You, me—the cream—we will always float to the top!" He raised suds in his hand to illustrate floating, getting little Lecter used to his movement.

"Dog tags don't float." Hannibal tossed Grutas' dog tag into the tub and it settled like a leaf to the bottom. "Alcohol floats." Hannibal threw the bottle and it smashed on the tile above Grutas, showering stinging fluid down on his head, pieces of glass falling in his hair. Hannibal took from his pocket a Zippo to light Grutas. As he flipped open the lighter, Mueller cocked a pistol behind his ear.

Gassmann and Dieter grabbed Hannibal's arms from both sides. Mueller pushed the muzzle of Hannibal's gun toward the ceiling and took it from his hand. Mueller stuck the gun in his waistband.

"No shooting," Grutas said. "Don't break the tile in here. I want to talk with him a little. Then he can die in a tub like his sister." Grutas got out of the tub and stood on a towel. He gestured to the woman, now desperate to please. She sprayed him with seltzer over his shaved body as he turned in place, his arms extended.

"Do you know how that feels, the fizzy water?" Grutas said. "It feels like being born again. I'm all new, in a new world with no room in it for you. I can't believe you killed Milko by yourself."

"Someone lent me a hand," Hannibal said.

"Hold him over the tub and cut him when I tell you."

The three men wrestled Hannibal to the floor and held his head and neck over the bathtub. Mueller had a switch knife. He put the edge to Hannibal's throat.

"Look at me, Count Lecter, my prince, twist your head and look at me, get your throat stretched tight and you'll bleed out fast. It won't hurt so long."

Through the steam room door, Hannibal could see the hand of the timer moving tick by tick.

"Answer this," Grutas said. "Would you have fed me to the little girl if she were starving? Because you loved her?"

"Of course."

Grutas smiled and tweaked Hannibal's cheek. "There. There you have it. Love. I love myself that much. I would never apologize to you. You lost your sister in the war." Grutas belched and laughed. "That burp is my commentary. Are you looking for sympathy? You'll find it in the dictionary between shit and syphilis. Cut him, Mueller. This is the last thing you will ever hear, I'll tell you what YOU did to live. You—"

The explosion shuddered the bathroom and the sink jumped off the wall, water spurting from the pipes, and the lights went out. Wrestling in the dark on the floor, Mueller, Gassmann, Dieter swarming on him and tangled up with the woman. The knife got into Gassmann's arm, him cursing and shrieking. Hannibal caught someone hard in the face with his elbow and was on his feet, a muzzle flash as a gun went off in the tiled room and splinters stung his face. Smoke, heavy smoke, curled out of the wall. A gun was sliding across the tiles, Dieter after it. Grutas picked up the gun, the woman jumping on him with her nails at his face and he shot her twice in the chest. Climbed to his feet, the gun coming up. Hannibal snapped the wet towel across Grutas' eyes. Dieter on Hannibal's back, Hannibal threw himself backward on top of him and felt the impact as the edge of the tub caught Dieter across the kidneys and Dieter let go. Mueller on him now before he could get up, trying to jam his big thumbs under Hannibal's chin. Hannibal butted Mueller in the face, slid his hand between them, finding a gun in Mueller's waistband, and pulled the trigger with the gun still in Mueller's pants, the big German rolling off him with a howl, and Hannibal ran with the gun. He had to slow in the dark bedroom, then fast into the corridor filling with smoke. He picked up the maid's pail in the corridor and carried it with him through the house, once hearing a gun go off behind him.

The gate guard was out of the blockhouse and halfway to the front door. "Get water!" Hannibal yelled to him. He handed the man the bucket as he rushed past. "I'll get the hose!" Running hard down the driveway, cutting into the trees as soon as he could. He heard shouts behind him. Up the hill to the orchard. Quick the ignition, feeling for the wire in the dark.

Compression release, twist a little gas, kick, kick. Kick, kick. Touch of choke. Kick. The BMW awakened with a growl and Hannibal exploded out of the brush, down an allée between the trees, knocking loose a muffler on a stump and then on the road, roaring off into the dark, the hanging pipe against the pavement leaving a trail of sparks.

The firemen stayed late into the night, hosing embers in the basement of Grutas' house, shooting water into the spaces in the walls. Grutas stood at the edge of his garden, smoke and steam rising into the night sky behind him, and stared in the direction of Paris.

53

THE NURSING STUDENT had dark red hair and maroon eyes about the same color as Hannibal's. When he stood back from the fountain in the medical school corridor so that she could drink first, she put her face close to him and sniffed. "When did you start smoking?"

"I'm trying to quit," he said.

"Your eyebrows are singed!"

"Careless lighting up."

"If you're careless with fire you shouldn't be cooking." She licked her thumb and smoothed his eyebrow. "My roommate and I are making a daube this evening, there's plenty if . . ."

"Thank you. Really. But I have an engagement."

His note to Lady Murasaki asked if he might visit. He found a branch of wisteria to go with it, suitably withered in abject apology. Her note of invitation was accompanied by two sprigs, watermelon crepe myrtle and a sprig of pine with a tiny cone. Pine is not sent lightly. Thrilling and boundless, the possibilities of pine.

Lady Murasaki's **poissonnier** did not fail her. He had for her four perfect sea urchins in cold seawater from their native Brittany. Next door the butcher produced sweetbreads, already soaked in milk and pressed between two plates. She stopped by Fauchon for a pear tart and last she bought a string bag of oranges.

She paused before the florist, her arms full. No, Hannibal would certainly bring flowers.

Hannibal brought flowers. Tulips and Casablanca lilies and ferns in a tall arrangement sticking up from the pillion seat of his motorcycle. Two young women crossing the street told him the flowers looked like a rooster's tail. He winked at them when the light changed and roared away with a light feeling in his chest.

He parked in the alley beside Lady Murasaki's building and walked around the corner to the entrance with his flowers. He was waving to the concierge when Popil and two beefy policemen stepped out of a doorway and seized him. Popil took the flowers.

"Those aren't for you," Hannibal said.

"You're under arrest," Popil said. When Hannibal was handcuffed, Popil stuck the flowers under his arm.

In his office at the Quai des Orfèvres, Inspector Popil left Hannibal alone and let him wait for a half-hour in the atmosphere of the police station. He returned to his office to find the young man placing the last stem in a flower arrangement in a water carafe on Popil's desk. "How do you like that?" Hannibal said.

Inspector Popil slugged him with a small rubber sap and he went down.

"How do you like that?" Popil said.

The larger of the two policemen crowded in behind Popil and stood over Hannibal. "Answer every question: I asked you how do you like that?"

"It's more honest than your handshake. And at least the club is clean."

Popil took from an envelope two dog tags on a loop of string. "Found in your room. These two were charged in absentia at Nuremberg. Question: Where are they?"

"I don't know."

"Don't you want to watch them hang? The hangman uses the English drop, but not enough to tear their heads off. He does not boil and stretch his rope. They yo-yo a lot. That should be to your taste."

"Inspector, you will never know anything about my taste."

"Justice doesn't matter, it just has to be you killing them."

"It has to be you too, doesn't it, Inspector? You always watch them die. It's to your taste. Do you think we could talk alone?" He took from his pocket a bloodstained note wrapped in cellophane. "You have mail from Louis Ferrat."

Popil motioned for the policemen to leave the room.

"When I cut the clothes off Louis' body, I found this note to you." He read aloud the part above the fold. **"Inspector Popil, why do you torment me with questions you will not answer yourself? I saw you in Lyons.** And he goes on." Hannibal passed the note to Popil. "If you want to open it, it's dry now. It doesn't smell."

The note crackled when Popil opened it, and dark flakes fell out of the fold. When he had finished he sat holding the note beside his temple.

"Did some of your family wave bye-bye to you

from the choo-choo?" Hannibal said. "Were you directing traffic at the depot that day?"

Popil drew back his hand.

"You don't want to do that," Hannibal said softly. "If I knew anything, why should I tell you? It's a reasonable question, Inspector. Maybe you'll get them passage to Argentina."

Popil closed his eyes and opened them again. "Pétain was always my hero. My father, my uncles fought under him in the First War. When he made the new government, he told us, 'Just keep the peace until we throw the Germans off. Vichy will save France.' We were already policemen, it seemed like the same duty."

"Did you help the Germans?"

Popil shrugged. "I kept the peace. Perhaps that helped them. Then I saw one of their trains. I deserted and found the Resistance. They wouldn't trust me until I killed a Gestapo. The Germans shot eight villagers in reprisal. I felt like I had killed them myself. What kind of war is that? We fought in Normandy, in the hedges, clicking these to identify each other." He picked up a cricket clicker from his desk. "We helped the Allies coming in from the beachheads." He clicked twice. "This meant I'm a friend, don't shoot. I don't care about Dortlich. Help me find them. How are you hunting Grutas?"

"Through relatives in Lithuania, my mother's connections in the church."

"I could hold you for the false papers, just on the con's testimony. If I let you go, will you swear to tell me everything you find out? Will you swear to God?"

"To God? Yes, I swear to God. Do you have a Bible?" Popil had a copy of the **Pensées** in his bookcase. Hannibal took it out. "Or we could use your Pascal, Pascal."

"Would you swear on Lady Murasaki's life?"

A moment's hesitation. "Yes, on Lady Murasaki's life." Hannibal picked up the clicker and clicked it twice.

Popil held out the dog tags and Hannibal took them back.

When Hannibal had left the office, Popil's assistant came in. Popil signaled from the window. When Hannibal emerged from the building a plainclothes policeman followed him.

"He knows something. His eyebrows are singed. Check fires in the Ile de France for the last three days," Popil said. "When he leads us to Grutas, I want to try him for the butcher when he was a child."

"Why the butcher?"

"It's a juvenile crime, Etienne, a crime of passion. I don't want a conviction, I want him declared insane. In an asylum they can study him and try to find out what he is."

"What do you think he is?"

"The little boy Hannibal died in 1945 out there in the snow trying to save his sister. His heart died with Mischa. What is he now? There's not a word for it yet. For lack of a better word, we'll call him a monster."

54

AT LADY MURASAKI'S building in the Place de Vosges, the concierge's booth was dark, the Dutch door with its frosted window closed. Hannibal let himself into the building with his key and ran up the stairs.

Inside her booth, seated in her chair the concierge had the mail spread before her on her desk, stacked tenant by tenant as though she were playing solitaire. The cable of a bicycle lock was buried nearly out of sight in the soft flesh of her neck and her tongue was hanging out.

Hannibal knocked on Lady Murasaki's door. He could hear the telephone ringing inside. It sounded oddly shrill to him. The door swung open when he pushed his key into the lock. He ran through the apartment, looking, looking, flinching when he pushed open her bedroom door, but the room was empty. The telephone was ringing, ringing. He picked up the receiver.

In the kitchen of the Café de L'Este, a cage of ortolans waited to be drowned in Armagnac and scalded in the big pot of boiling water on the stove. Grutas gripped Lady Murasaki's neck and held her face close to the boiling pot. With his other hand he held the telephone receiver. Her hands were tied behind her. Mueller gripped her arms from behind.

When he heard Hannibal's voice on the line, Grutas spoke into the phone. "To continue our conversation, do you want to see the Jap alive?" Grutas asked.

"Yes."

"Listen to her and guess if she still has her cheeks."

What was that sound behind Grutas' voice? Boiling water? Hannibal did not know if the sound was real; he heard boiling water in his dreams.

"Speak to your little fuckboy."

Lady Murasaki said, "My dear, DON'T—" before she was snatched away from the telephone. She struggled in Mueller's grip and they banged into the cage of ortolans. The birds screeched and twittered among themselves.

Grutas spoke to Hannibal. "'My DEAR,' you have killed two men for your sister and you have blown up my house. I offer you a life for a life. Bring everything, the dog tags, Pot Watcher's little inventory, every fucking thing. I feel like making her squeal."

"Where—"

"Shut up. Kilometer thirty-six on the road to Trilbardou, there is a telephone kiosk. Be there at sunrise and you'll get a call. If you are not there you get her cheeks in the mail. If I see Popil, or any policeman, you get her heart parcel post. Maybe you can use it in your studies, poke through the chambers, see if you can find your face. A life for a life?"

"A life for a life," Hannibal said. The line went dead.

Dieter and Mueller brought Lady Murasaki to a van outside the café. Kolnas changed the license plate on Grutas' car.

Grutas opened the trunk and got out a Dragunov sniper rifle. He gave it to Dieter. "Kolnas, bring a jar." Grutas wanted Lady Murasaki to hear. He watched her face with a kind of hunger as he gave instructions.

"Take the car. Kill him at the telephone,"

Grutas told Dieter. He handed him the jar. "Bring his balls to the boat below Nemours."

Hannibal did not want to look out the window; Popil's plainclothesman would be looking up. He went into the bedroom. He sat on the bed for a moment with his eyes closed. The background sounds rang on in Hannibal's head. **Chirp chirp. The Baltic dialect of the ortolan.**

Lady Murasaki's sheets were lavender-scented linen. He gripped them in his fists, held them to his face, then stripped them off the bed and soaked them quickly in the tub. He stretched a clothesline across the living room and hung a kimono from it, set an oscillating fan on the floor and turned it on, the fan turning slowly, moving the kimono and its shadow on the sheer curtains.

Standing before the samurai armor, he held up the tanto dagger and stared into the mask of Lord Date Masamune.

"If you can help her, help her now."

He put the lanyard around his neck and slipped the dagger down the back of his collar.

Hannibal twisted and knotted the wet sheets

like a jail suicide, and when he had finished the sheets hung from a terrace railing to within fifteen feet of the alley pavement.

He took his time going down. When he let go of the sheet the last drop through the air seemed to take a long time, the bottoms of his feet stinging as he hit and rolled.

He pushed the motorcycle down the alley behind the building and out into the back street, dropped the clutch and swung aboard as the engine fired. He needed enough of a lead to retrieve Milko's gun.

55

IN THE AVIARY OUTSIDE the Café de L'Este the ortolans stirred and murmured, restive under the bright moon. The patio awning was rolled up and the umbrellas folded. The dining room was darkened, but the lights were still on in the kitchen and the bar.

Hannibal could see Hercule mopping the bar floor. Kolnas sat on a barstool with a ledger. Hannibal stepped further back into the darkness, started his motorcycle and rode away without turning on his lights.

He walked the last quarter-mile to the house on the Rue Juliana. A Citroën Deux Cheveaux was parked in the driveway; a man in the driver's seat took the last drag off a cigarette. Hannibal watched the butt arc away from the car and splash sparks in the street. The man settled himself in the seat and laid back his head. He may have gone to sleep.

From a hedge outside the kitchen, Hannibal could look into the house. Madame Kolnas passed a window talking to someone who was too short to see. The screened windows were open to the warm night. The screen door to the kitchen opened onto the garden. The tanto dagger slid easily through the mesh and disengaged the hook. Hannibal wiped his shoes on the mat and stepped into the house. The kitchen clock seemed loud. He could hear running water and splashing from the bathroom. He passed the bathroom door, staying close to the wall to keep the floor from squeaking. He could hear Madame Kolnas in the bathroom talking to a child.

The next door was partly open. Hannibal could see shelves of toys and a big plush elephant. He looked into the room. Twin beds. Katerina Kolnas was asleep on the nearer one. Her head was turned to the side, her thumb touching her forehead. Hannibal could see the pulse in her temple. He could hear his heart. She was wearing Mischa's bracelet. He blinked in the warm lamplight. He could hear himself blink. He could hear the child's breathing. He could hear Madame Kolnas' voice from down the hall. Small sounds audible over the great roaring in him.

"Come, Muffin, time to dry off," Madame Kolnas said.

Grutas' houseboat, black and prophetic-looking, was moored to the quay in a layered fog. Grutas and Mueller carried Lady Murasaki bound and gagged up the gangway and down the companionway at the rear of the cabin. Grutas kicked open the door of his treatment room on the lower deck. A chair was in the middle of the floor with a bloody sheet spread beneath it.

"Sorry your room isn't quite ready," Grutas said. "I'll contact room service. Eva!!" He went down the passageway to the next cabin and shoved open the door. Three women chained to their bunks looked at him with hate in their faces. Eva was collecting their mess gear.

"Get in here."

Eva came into the treatment room, staying out of Grutas' reach. She took up the bloody sheet and spread a clean sheet beneath the chair. She started to take the blood-stained sheet away, but Grutas said, "Leave it. Bundle it there where she can see it."

Grutas and Mueller bound Lady Murasaki to the chair.

Grutas dismissed Mueller. He lounged on a chaise against the wall, his legs spread, rubbing his thighs. "Do you have any idea what will happen if you don't find me some bliss?" Grutas said.

Lady Murasaki closed her eyes. She felt the boat tremble and begin to move.

Hercule made two trips out of the café with the garbage cans. He unlocked his bicycle and rode away.

His taillight was still visible when Hannibal slipped into the kitchen door. He carried a bulky object in a bloodstained bag.

Kolnas came into the kitchen carrying his ledger. He opened the firebox of the wood-burning oven, put in some receipts and poked them back into the fire.

Behind him, Hannibal said, "Herr Kolnas, surrounded by bowls."

Kolnas spun around to see Hannibal leaning against the wall, a glass of wine in one hand and a pistol in the other.

"What do you want? We are closed here."

"Kolnas in bowl heaven. Surrounded by bowls. Are you wearing your dog tag, Herr Kolnas?"

"I am Kleber, citizen of France, and I am calling the police."

"Let me call them for you." Hannibal put down his glass and picked up the telephone.

"Do you mind if I call the War Crimes Commission at the same time? I'll pay for the call."

"Fuck you. Call who you please. You can call them, I'm serious. Or I'll do it. I have papers, I have friends."

"I have children. Yours."

"What is that supposed to mean?"

"I have both of them. I went to your home on the Rue Juliana. I went into the room with the big stuffed elephant and I took them."

"You are lying."

" 'Take her, she's going to die anyway,' that's what you said. Remember? Tagging along behind Grutas with your bowl.

"I brought something for your oven." Hannibal reached behind him and threw onto the table his bloody bag. "We can cook together, like old times." He dropped Mischa's bracelet onto the kitchen table. It rolled around and around before it settled to a stop.

Kolnas made a gagging sound. For a moment he could not touch the bag with his trembling hands and then he tore at it, tore at the bloody butcher paper inside, tore down to meat and bones.

"It's a beef roast, Herr Kolnas, and a melon. I got them at Les Halles. But do you see how it feels?"

Kolnas lunged across the table, bloody hands

finding Hannibal's face, but he was off his feet stretched over the table and Hannibal pulled him down, and he brought the pistol down on the base of Kolnas' skull, not too hard, and Kolnas' lights went out.

Hannibal's face, smeared with blood, looked like the demonic faces in his own dreams. He poured water in Kolnas' face until his eyes opened.

"Where is Katerina, what have you done with her?" Kolnas said.

"She is safe, Herr Kolnas. She is pink and perfect. You can see the pulse in her temple. I will give her back to you when you give me Lady Murasaki."

"If I do that I am a dead man."

"No. Grutas will be arrested and I will not remember your face. You get a pass for the sake of your children."

"How do I know they are alive?"

"I swear on my sister's soul you will hear their voices. Safe. Help me or I will kill you and leave the child to starve. Where is Grutas? Where is Lady Murasaki?"

Kolnas swallowed, choked on some blood in his mouth. "Grutas has a houseboat, a canal boat, he moves around. He's in the Canal de Loing south of Nemours."

"The name of the boat?"

"**Christabel.** You gave your word, where are my children?"

Hannibal let Kolnas up. He picked up the telephone beside the cash register, dialed a number and handed Kolnas the receiver.

For a moment Kolnas could not recognize his wife's voice, and then "Hello! Hello! Astrid?? Check on the children, let me speak to Katerina! Just do it!"

As Kolnas listened to the puzzled sleepy voice of the awakened child, his face changed. First relief and then curious blankness as his hand crept toward the gun on the shelf beneath the cash register. His shoulders slumped. "You tricked me, Herr Lecter."

"I kept my word. I will spare your life for the sake of your—"

Kolnas spun with the big Webley in his fist, Hannibal's hand slashing toward it, the gun going off beside them, and Hannibal drove the tanto dagger underneath Kolnas' chin and the point came out the top of his head.

The telephone receiver swung from its wire. Kolnas fell forward on his face. Hannibal rolled him over and sat for a moment in a kitchen chair looking at him. Kolnas' eyes were open, already glazing. Hannibal put a bowl over his face.

He carried the cage of ortolans outside and

opened it. He had to grab the last one and toss it into the moonbright sky. He opened the outdoor aviary and shooed the birds out. They formed up in a flock and circled once, tiny shadows flicking across the patio, climbing to test the wind and pick up the polestar. "Go," Hannibal said. "The Baltic is that way. Stay all season."

56

THROUGH THE VAST NIGHT a single point of light shot across the dark fields of Ile de France, the motorcycle flat out, Hannibal down on the gas tank. Off the concrete south of Nemours and following an old towpath along the Canal de Loing, asphalt and gravel, now a single lane of asphalt overgrown on both sides, Hannibal once zigging at speed through cows on the road and feeling a tail-brush sting him as he passed, swerving off the pavement, gravel rattling under the fenders, and back on again, the motorcycle shaking its head and catching itself, settling into speed again.

The lights of Nemours dimming behind him, flat country now, and only the darkness ahead, the details of the gravel and the weeds absurdly sharp, insistent in his headlight, and the dark ahead swallowed up the yellow beam. He wondered if he joined the canal too far south—was the boat behind him?

He stopped and turned off his lights, to sit in darkness and decide, the motorcycle shivering under him.

Far ahead, far into the dark, it appeared that two little houses moved in tandem across the meadow, deckhouses just visible above the banks of the Canal de Loing.

Vladis Grutas' houseboat was wonderfully quiet as it motored southward sending a soft ripple against the sides of the canal, cows asleep in the fields on both sides. Mueller, nursing stitches in his thigh, sat in a canvas chair on the foredeck, a shotgun propped against the railing of the companionway beside him. At the stern, Gassmann opened a locker and took out some canvas fenders.

Three hundred meters back, Hannibal slowed, the BMW burbling along, weeds brushing his shins. He stopped and took his father's field glasses from the saddlebag. He could not read the name of the boat in the darkness.

Only the boat's running lights showed and the

glow from behind the window curtains. Here the canal was too wide to be sure of making a jump onto the deck.

From the bank he might be able to hit the captain in the wheelhouse with the pistol—he could surely drive him from the helm—but then the boat would be alerted, he would have to face them all at once as he came aboard. They could be coming from both ends at once. He could see a covered companionway at the stern and a dark lump near the bow that was probably another entrance to the lower deck.

The binnacle light glowed in the wheelhouse windows near the stern, but he could not make out anyone inside. He needed to get ahead of them. The towpath was close beside the water and the fields too rough for a detour.

Hannibal rode past the canal boat on the towpath, feeling his side toward the boat tingling. A glance at the boat. Gassmann on the stern was pulling canvas fenders out of a locker. He looked up as the motorcycle passed. Moths fluttered above a cabin skylight.

Hannibal held himself to a moderate pace. A kilometer ahead he saw the lights of a car crossing the canal.

The Loing narrowed to a lock not more than twice the beam of a canal boat. The lock was integral with a stone bridge, its upstream doors set into the stone arch, the lock's enclosure like a box beyond the bridge, not much longer than the **Christabel.**

Hannibal turned left along the bridge road in case the boat captain was watching him and drove a hundred yards. He turned off his lights, turned around and returned near the bridge, putting the motorcycle in brush beside the road. He walked forward in the dark.

A few rowboats were upside down on the canal bank. Hannibal sat on the ground among them and peered over the hulls at the boat coming on, still a half-kilometer away. It was very dark. He could hear a radio in a small house at the far end of the bridge, probably the house of the lockkeeper. He buttoned the pistol into the pocket of his jacket.

The tiny running lights of the canal boat came very slowly, the red portside light toward him and behind it the high white light on a folding mast above the cabin. The boat would have to stop and lower itself a meter in the lock. He lay beside the canal, weeds all around him. It was too early in the year for the crickets to sing.

Waiting as the canal boat came, slowly slowly. Time to think. Part of what he did at Kolnas' café was unpleasant to remember: It was difficult to spare Kolnas' life even for that short time, and distasteful to allow him to speak. Good, the crunch he felt in his hand when the tanto blade broke out the top of Kolnas' skull like a little horn. More satisfying than Milko. Good things to enjoy: the Pythagorean proof with tiles, tearing off Dortlich's head. Much to look forward to: He would invite Lady Murasaki for the jugged hare at Restaurant Champs de Mars. Hannibal was calm. His pulse was 72.

Dark beside the lock, and the sky clear and frosted with stars. The mast light of the canal boat should just be among the low stars when the boat reached the lock.

It had not quite reached the low stars when the mast folded back, the light like a falling star descending in an arc. Hannibal saw the filament glow in the boat's big searchlight and flung himself down as the light gathered its beam and swept over him to the gates of the lock and the horn of the canal boat sounded. A light came on in the lockkeeper's cabin and in less than a minute the man was outside pulling on his galluses. Hannibal screwed the silencer onto Milko's gun.

Vladis Grutas came up the front companionway and stood on the deck. He stretched and threw a cigarette into the water. He said something to Mueller and put the shotgun on the deck among the planters, out of sight of the lockkeeper, and went below again.

Gassmann at the stern put out fenders and readied his line. The upstream lock doors stood open. The lockkeeper went into his booth beside the canal and turned on bollard lights at each end of the lock. The canal boat slid under the bridge into the lock, the captain reversing his engine to stop. At the sound of the motor, Hannibal sprinted onto the bridge in a low crouch, keeping below the stone railing.

He looked down into the boat as it slid beneath him, down on the deck and through the skylights. Skylight sliding under, a glimpse of Lady Murasaki bound to a chair, visible only for an instant from directly above.

It took about ten minutes to equalize the level of the water with the downstream side, the heavy doors rumbling open, Gassmann and Mueller gathering in the lines. The lockkeeper turned back toward his house. The captain advanced the throttle and the water boiled behind the canal boat.

Hannibal leaned over the railing. At a range of two feet he shot Gassmann in the top of the head, up on the railing now and jumping, landing on Gassmann and rolling to the deck. The captain felt the thud of Gassmann falling, and looked first to the stern lines, saw they were clear.

Hannibal tried the stern companionway door. Locked.

The captain leaned out of the wheelhouse. "Gassmann?"

Hannibal crouched beside the body on the stern, patted the waist. Gassmann was not armed. Hannibal would have to pass the wheelhouse to go forward, and Mueller was on the bow. He went forward on the right side. The captain came out of the wheelhouse on the left and saw Gassmann sprawled there, his head leaking into the scuppers.

Hannibal scuttling forward fast, bent over beside the low deck cabins.

He felt the boat go into neutral, and running now he heard a gun go off behind him, the bullet screaming off a stanchion and fragments stinging his shoulder. He turned and saw the captain duck behind the aft cabin. Near the forward companionway a tattooed hand and arm were visible for a second, grabbing the shotgun from beneath the bushes. Hannibal fired to no effect. His upper arm felt hot and wet. He ducked between the two deck cabins and out onto the portside deck, running forward low, up beside the forward cabin to the foredeck, Mueller crouched on the foredeck, standing when he heard Hannibal, swinging the shotgun, the muzzle hitting the corner of the companionway for a half-instant, swinging again, and Hannibal shot him four times in the chest as fast as he could pull the trigger, the shotgun going off blowing a ragged hole in the woodwork beside the companionway door. Mueller staggered and looked at his chest, collapsed backward and sat dead against the railing. The companionway door was unlocked. Hannibal went down the stairs and locked the door behind him.

At the stern, the captain, crouched on the afterdeck beside Gassmann's body, fumbled in his pocket for the keys.

Fast down the stairs and along the narrow passage of the lower deck. He looked into the first cabin, empty, nothing but cots and chains. He slammed open the second door, saw Lady Murasaki tied to the chair and rushed to her. Grutas shot Hannibal in the back from behind the door, the bullet striking between his shoulder blades and he went down on his back, blood spreading from under him.

Grutas smiled and came to him. He put his pistol under Hannibal's chin and patted him down. He kicked Hannibal's gun away. Grutas took a stiletto from his belt and poked the tip into Hannibal's legs. They did not move.

"Shot in the spine, my little Mannlein," Grutas said. "Can't feel your legs? Too bad. You won't feel it when I cut off your balls." Grutas smiled at Lady Murasaki. "I'll make you a coin purse to keep your tips."

Hannibal's eyes opened.

"You can see?" Grutas wagged the long blade before Hannibal's face. "Excellent! Look at this." Grutas stood before Lady Murasaki and trailed the point lightly down her cheek, barely dimpling the skin. "I can put some color in her cheeks." He drove the stiletto into the back of the chair beside her head. "I can make some new places for sex."

Lady Murasaki said nothing. Her eyes were fixed on Hannibal. His fingers twitched, his hand moved slightly toward his head. His eyes moved from Lady Murasaki to Grutas and back again. Lady Murasaki looked up at Grutas, excitement in her face along with anguish. She could be as beautiful as she chose to be. Grutas bent and kissed her hard, cutting her lips against her teeth, his face crushed over hers, his hard empty face paling, his pale eyes unblinking as he groped inside her blouse.

Hannibal got his hand behind his head, pulled from behind his collar the tanto knife, bloody, bent and dimpled by Grutas' bullet.

Grutas blinked, his face convulsed in agony,

his ankles buckled and he fell hamstrung, Hannibal twisting from under him. Lady Murasaki, her ankles bound together, kicked Grutas in the head. He tried to raise his gun, but Hannibal seized the barrel, twisting up, the gun went off and Hannibal slashed Grutas' wrist, the gun falling away and sliding on the floor. Grutas crawled toward the gun, pulling himself on his elbows, then up on his knees, knee-walking, and falling again, pulling himself on his elbows like a broken-backed animal in the road. Hannibal cut Lady Murasaki's arms free and she jerked the stiletto out of the back of the chair to cut free her ankles and moved into the corner beside the door. Hannibal, his back bloody, cut Grutas off from the gun.

Grutas stopped and on his knees he faced Hannibal. An eerie calm came over him. He looked up at Hannibal with his pale Arctic eyes.

"Together we sail deathward," Grutas said. "Me, you, the stepmother that you fuck, the men you have killed."

"They were not men."

"What did Dortlich taste like, a fish? Did you eat Milko too?"

Lady Murasaki spoke from the corner. "Hannibal, if Popil takes Grutas he may not take you. Hannibal, be with me. Give him to Popil."

"He ate my sister."

"So did you," Grutas said. "Why don't you kill yourself?"

"No. That's a lie."

"Oh, you did. Kindly Pot Watcher fed her to you in the broth. You have to kill everyone who knows it, don't you? Now that your woman knows it, you really should kill her too."

Hannibal's hands are over his ears, holding the bloody knife. He turns to Lady Murasaki, searching her face, goes to her and holds her against him.

"No, Hannibal. It's a lie," she said. "Give him to Popil."

Grutas scuttled toward the gun, talking, talking. "You ate her, half-conscious, your lips were greedy around the spoon."

Hannibal screamed at the ceiling, "NOOOOO!" and ran to Grutas raising the knife, stepped on the gun and slashed an "M" the length of Grutas' face screaming "'M' for Mischa! 'M' for Mischa! 'M' for Mischa," Grutas backward on the floor and Hannibal cutting great "M"s in him.

A cry from behind him. Dimly in the red mist a gunshot. Hannibal felt the muzzle blast above him. He did not know if he was hit. He turned. The captain stood behind him, his back to Lady Murasaki, the handle of the stiletto standing behind his clavicle, the blade through his aorta;

the gun slipped from the captain's fingers and he pitched forward on his face.

Hannibal weaving on his feet, his face a mask of red. Lady Murasaki closed her eyes. She was shaking.

"Are you hit?" he said.

"No."

"I love you, Lady Murasaki," he said. He went to her.

She opened her eyes and held his bloody hands away.

"What is left in you to love?" she said and ran from the cabin, up the companionway and over the rail in a clean dive into the canal.

The boat bumped gently along the edge of the canal.

On the **Christabel,** Hannibal was alone with the dead, their regard fast glazing. Mueller and Gassmann are belowdecks now, at the foot of the companionways. Grutas, herringboned with red, lies in the cabin where he died. Each of them holds in his arms a Panzerfaust like a big-headed doll. Hannibal took from the arms rack the final Panzerfaust and lashed it down in the engine room, its fat anti-tank missile two feet from the fuel tank. From the boat's ground tackle he took a grapnel and tied the line around the top-mounted trigger of the Panzer-faust. He stood on deck with the grapnel hook in his hand as the boat inched along, bumping gently against the stone border of the canal. From the deck he could see flashlights on the bridge. He heard yelling and a dog was barking.

He dropped the hook into the water. The line snaked slowly over the side as Hannibal stepped onto the bank and set off across the fields. He did not look back. At four hundred meters the explosion came. He felt the shock wave on his back and the pressure rolled over him with the noise. A piece of metal landed in the field behind him. The boat blazed fiercely in the canal and a column of sparks rose into the sky, whipped into spirals by the fire's draft. More explosions blew the burning timbers wheeling into the sky as the charges in the other Panzer-fausts went off.

From a mile distant he saw the flashing lights of police cars at the lock. He did not go back. He walked across the fields and they found him at daylight.

57

THE EAST WINDOWS at Paris police headquarters during the warm months were crowded at breakfast time with young policemen hoping to see Simone Signoret take coffee on her terrace in the nearby Place Dauphin.

Inspector Popil worked at his desk, not looking up even when the actress's terrace doors were reported to be opening, and remained undisturbed at the groaning when only the housekeeper came out to water the plants.

His window was open and he could hear faintly the Communist demonstration on the Quai des Orfèvres and the Pont Neuf. The demonstrators were mostly students, chanting "Free Hannibal, Free Hannibal." They carried placards reading DEATH TO FASCISM and demanding the immediate release of Hannibal

Lecter, who had become a minor cause célèbre. Letters in **L'Humanité** and **Le Canard Enchaîné** defended him and **Le Canard** ran a photo of the burning wreckage of the **Christabel** with the caption "Cannibals Cooked."

A moving childhood reminiscence of the benefits of collectivization ran in **L'Humanité** as well, in a piece under Hannibal's own byline, smuggled out of the jail, further bolstering his Communist supporters. He would have written as readily for the extreme right fringe publications, but the rightists were out of fashion and could not demonstrate on his behalf.

Before Popil was a memorandum from the public prosecutor asking what could positively be proved against Hannibal Lecter. In the spirit of retribution, **l'épuration sauvage,** remaining from the war, a conviction for the murder of fascists and war criminals would have to be airtight and, even justified, it would be politically unpopular.

The murder of the butcher Paul Momund was years ago, and the evidence consisted of the smell of oil of cloves, the prosecutor pointed out. Would it help to detain the woman Murasaki? Might she have colluded? the prosecutor asked. Inspector Popil advised against the detention of the woman Murasaki.

The exact circumstances surrounding the death of the restaurateur Kolnas, or **Cryto-Fascist Restaurateur and Black-Marketeer Kolnas,** as he was known in the papers, could not be determined. Yes, there was a hole of unknown origin in the top of his skull and his tongue and hard palate were pierced by persons unknown. He had fired a revolver, as a paraffin test proved.

The dead men in the canal boat were reduced to grease and soot. They were known to be kidnappers and white slavers. Was not a van recovered containing two captive women, by dint of a license number provided by the woman Murasaki?

The young man had no criminal record. He led his class at medical school.

Inspector Popil looked at his watch and went down the corridor to **Audition 3,** the best of the interrogation rooms because it received some sunlight and the graffiti had been painted over with thick white paint. A guard stood outside the door. Popil nodded to the guard and he pulled the bolt to admit him. Hannibal sat at the bare table in the center of the room. His ankle was shackled to the table leg and his wrists to a ring in the table.

"Take off the iron," Popil told the guard.

"Good morning, Inspector," Hannibal said.

"She's here," Popil said. "Dr. Dumas and Dr. Rufin are coming back after lunch." Popil left him alone.

Now Hannibal could stand when Lady Murasaki came into the room.

The door closed behind her and she reached behind her and put her hand flat on the door.

"Are you sleeping?" she said.

"Yes. I sleep well."

"Chiyoh sends her good wishes. She says she is very happy."

"I'm glad."

"Her young man has graduated and they are betrothed."

"I couldn't be more pleased for her."

A pause.

"Together they are manufacturing motor scooters, small motorcycles, in partnership with two brothers. They have made six of them. She hopes they will catch on."

"Surely they will—I'll buy one myself."

Women pick up surveillance faster than men do, as part of their survival skills, and they at once recognize desire. They also recognize its absence. She felt the change in him. Something was missing behind his eyes.

The words of her ancestor Murasaki Shikibu came to her and she said them:

**"The troubled waters
Are frozen fast.
Under clear heaven
Moonlight and shadow
Ebb and flow."**

Hannibal made Prince Genji's classic reply:

**"The memories of long love
Gather like drifting snow.
Poignant as the mandarin ducks
Who float side by side in sleep."**

"No," Lady Murasaki said. "No. Now there is only ice. It's gone. Is it not gone?"

"You are my favorite person in the world," he said, quite truthfully.

She inclined her head to him and left the room.

In Popil's office she found Dr. Rufin and Dr. Dumas in close conversation. Rufin took Lady Murasaki's hands.

"You told me he might freeze inside forever," she said.

"Do you feel it?" Rufin said.

"I love him and I cannot find him," Lady Murasaki said. "Can you?"

"I never could," Rufin said.

She left without seeing Popil.

Hannibal volunteered to work in the jail dispensary and petitioned the court to allow him to return to medical school. Dr. Claire DeVrie, the head of the fledgling Police Forensics Laboratory, a bright and attractive woman, found Hannibal extremely useful in setting up a compact qualitative analysis and toxin identification unit with the minimum of reagents and equipment. She wrote a letter on his behalf.

Dr. Dumas, whose relentless cheer irritated Popil beyond measure, submitted a ringing endorsement of Hannibal, and explained that Johns Hopkins Medical Center in Baltimore, America, was offering him an internship, after reviewing his illustrations for the new anatomy text. Dumas addressed the morals clause in no uncertain terms.

In three weeks' time, over the objections of Inspector Popil, Hannibal walked out of the Palace of Justice and returned to his room above the medical school. Popil did not say goodbye to him, a guard simply brought him his clothes.

He slept very well in his room. In the morning he called the Place de Vosges and found Lady Murasaki's telephone had been disconnected. He went there and let himself in with his key. The apartment was empty except for the telephone stand. Beside the telephone was a letter for him. It was attached to the blackened twig from Hiroshima sent to Lady Murasaki by her father.

The letter said **Goodbye, Hannibal. I have gone home.**

He tossed the burnt twig into the Seine on his way to dinner. At the Restaurant Champs de Mars he had a splendid jugged hare on the money Louis left to buy Masses for his soul. Warmed with wine, he decided that in strict fairness he should read some prayers in Latin for Louis and perhaps sing one to a popular tune, reasoning that his own prayers would be no less efficacious than those he could buy at St.-Sulpice.

He dined alone and he was not lonely.

Hannibal had entered his heart's long winter. He slept soundly, and was not visited in dreams as humans are.

III

I'd yield me to the Devil instantly,
Did it not happen that myself am he!

——J. W. VON GOETHE: **Faust: A Tragedy**

58

IT SEEMED TO SVENKA that Dortlich's father was never going to die. The old man breathed and breathed, two years of breathing while the coffin draped with a tarpaulin waited on sawhorses in Svenka's cramped apartment. It took up most of the parlor. This occasioned a lot of griping by the woman living with Svenka, who pointed out that the coffin's rounded top prevented its use even as a sideboard. After a few months she began to keep in the coffin contraband canned goods Svenka extorted from people returning from Helsinki on the ferries.

In the two years of Joseph Stalin's murderous purges, three of Svenka's fellow officers were shot and a fourth was hanged in Lubyanka Prison.

Svenka could see that it was time to go. The

art was his and he was not leaving it. Svenka did not inherit all of Dortlich's contacts, but he could get good papers. He did not have contacts inside Sweden, but he had plenty on the boats between Riga and Sweden who could deal with a package once it was at sea.

First things first.

On Sunday morning at six forty-five a.m., the maid Bergid emerged from the Vilnius apartment building where Dortlich's father lived. She was bareheaded to avoid the appearance of going to church, and carried a sizable pocketbook with her scarf and her Bible in it.

She had been gone about ten minutes when, from his bed, Dortlich's father heard the footsteps of a person heavier than Bergid coming up the stairs. A clicking and a rasping came from the apartment door as someone raked the tumblers of the lock.

With an effort, Dortlich's father pushed himself up on his pillows.

The outside door dragged on the threshold as it was pushed open. He fumbled in the drawer beside his bed and took out a Luger pistol. Faint with the effort, he held the gun in both hands and brought it under the sheet.

He closed his eyes until the door of his room opened.

"Are you sleeping, Herr Dortlich? I hope I'm

not disturbing you," said Sergeant Svenka, in civilian clothes with his hair slicked down.

"Oh, it's you." The old man's expression was as fierce as usual, but he looked gratifyingly weak.

"I came on behalf of the Police and Customs Brotherhood," Svenka said. "We were cleaning out a locker and we found some more of your son's things."

"I don't want them. Keep them," the old man said. "Did you break the lock?"

"When no one came to the door I let myself in. I thought I'd just leave the box if no one was home. I have your son's key."

"He never had a key."

"It's his skeleton key."

"Then you can lock the door on your way out."

"Lieutenant Dortlich confided to me some details about your . . . situation and your eventual wishes. Have you written them down? You have the documents? The brotherhood feels it's our responsibility now to see your desires carried out to the letter."

"Yes," Dortlich's father said. "Signed and witnessed. A copy sent to the Klaipeda. You won't need to do anything."

"Yes, I do. One thing." Sergeant Svenka put down the box.

Smiling as he approached the bed, he picked up a cushion off a chair, scuttling sideways spiderlike to put it over the old man's face, climbing astride him on the bed, knees on his shoulders, and leaned with his elbows locked, his weight on the cushion. How long would it take? The old man was not thrashing.

Svenka felt something hard pressing in his crotch, the sheet tented under him and the Luger went off. Svenka felt the burn on his skin and the burn deep up inside him and fell away backward, the old man raising the gun and shooting through the sheet, hitting him in the chest and chin, the muzzle drooping, and the last shot hit his own foot. The old man's heart beat faster and faster faster stop. The clock above his bed struck seven, and he heard the first four strokes.

59

SNOW ABOVE THE 50th Parallel dusting the high forehead of the hemisphere, Eastern Canada, Iceland, Scotland, and Scandinavia. Snow in flurries in Grisslehamn, Sweden, snow falling into the sea as the ferry carrying the coffin came in.

The ferry agent provided a four-wheeled trolley to the men from the funeral home and helped them load the coffin on it, getting up a little speed on the deck to bump up the ramp onto the dock where the truck waited.

Dortlich's father died without immediate family and his wishes were clearly expressed. The Klaipeda Ocean and River Workers Association saw to it his wishes were carried out.

The small procession to the cemetery consisted of the hearse, a van with six men from the funeral home, and a car carrying two elderly relatives.

It is not that Dortlich's father was entirely forgotten, but most of his childhood friends were dead and few relatives survived. He was a maverick middle son, and his enthusiasm for the October Revolution estranged him from his family, and took him to Russia. The son of shipbuilders spent his life as an ordinary seaman. Ironic, agreed the two old relatives riding behind the hearse through the falling snow in the late afternoon.

The Dortlich family mausoleum was grey granite with a cross incised above the door and a tasteful amount of stained glass in clerestory windows, just colored panes, not figurative.

The cemetery warden, a conscientious man, had swept the path to the mausoleum door and swept the steps. The great iron key was cold through his mittens and he used both hands to turn it, the tumblers squealing in the lock. The men from the funeral home opened the big double doors and carried the coffin in. There was some muttering from the relatives about the Communist labor union emblem on the lid being displayed in the mausoleum.

"Think of it as a brotherly farewell from those

who knew him best," the funeral director said, and coughed against his glove. It was an expensive-looking coffin for a Communist, he reflected, and speculated about the markup.

The warden had in his pocket a tube of white lithium grease. He made paths on the stone for the feet of the coffin to slide on as it went sideways into its niche, and the pallbearers were glad when they had to slide it into place, pushing from only one side and unable to lift.

The party looked around among themselves. No one volunteered to pray, and so they locked the building and hurried back to their vehicles in the blowing snow.

Upon his bed of art Dortlich's father lies still and small, ice forming in his heart.

The seasons will come and go. Voices come in faintly from the gravel paths outside, and occasionally the tendril of a vine. The colors of the stained glass grow softer as the dust accumulates. The leaves blow and then the snow, and around again. The paintings, their faces so familiar to Hannibal Lecter, are rolled up in the dark like the coils of memory.

60

GREAT SOFT FLAKES fall in still morning air along the Lievre River, Quebec, and lie feathery on the sills of the Caribou Corner Outdoor and Taxidermy shop.

Big flakes like feathers fall in Hannibal Lecter's hair as he hikes up the wooded lane to the log building. It is open for business. He can hear "O Canada!" coming from a radio in the back as a high school hockey game is about to begin. Trophy heads cover the walls. A moose is at the top and arranged in Sistine fashion below it are tableaus of Arctic fox and ptarmigan, soft-eyed deer, lynx and bobcat.

On the counter is a partitioned tray of taxidermy eyes. Hannibal sets down his bag and pokes through the eyes with a finger. He finds a pair of the palest blue intended for a dear and deceased husky. Hannibal takes them out of the tray and places them side by side on the countertop.

The proprietor is coming out. Bronys Grentz's beard is grizzled now, his temples are greying.

"Yah? I can help you?"

Hannibal looks at him, pokes in the tray and finds a pair of eyes that match Grentz's bright brown eyes.

"What is it?" Grentz asks.

"I've come to collect a head," Hannibal said.

"Which one, have you got your ticket?"

"I don't see it up there on the wall."

"It's probably in the back."

Hannibal has a suggestion. "May I come? I'll show you which one."

Hannibal brings his bag with him. It contains a few clothes, a cleaver and a rubber apron marked **Property of Johns Hopkins.**

It was interesting to compare Grentz's mail and his address book to the roster of the wanted Totenkopfs circulated by the British after the war. Grentz had a number of correspondents in Canada and Paraguay and several in the United States. Hannibal examined the documents at his leisure on the train, where he enjoyed a private compartment, courtesy of Grentz's cash box.

On the way back to his internship in Baltimore, he broke his trip in Montreal, where he mailed Grentz's head to one of the taxidermist's pen pals and put as a return address the name and address of another.

He was not torn with anger at Grentz. He was not torn at all by anger anymore, or tortured by dreams. This was a holiday and killing Grentz was preferable to skiing.

The train rocking southward toward America, so warm and well sprung. So different from his long train trip to Lithuania as a boy.

He would stop in New York overnight, stay at the Carlyle as the guest of Grentz, and see a play. He had tickets for both **Dial M for Murder** and **Picnic.** He decided to see **Picnic** as he found stage murders unconvincing.

America fascinated him. Such abundant heat and electricity. Such odd, wide cars. American faces, open but not innocent, readable. In time he would use his access as a patron of the arts to stand backstage and look out at audiences, their rapt faces glowing in the stage lights, and read and read and read.

Darkness fell and the waiter in the dining car brought a candle to his table, the blood-red claret shivering slightly in his glass with the movement of the train. Once in the night he woke at a station to hear the railroad workers blasting ice off the undercarriage with a steam hose, great clouds of steam sweeping past his window on the wind. The train started again with a tiny jerk and then a liquid glide away from the station lights and into the night, stroking southward toward America. His window cleared and he could see the stars.

ACKNOWLEDGMENTS

My thanks to the Brigade Criminelle of the Paris police, who welcomed me into the world of the Quai des Orfèvres and shared with me both their harrowing knowledge and their excellent lunch.

Lady Murasaki is the namesake of Murasaki Shikibu, who wrote the first great novel in the world, **The Tale of Genji.** Our own Lady Murasaki quotes Ono no Komachi and hears in her mind a poem by Yosano Akiko. Her farewell to Hannibal is from **The Tale of Genji**. Noriko Miyamoto helped me greatly with literature and music.

As you see, I have borrowed S. T. Coleridge's dog."

For a better understanding of France during the occupation and in the post-war period, I am indebted to Robert Gildea's **Marianne in Chains,** to Antony Beevor and Artemis Cooper's **Paris After the Liberation, 1944–1949,** and to **The Rape of Europa** by Lynn H. Nicholas. Susan Mary Alsop's remarkable letters to Marietta Tree, collected in **To Marietta from Paris, 1945–1960,** were helpful as well.

Most of all, my thanks to Pace Barnes for her unfailing support, and her love and her patience.

—T.H.

ABOUT THE AUTHOR

Thomas Harris began his writing career covering crime in the United States and Mexico, and was a reporter and editor for the Associated Press in New York City. His first novel, **Black Sunday,** was published in 1975, followed by **Red Dragon** in 1981, **The Silence of the Lambs** in 1988, and **Hannibal** in 1999.